L.C. FENTON

OMNIFIC PUBLISHING
LOS ANGELES

Saint Kate of the Cupcake: The Dangers of Lust and Baking,
Copyright © L.C. Fenton, 2014

Omnific Publishing
1901 Avenue of the Stars, 2nd floor
Los Angeles, CA 90067
www.omnificpublishing.com

First Omnific eBook edition, March 2014
First Omnific trade paperback edition, March 2014

The characters and events in this book are fictitious.
Any similarity to real persons, living or dead,
is coincidental and not intended by the author.

Library of Congress Cataloguing-in-Publication Data

Fenton, L.C.
Saint Kate of the Cupcake: The Dangers of Lust and Baking / L.C. Fenton – 1st ed.
    ISBN: 978-1-623420-84-0
    1. Romance — Fiction. 2. Baking — Fiction.
    3. Divorce — Fiction. 4. London — Fiction. I. Title

10 9 8 7 6 5 4 3 2 1

Cover Design by Micha Stone and Amy Brokaw
Interior Book Design by Coreen Montagna

Printed in the United States of America

*To my wonderful husband, Sean, who looked after the kids
while I gallivanted around the UK doing research.
I think we are both very happy that this book
is a product of my imagination and not reality.*

"Regret is the price we pay for choice."

~Alain De Botton

(who in no way endorsed this book and would probably be rather shocked)

Prologue

How do you create a fabulous chocolate cake? That I know, and several ways of varying complexity to do it. How do you implode a marriage? That's a much more difficult question. I think there are even more ways to do it than there are chocolate cake recipes, and there are more than enough of those. I do know how I successfully blew up my own. I can't take exclusive credit for it, nothing that spectacular is a solo job, but I certainly laid my share of the explosives and lit the fuse that finally set it off. Taking a lover would generally be enough, but as usual, I had to go that little bit further. Why burn the bridge when you can use a nuclear weapon to reduce it to its component atoms?

This is not a how-to guide — I cannot recommend my own course of action as a good way to go about it; this is merely my attempt to justify the unjustifiable. After all, monogamy is supposed to be the correct and honorable way to conduct a marriage, and there are no excuses, never ever. If you are unhappy, you are supposed to realize it and face it head-on like an adult, opening up all the dark, dank crevasses of your soul for examination at marriage counseling and allow the bitter healing to commence. No one is supposed to lie or cheat or fall out of love. But outside the hundred-odd minutes of a formulaic Hollywood movie, it's hard to distinguish the goodies from the baddies, and few things are that black and white.

As a cautionary tale, this may have some merit, or would if I was a better wife and there wasn't a small part of me that was secretly, nihilistically, unrepentant of my part in it. I look back at my decisions, and there are few that I wouldn't have made again, and again, a hundred times over. Even those truths we both tried to hide that were so brutally exposed, for my part I'd rather have known than still be in the dark, though surely my husband wishes the opposite. It all seems so inevitable, really; the start of our decline began almost from the start, so many years ago. The dance just had to be completed for the music to stop.

My job, ironically, is as a beacon of conservative domesticity. I write popular books on baking, selling a version of my life that is glossy and perfect, an air-brushed hologram of reality, with a nice sideline in kitchenware. But it is work, and I find it fulfilling, and despite the weariness I feel at maintaining what is a fragile façade of a life, I have little choice. If this became public, it would not only be humiliating, but potentially financially ruinous. Our twin boys are also at a terrifyingly expensive public school, which we can only manage with the help of my mother-in-law, who would not countenance a divorce. My husband wants to stay married for them, and to maintain our lifestyle, but in name only because he can never forgive me. So, that is my choice: stay married to the man who cannot stand me, or leave and try to salvage some self-respect but disrupt the lives of everyone. What price should have to be paid for being able to meet your own eyes in the mirror each day?

Perhaps I should start with how my husband and I met, when we were young and sure of the world and where we fit into it.

Chapter One

1993

In my last year of school, I'd had my life worked out. I knew exactly what I wanted. I was confident and certain that I would have a brilliant career in my chosen field. In the way of these things, though, they are never quite as you imagine them. I studied hard for my school-leaving exams, made the entry into an Arts/Law degree at university, and set off down the path that would, of course, lead to a stellar and satisfying career as a lawyer and, ultimately, partner in a first-tier law firm. My law results were good, though not outstanding, but enough to land me a job with the firm of my choice before I had even finished.

Then I graduated and started work in my dream job. I was so excited, and I certainly looked the part in my black pinstripe suit and Prada glasses. But all too soon I began to feel the creeping disillusionment of working in a big law office. The long hours, the pressure and the monotony of it, along with the lingering whiff of misogyny left a bad taste in my mouth. Even in a room of my peers, I was expected to pour the coffee, and several of the partners felt free to leer at me at Friday night drinks and, after a few too many whiskys, would go for the grope if they thought no one would see it. There was no point in complaining about it, unless you wanted a fast end to your career. You might win the sexual harassment suit, but you'd never get another job. They couldn't fire you, but there were corners they could push you into so deep and work so awful you would be forced to leave before it destroyed your soul.

It took only six months of being a lawyer until I couldn't think of anything I'd less like to do for the rest of my life, but by then I was trapped. I had worked too long and hard to get to where I was, and I had never envisioned a Plan B, but I needed to escape. As many Australians do when faced with this exact situation, I moved to London as soon as I could.

The plan was to work for a few years and travel whenever possible to make being a lawyer bearable, together with the vain hope that things might be different in another country. I lived in a tiny flat in Kensington with a friend from university, Megan. We were both working in the legal departments of large multi-nationals in unexciting fields, drones rather than queen bees — or even queen bees in the making. The hours were long, but not exceptionally so, little was urgent or innovative, and most of my work involved looking over contracts which differed only minutely from each other.

While I had many friendly acquaintances, mostly through work, I hadn't made too many friends amongst the natives. There wasn't a huge amount in it for them, given that everyone understood that the migration was temporary and the Australians and South Africans would eventually go home to roost and breed. There were also so many of us around that there was nothing exciting or exotic to pique the interest of the locals. The exception was the occasional male, interested in relations of the brief but intimate kind, which was how, in a roundabout way, I came to meet my husband, Jack.

Andrew Plimpton worked in the property division of the same company and had been making overtures so subtle, it took me a while to realize that was what he was doing.

"More rain today, eh, Kate?" he asked pleasantly.

"Umm…yes. Same as yesterday," I answered, my voice cheerful as I kept going with my work. It's not like I needed to give all my attention to a conversation about the weather, which this summer was all gray and rain every day. The weather forecast spoke of "periods of lightening," which I when I first arrived I thought meant there was going to be an electrical storm, but turns out just meant that the clouds lifted a little. I guess when the weather is so monotonous, even that is noteworthy.

"That's London for you!" He laughed with forced enthusiasm.

"Yup." Usually this was the part of the conversation where he stopped talking and walked off. He wasn't bad looking, but he didn't have any outstanding features that caused one to immediately notice him. He was pale and blondish with glasses and was slightly shorter than me. I'm quite tall at five foot ten, so I tend to either intimidate or attract shorter men. Most women like to date taller men, but it's not so easy and tends to restrict the dating pool somewhat when one is six foot in moderate heels.

I looked up at him because he still hadn't left my desk. He cleared his throat a few times, and I watched, fascinated. I had never seen someone so uncomfortable. I could have been inserting wooden splinters under his fingernails, and he couldn't have looked more tortured.

"A friend of mine is having a party this weekend. Would you like to go? If you've nothing on, of course." He looked around the room, anywhere but at me. This was by far the most overt he had ever been, actually coming out and asking me somewhere directly, and the strain of it caused him to nervously clear his throat again and fidget with his tie. I had no better offers at the moment, so I decided to take a chance on him. He seemed quite nice, and sometimes it pays to give the quiet ones a go.

"Sure. That would be lovely," I said. He looked at me, genuinely surprised and even more anxious, if possible. My estimation of the night declined slightly from its already low position. I think I just agreed to put both of us through many hours of awkwardness, though with music and alcohol, it might be easier.

"Perhaps you could write down the details for me?" I prompted, pushing a notepad and pen toward him, trying to be helpful.

"Yes. Shall I pick you up? It's a longish drive, and we'll stay overnight. Separate rooms, of course."

"Where are we going?" I tried to keep the slight panic from my voice. *Oh, God!* I thought. *It's not even in London! What if it's really dire? There'll be no escape.* I really should have asked for more information before saying yes.

"Pool party at a friend's country house. If we leave Saturday morning, we should get there by lunch."

"Lovely," I repeated for lack of a better response and forced a smile and tried to inject some cheer into my voice. I wasn't worried about being alone with Andrew for the weekend on a physical level. He was the harmless type and hardly likely to force himself on anyone. I wasn't exactly sure what we'd talk about on a long drive there and back, but I should let myself be open to the experience. He seemed nice enough, and getting to know him better wouldn't be a hardship, though I had a feeling that this "pool party" wouldn't be exactly the same as the ones back home which were usually very casual and involved blackening meat of various types and throwing together a few salads while everyone drank a lot and tried to keep cool.

Chapter Two

How right I was! The "country house" was a spectacular and famous Grade 11-listed mansion in Gloucestershire and by far the largest house I had ever seen that wasn't operated by the National Trust. It was vast, with pale creamy yellow stone and a gray roof. From this approach, I couldn't see if it was a square or three-sided. Either way, it was something straight out of Austen. *It could have been Pemberley,* I thought, my brain slightly addled.

"My God! It's beautiful!" I gasped, unable to contain myself.

"Yes, Clouston Hall is one of the finest examples of the period still in private hands," said Andrew. "It's been in the family since the seventeenth century, though this house was mostly built in the eighteenth. It's perfectly symmetrical. There are even false windows built in to maintain the lines." The wide stone steps leading up to the large columned pediment over the central bay added to its already impressive grandeur. If it had been a person, it would have been a supermodel. I had never seen something so glorious, and it seemed to bask in the dusty summer sunshine surrounded by its blanket of checkered green lawns.

"Wow!" I said as we drove past the front entrance. "This is your friend's place?" I was awestruck. I couldn't believe people actually lived in something this magnificent.

"Well, it's his parents but will eventually be his. We were at school together, so I used to come here for holidays sometimes. Jack throws a great party when his parents go away on their annual summer holiday. I think they know about it, but everyone pretends they don't." That sounded slightly odd to me, but what did I know? It's not like I hadn't thrown the odd party at my parents' place in Vaucluse when they went away, but they had known about it and even helped organize on occasion. Mind you, they didn't live in a house like *this*.

We drove around to the back of the house, parking near the garages where there were already nearly forty cars abandoned in varying degrees of neatness. It would be chaos getting out again. Feeling uncommonly nervous, I smoothed the skirt of my yellow sundress and adjusted the straps on my white low-heeled sandals. It wasn't like I was from an impoverished background, but this was another level.

"Let's leave the bags here for the moment. We can get them later." Andrew put a hand on my elbow, guiding me toward the house. Instead of going inside, though, we went past it, down the white stone path through the formal gardens to the pool, where festivities had clearly commenced. I could hear the babble of many people talking, the occasional louder bark of laughter, and the clink of glasses over the top. As we climbed the stone steps to the raised pool area, I could see roughly eighty people gathered around the light blue water.

A band was playing on the far side, and people were dancing with varying degrees of success. I'm not generally socially awkward, but walking into a party at a house like this, with that many people and knowing no one but my date, and him not particularly well, was incredibly nerve wracking. I had the insane notion to turn around and walk out, but not only would that have been a ridiculous thing to do, there was no way of getting back to London other than the car I came in, which wasn't mine. *Suck it up*, I told myself sternly, *you might have fun*. Putting a smile on my face, I indicated to Andrew to lead on.

"There can't possibly be enough rooms for everyone at the party?" I asked. The house was huge, but nearly eighty people? Andrew shook his head.

"We're some of the lucky ones who are staying in the house. Everyone else will be camping on the lawn." He pointed to the large lawn behind the pool, and I could see some tents already set up in the corner. I'd love to say I was a down-to-earth kind of girl who would be happy camping, but frankly, I was glad I had a room with a bathroom handy.

"Let's go and say hello to Jack. I think he's over by the table," Andrew said loudly into my ear so he could be heard over the noise of the party. I looked over to the table with the drinks but could see only women standing there. Maybe I had misheard him and Jack was a Jacqueline? I couldn't pick which person he was talking about.

As we reached the table, I was still puzzled as to the identity of our host, until Andrew excused his way past two of the women, and in the break I could see a man sitting down, his leg in plaster. Andrew reached back past the wall of women who had closed around him and guided me through. My first impression was of a foppish young man, more of a boy really. He was tall, or would have been if he was standing up, with broad shoulders but a slightness of build that indicated it would take a few more years yet for him to fill out completely. His leg was encased in a cast to the knee, which was propped awkwardly on a stool. His chestnut brown hair flopped into his eyes, and he pushed it away distractedly.

From his fresh face, I guessed his age at around twenty-one, probably two or three years younger than me. He had preppy, particularly English good looks, with rosy cheeks and soft hair. The amused expression in his eyes, though, was too old for his face and spoke of devilish deeds done in the name of "fun," and the swarms of women around him screamed "spoiled and privileged." It may have been wrong to take an instant dislike and assume all these things, but I did.

"Jack, this is Katherine Winters. Kate, Jack Preedy, our host."

"Pleased to meet you," I said politely, holding out my hand. He took it awkwardly and, instead of shaking it, planted a wet kiss on the back of my fingers. I swore I could feel a bit of tongue. I pulled away quickly, putting my hands behind my back so I could surreptitiously wipe my fingers on the back of my dress. If I hadn't already decided within the first two seconds, this would have confirmed it. Even if someone was good-looking and had an amazing house, they could still be definitely not my type. Too young, too indulged, and with a weird hand-kissing thing. I generally liked my men a bit tougher as well as older (even Andrew was a bit of a departure for me, and he could have taken Jack with his eyes closed). I know it is a bit primitive to look for that in a man; besides, it's not like I was living in a cave and surviving on my ability to forage either, but the body wants what it wants.

"Welcome! Please help yourself to a drink. I'd get you one myself, but I'm a bit incapacitated at the moment," Jack said with what he probably thought was an endearingly self-deprecating grin and indicated his leg.

"Is it broken?" I asked, attempting to summon up some sympathy. Maybe he was on painkillers that were affecting his behavior and he didn't usually lick people's hands. I was a guest, after all, so I shouldn't be bad mannered, no matter how tempting.

"Yes. Stupid pedestrian walked out onto the road without looking and made me crash my bicycle to avoid him. Maybe I should sue. Andrew tells me you're a lawyer? You could take my case. It is a ridiculous place to have a crossing." Wow, this guy just got better and better!

"I'm not that sort of lawyer," I said, not sure what else to say. At that moment, a beautiful dark-haired waif model-type came up and threw her arms around him, giving him a big smacking kiss on the lips. I took that as a sign the conversation was over and made my escape, heading off toward the drinks table with Andrew following.

"What would you like?" he asked, catching up with me.

"Gin and tonic please."

He ordered and collected our drinks from the bartender and introduced me to some people. The afternoon wore on, people getting more inebriated and consequently more guests ending up in the pool. Andrew kept us both well-supplied and very mellow.

"Fancy a swim?" Andrew asked.

"Sure." I smiled, pleasantly buzzed. This party was far more fun than I had thought it would be. Despite the location, no one seemed pretentious, and all the people I spoke to were lovely.

"I'll go get the bags and meet you in the pool house."

I took the opportunity to use the bathroom before he returned, but the door was locked when I tried the handle. After waiting for ages, I was about to go and look for another one when the door opened and Jack hobbled out, followed by the waif, who was adjusting her clothing. *Classy*, I thought. Smiling at them both, I entered the bathroom and closed the door behind me. "With the entire house at your disposal," I muttered, "why would you have sex in a bathroom?" I shrugged mentally. *Better than the bushes, maybe.* Bathrooms didn't do much for me, but to each their own.

I met back up with Andrew, who was waiting outside when I came out, and we went into the change rooms provided. I wriggled into my white one-piece suit with a plunging V-neck and twisted my hair up into a knot, securing it with a bar clip. Grabbing the towel from my bag and draping it over one arm, I went to meet up with Andrew. His stunned expression at seeing me in my swimming costume was a reminder of how camouflaging work clothes can be. He clearly hadn't expected the large breasts that were well-concealed in our ultra-conservative work environment and hadn't been particularly obvious from the sundress I wore earlier. The swimming costume lifted and enhanced rather than hid, so they looked like something out of a men's magazine. I'm not a hermit, though, and sometimes it's fun to show off what you've got, and I hadn't thought about it being in front of someone from work. Still, it's not like Andrew was my boss or this was the office Christmas party. He recovered fairly quickly, though he struggled to raise his eyes from my chest as we returned to the party. *At least he's definitely heterosexual,* I thought with a wince. (Every girl made that mistake at least once, and it was one particular university "experience" I was not planning on repeating. Unrequited love may fuel the creative process for the philosophers and poets, but it doesn't help the law students. I nearly failed that semester.)

Andrew dove straight in and swam efficiently to the other end, showing off a good swimming style. Goose bumps raced up my leg from the first step into the water, so clearly I hadn't had enough to drink. Everyone else was seemingly oblivious to the temperature and splashed about happily. Unwilling to seem the soft Antipodean unable to stand the cold, I forced myself to get into the water, clamping down on the high-pitched squeal wanting to escape as I went in up to my shoulders. I swam around for a while, hoping my body would adjust and it would no longer feel cold, but to no avail. After ten minutes, I was completely numb and gave up and raced for my towel, huddling gratefully in its warmth. I looked around for Andrew and saw him by the side of the pool, talking to Jack, who was sitting with his good leg dangling in the water. He looked comfortable, unlike me, and both of them held drinks in their hands, which Jack was topping up from the bottle of whisky sitting on the other side of him. Cold, I went inside for a shower to warm up and change back into my clothes.

It was a while before I got back to the party, and I couldn't see Andrew anywhere. I asked a few people I had met earlier, but no one could tell me where they had last seen him except by the side of the pool where I had seen him last too. I assumed that he'd possibly gone for a shower now, as they were all occupied, and I would see him when he got out. Food was being served at the buffet that had been set up, and I followed the other guests to get dinner. I started chatting and lost track of time for a bit. It was getting dark, and Andrew still hadn't emerged, so I went to look for him. He wasn't in the change rooms or the pool. I was about to search the surrounding gardens when I ran into Jack.

"Hi! Have you seen Andrew?" I asked. "I haven't seen him in a while."

"No, but he was drinking pretty heavily, though, so…I'll help you look for him."

"It's okay. You probably have people you need to talk to. I can have a look for him." He was hobbling around on crutches, so he wasn't the most obvious person to enlist in a search party.

"Nonsense! It's the least I can do, Kate," he said, his smile charming though slightly smug. Not sure why he had the cat-that-got-the-cream look about him, I shrugged. I didn't want to waste any time wondering what was going on in his mind. We searched the gardens, calling out Andrew's name. We stumbled on a few people in the bushes, much to my embarrassment and Jack's amusement, before finding Andrew passed out in the rose garden.

"Oh dear," I said, looking him over and wondering how to extract him from the thorny plants. He was out cold and had a few scratches on his face and arms, though not as many as I would have thought, given he was still only wearing his swimming trunks.

"He never could drink whisky." Jack shook his head and smirked. Then he hobbled over to the pool house to call the main house and returned shortly. After a few minutes, a man came to help. Without any introduction and only the briefest of nods to me, we each took one of Andrew's legs and pulled. Then he took the heavier end under Andrew's shoulders while I took his legs, and together we carried him into the house and up the stairs to the first floor.

Concentrating on not falling over while supporting half of Andrew, I didn't pay attention to where we were going. Jack led the way to a room which I think was halfway down the upper left-hand hallway, and we plonked him on the bed. The silent man nodded again and left. I looked around the reasonably-sized room, which was furnished with gleaming dark-wood furniture and deep blues.

"We should get him out of his wet costume," I said, but I made no move to do it.

"Surely you'd be the best person to do that?" Jack said, looking at me inquiringly.

"No, not really. This is as close to naked as I've ever seen him," I said bluntly.

"I haven't seen him naked since we were at school and have no ambition to ever do so again," Jack said with a laugh.

"Wet swimmers are the least of it. Maybe we should spare him the embarrassment of waking up without them." His hangover was going to hurt, and he'd probably have some memory loss, so waking up naked was bound to freak him out, even if there turned out to be a completely innocent explanation.

"Good point. It's not like they're still wet anyway," he agreed. With that, I pulled the covers over him and followed Jack out of the room.

"Andrew said there would be a room for me?" I asked hopefully.

"Yes, yours is the one at the end of the hallway." He indicated the door four down from Andrew's.

"Well, thank you for having me to stay. I might bring our bags up now. I'm sure Andrew will want his in the morning."

"Don't bother yourself with that. I'll ask Daniels. Come." I had no idea who that was, but he had already hobbled off, and to prevent getting myself lost, I followed. He moved surprisingly fast on his crutches. We were just coming down the wide main stairs when we passed the butler.

"Daniels!" he called out.

"Yes, sir?" the man asked impassively.

"Could you please arrange to get Miss Winters' bag from the pool house and take it to the blue room? Get Andrew's too, if you will. He's in the first bachelor room. What do they look like?" he asked me. I gave a brief description of our bags.

"Very well, sir, madam." Daniels bowed slightly and walked off.

"Now, let's have a drink without everyone bothering us so I can get to know you better."

"Lovely," I murmured, wondering when that became my default response. For some reason, Jack didn't seem that keen to get back to the party. He led us into the library, which was on the ground floor and down another long hallway. It was a large and luxurious room, softly lit by scattered table lamps. Beautiful leather-bound books in gleaming wood bookshelves encased the room on all sides. Paintings of graceful people reclining or looking into the distance adorned the spaces between the books and over the fireplace.

We sunk down into the opposite ends of a deep pillowy couch covered in a red stripy fabric. Jack hefted his injured leg up onto the pouf covered with a different, though tonally similar, floral material. I looked around the room at the tables full of knickknacks and framed photographs, amazed that nothing matched but produced a busy-but-harmonious effect. Nothing like the polished minimalism of my parents' home in Sydney.

"So, what's your poison? Wine, whisky, port?" he asked.

"I'll drink anything. Bit of a lush that way," I replied, only half-joking.

"Whisky it is." He raised himself again, clattered off to one of the cupboards, and returned very efficiently with a bottle and two glasses, gripped precariously in the fingers he could spare from the crutches.

"Well done," I said, indicating his balancing act.

"Glad you're impressed." He sat back down and poured us a dram each. "Bottoms up." He shotted it. I shrugged and did the same.

We talked of inconsequential things and kept drinking. It turned out he was older than I had first thought and had just finished his degree in Physics at Oxford and was interviewing for jobs in merchant banking in London. He had one sibling, a younger brother who was in his final year at Harrow. Before long, the conversation became more philosophical and intimate. He revealed that his choice of degree and subsequent career were solely to keep his parents happy.

"*One must study a discipline, not a vocation!*" he said in a high voice, imitating someone who sounded a bit like the Queen.

"But you were able to choose what you studied?"

"It was that or Geography."

"That was your only choice? What about universities? Surely you could pick that?"

"No, it was Oxford or nothing," he said with a shake of his head.

"If you could have done anything, what would you have done?" I asked curiously.

He looked at me, thinking.

"No idea." He shrugged. "Why think about something that's not even an option?" Beneath the posh and careless manner, in odd moments, there was a flash of deep sadness which intrigued me, though his flirting was a bit heavy-handed.

"I liked your swimsuit," he said, raising his eyebrows suggestively, but the evenness of his smile took away some of the leering.

"I didn't realize you'd even seen me. I wasn't in for long. It was way too cold!"

"I don't think there was a man there who missed it. Some of the girls were looking too."

"They're just breasts," I said dryly. "I don't see what all the fuss is about."

"It's not just the breasts; it's the whole package. Great legs, beautiful face, tall. You could be Elle McPherson's younger, better-looking sister. You could be a model."

Hmm…Why was it guys thought all women wanted to be told they could be a model? Clearly I wasn't, and I wasn't deluded enough to believe I had simply been overlooked by model scouts all these years. I knew I was tall, but I was nowhere near narrow enough to have been an actual model. Besides, this was the nineties, and the waif look was in. Kate Moss I was not.

"Right, and you're also forgetting that my date got so drunk, he passed out in the bushes at the start of the night. Apparently, my company was not very riveting," I said ruefully, deciding to not take issue with the model comment. I simply couldn't be bothered explaining why it was a stupid thing to say when he obviously thought it was a compliment.

"I don't know what Andrew's problem is, but it's not you." He waved his hand dismissively. "I'm just glad to have you alone so I don't have to fight off the admiring hordes to talk to you."

"That's very flattering and all, but what about your girlfriend? Won't she be looking for you?"

"Not my girlfriend, just someone I see sometimes. Nothing serious."

Nice! He had a fuck-buddy. I wondered if she thought it was as casual as he did. I was betting not. Still, it was none of my business; I wasn't trying to date him.

"Um, you should probably get back to the party. Your guests will be wondering where you are," I said, putting my glass down and moving to rise.

"No, stay," he said softly, his hand on my arm. "Everyone is enjoying themselves, and they don't need me there for that. I can't even dance with my leg in the cast. I have to rely on everyone coming to talk to me, or I'd be left there on my own. At least here I'm comfortable, and I'm sure you're too polite to leave me on my own." He looked at me pointedly.

I was stuck, unless I wanted to put up a fuss or could think of a plausible excuse. For want of a good reason to leave, I ended up talking to Jack until four in the morning.

Chapter Three

Jack started turning up in my life while at the same time Andrew completely disappeared from it. After a tense and silent drive back from the party, he no longer came to my desk to chat and averted his eyes if I ran into him at work. I figured he was embarrassed by what happened and seeing me reminded him of it. I tried to talk to him, but he clearly didn't want to be anywhere near me. It bothered me a bit, but I let it go as I couldn't force him to talk to me, and Jack was soon taking up all my free time and headspace anyway.

"Come with me, Katie. You're the only thing that will make it bearable. Otherwise I will be terribly bored," he complained, playing with my fingers as we sat in the café, waiting for our lunch.

"But I feel like I'm taking advantage of you. You take me to all these great places, and we're not even together."

"I *like* spending time with you."

"Everyone thinks we're dating."

"I don't care what they think. We know we're friends, and that's what matters. You're my best female friend, and I'd rather take you and have fun than someone else who bores me to tears and whose mother is whispering in her ear, trying to marry us off." His fingers tightened around my hand, and his gaze was just slightly too intense.

"Okay." I squeezed his hand back. It seemed we were touching a lot, but it didn't feel weird. I was a tactile person, and he was too. *It didn't mean anything*, I assured myself and anyone else who would listen.

We went to the Chelsea Flower Show, Wimbledon, Henley Royal Regatta, Glyndebourne, Glorious Goodwood, and Cowes Week. There didn't seem to be a social event that we didn't go to. Jack provided an entry that I would never, ever have been accorded on my own. I felt guilty about going, even though he insisted that I was doing him the favor by accompanying him. It wasn't that I didn't like Jack; I did, but part of me wasn't sure what we were doing. We were friends, but closer than that, seeing each other almost every day. He kept asking me to things, not taking no for an answer. He didn't push things on a physical level, which I was expecting, and that threw me off balance.

Then August came around, and I received a crash course in hunting and shooting. Culturally, England and Australia are not dissimilar, but Jack found it mind-boggling that I had never done these things and that they weren't organized activities back home. The only time I'd been hunting was on a friend's farm when we were teenagers, and we literally just grabbed some guns and went walking. I didn't see any wild boar (thankfully) or shoot anything apart from a large tree. The English system seemed far more involved, though only nine people, usually men, actually shot at things. Everyone else was along for the more casual Friday night and formal Saturday night dinners and a relaxing and fun weekend. Well, that was the theory.

The first time was a lesson in humiliation.

The Friday night dinner was fairly casual and largely unremarkable. The next day was horrific. Only the men were shooting, so everyone else was floating around the house for the day. It was raining, so lunch was served inside. I was one of the first to arrive, so I sat down at one end. After ten minutes, the other women turned up and, seeing me, pointedly sat at the other end of the table. No one even spoke to me, and I felt like *that* kid at school, the one who, for no particular reason, gets treated like a leper.

I had that same tightness in my chest and slightly sick feeling in my stomach that I associated with the excruciating self-awareness of my teenage years, where every social contact was fraught with embarrassment and endless possibilities for recriminations and self-loathing. I took a deep breath, reminding myself that I was no longer an awkward teen who didn't make new friends easily. I was a lawyer, damn it, which was more than these spoiled princesses had ever managed to achieve. They faffed around, playing at working as PR girls or legal secretaries. They came in late, went for a smoke, and generally believed they were there solely for decoration, biding their time until they married one of the men they knew.

I looked over at their leader, Caroline Pennington-Smyth, a skinny, Sloane Ranger-styled heavily-streaked blonde who had known Jack since they were born. They had grown up going to each other's country houses for holidays. The other girls with her were just variations of the same, with fluctuating degrees of horsiness. They had grown up in the same areas, gone to the same schools, and families interbred so much they could have been cousins. *Probably were*, I thought bitchily.

I had met Caroline once before at a night out at the Builders' Arms in Chelsea, but we hadn't really spoken much, apart from the introduction. Something about her dismissive manner, however, alerted me to the fact that we wouldn't be buddying up any time soon even then. She caught me looking at her and returned the look disdainfully. Addressing her best friend, Olympia, she spoke with deliberate rudeness.

"I'm all for travel, darling, but there's something to be said for leaving your Aussie adventures where you found them." The other girls tittered with laughter, encouraging her.

"Jack's always had a weakness for fast food. He's just extending it to fast women now." Ha, ha. So frigging witty.

It went on, but I refused to give her the satisfaction of reacting.

"Oh, no, she's looking a bit constipated. Maybe she needs to go to the *toilet* before *dessert* is served." *Hilarious, she should be a comedienne*, I thought.

I could have handled being ignored and insulted, but their behavior after the men returned was even worse. I declined every invitation after that one.

"Kaaatieeee, why won't you come to Kent this weekend?" Jack asked pleadingly, his arm across my shoulders as we sat snuggled up watching television on my couch one night. He always smelled so good, and I surreptitiously turned my head to bring my nose closer to his arm. He wore a clean-smelling cologne, and underneath was a slightly musky male smell that was particular to him.

"You were there the last shooting weekend I came to, weren't you?" I asked sarcastically, my lips brushing the skin of his arm as I spoke. "Absolutely no way."

"I'm sorry about Caroline. She's just a bit possessive at times. She has no reason to be, though!" he added hastily, twining his fingers in mine and lifting them to his lips. The simple gesture caused a fluttering in my stomach, and I struggled to keep from being distracted.

"She refused to speak to me the whole weekend, just insulted me constantly so I could hear it, particularly about your propensity for 'low' women." Actually, none of the other women there had spoken to me either, though none of the others had had the overt hostility exhibited by Caroline, either.

"She's a bit insecure, that's all. Her grandfather had to buy their estate, so she's a bit more worried about all that new money/old money palaver. Plus, their family was from the North." I had only a vague understanding what he meant by that, and the greater part of me just didn't want to know. The English class system made my head hurt.

"What am I? *No* money?" I asked wryly.

"You're Australian. That means that you're outside it all," he said, waving it off. But that wasn't my only issue. The girls all spoke to the boys in a really flirty way, which I found particularly disturbing.

"Okay. So, why do Caroline and Olympia act like they are coming on to all the guys?" I named the two worst offenders. "I realize they've dated pretty much everyone at some point, but the excessive touching and suggestive comments seems a bit inappropriate."

"It's just the way they are. It doesn't mean anything," he said dismissively.

"But how would you know if they actually like you, if they do it with everyone?" I asked, genuinely interested.

Jack laughed.

"You don't. Everyone drinks a lot, and then you hope for the best!" he said flippantly. I had already learned that they all got drunk together and hooked up, and after three years they had all slept with each other at some stage. Cheating was rife, and you could pick the former couples by the lingering awkwardness between them. From what Jack told me, rumors of cheating would fly around, and then one of the friends would have to tell the person, who would confront their partner, who in turn would deny it, but they usually broke up anyway.

"But surely it causes a lot of problems? What if someone misinterpreted it?"

"It can be a bit confusing, but that's why I prefer you. I know where I stand, and it's refreshing." He leaned over and gave me a kiss on the lips, which was enough to get me off the topic and on to what the hell I was doing with Jack.

His lips on mine were firm and playful, but not demanding. He pushed me onto my back on the couch, lying on top of me, his weight taken on his forearms. He raised our entwined fingers above my head, pinning me there lightly, as his tongue entered my mouth to play with mine. Long slow kisses until I was wet and ready, but he just kept up the tormentingly leisurely pace. We kept kissing for hours, and it was wonderful but confusing as it didn't go any further. When we reached the point where we were both breathing hard, he stopped and, rolling over, hugged me to his chest. I would have thought he wasn't interested, but the evidence that he was could be felt clearly against my leg.

This repeated every time we hung out, which was often.

I had put him in the "non-boyfriend" pile when we first met, and it's hard to make the move to the "relationship material" pile without something major happening to make you reassess. He was still largely who I thought he was at the start, though better company and more fun than I had given him credit for. However, I wasn't sure I wanted his life. The stately homes and social events were fun at first, but the enjoyment I had was ebbing as I saw more of the dark underside of it. The bright glossy exterior was just that: the surface. Underneath was bitchiness, desperation, and a rigidity that bordered on brittle.

They guarded their perceived positions so fiercely it seemed like they might just snap at the slightest breeze. Only Jack's foot in the door kept it from closing on me entirely. I might have had Jack on my side, but would that be enough? I had no friends amongst them, and I despaired that I ever would. He wouldn't be glued to my side the whole time we were with them, and that left me with a whole lot of alone time. The other part I didn't enjoy was the lack of privacy. Everything we did was observed and noted. There were always people around—friends, family, and staff. The only time I could relax was when we were at my flat, when I knew no one was watching.

Despite the fact that he wasn't what I thought I wanted, and all the reasons I should run a mile from his scary friends, I found myself looking forward to seeing him, calling him to tell him funny or absurd things that happened in my day, and slowly sharing things that let you know without a doubt you are in a relationship. Or would be, but now I was unsure about what he wanted. We shared so much of our lives — not even one's closest friends needed that much detail — but something held us both back from going that next step.

So, I seemed to be in a quasi-platonic relationship with Jack. We would kiss, but that's it. I hadn't pushed for anything more, not sure if I wanted it to go any further, but he would be angling for it, right? That's what guys did. I was so confused. Maybe he shared my ambivalence. It was strange kissing someone, enjoying it, but not sure. I wanted him, but only if we were on a desert island and all the rest of the surrounding stuff wasn't there. It was as though I wanted to push him away equally as much as I wanted to draw him closer.

If I thought he had given up about shooting weekends, I was mistaken. Any refusal to Jack seemed to just be a starting point for further negotiations.

"Come to Wiltshire this weekend," he urged the following week. "There's only a few of us so you can shoot if you want to."

I thought about it. I had sworn I would never go to one of those things again, but if I wasn't stuck in the house with the other women all day, the weekend might just be bearable. As if he could sense my wavering, Jack dropped to his knees at my feet and raised his entwined hands in the classic begging position.

"Please?" he entreated. "I'll make sure you have fun. *Please!*"

"All right," I said with a sigh, reneging on my vow that the first one would be my last. Jack jumped up and gave me a big kiss, his tongue suddenly invading my mouth. I was just starting to get into it when he pulled away and, laughing, gave me a smack on the rump. Jack really wanted me to come, and these things were obviously part of his life and more important than I had initially realized. I was increasingly aware that it was part of Jack's package. If I wasn't willing to make the hard decision to cut Jack out of my life, then I needed to make an effort with this and with his friends.

On the drive down, Jack issued almost non-stop instructions while I drove.

"Remember, Katie, you are not here to massacre the wildlife. Shooting is about enjoying the sport and providing food."

"Great, thanks. I needed some more pressure." I already had nervous cramping in my stomach. I was a pretty good shot, as long as it was a tin can sitting on a fence. I'd never tried to shoot something alive and moving.

"Never point your gun, whether it's loaded or not, at anyone else. When you're walking in line, or standing at your peg, keep your barrels high in the air or pointed directly at the ground."

"Got it."

"Only load your gun just before you're going to shoot. This is going to be a driven day, so wait for the signal that the drive has started before loading. When you're aiming, don't ever swing the barrels through the line of guns and make sure you know where everybody else is. Never shoot in a direction that could potentially endanger anyone else."

"Don't shoot other people. Got it," I answered, keeping my voice serious. Jack looked at me and rolled his eyes before continuing his lecture.

"Don't stand with the gun over your arm horizontally, and make sure it's broken before you hand it to someone else. Check that the barrels are clear before loading the gun, and never keep mixed-caliber cartridges in your pockets. Putting a twenty-bore cartridge into a twelve-bore and then placing another twelve-bore cartridge over the top of it is one of the most common shooting accidents. You could kill yourself or lose a few fingers. It happens every year."

"Try not to blow myself up. Check."

Jack smiled despite himself. "It's mostly common sense. Everyone knows that you haven't done this before, and I'll be there with you to make sure you don't do anything dangerous."

"You don't think a bunch of people with loaded guns is inherently dangerous?"

"Not if you're careful," he said sternly.

"Just for the birds," I muttered to myself. I did have a few qualms about shooting things. I hadn't grown up with it, so it wasn't something I thought of as a normal activity. On the other hand, I ate meat frequently, and the conditions in a chicken farm were much worse. These birds grew up in the forest, being fed by gamekeepers and kept in good condition, unlike those poor birds in cages with no room to move. Still, I didn't have to kill the chicken I ate, so there was that deniability there. I didn't know if I could actually do it, though I didn't say that to Jack, who I don't think would have understood.

Lost in my anxiety, I didn't see the pheasant crossing the road until after I hit it with the car. Turned out my first kill happened before I'd even loaded a gun.

"Oh my God!" I braked the car as colorful feathers fluttered up over the windscreen.

"That happens. They're not the brightest bird." Jack shook his head sadly. "Don't worry; we can clean the car when we get there." I just looked at him for a moment, wondering which planet I had landed on.

Dinner that night was actually fun. Caroline and Olympia were fortunately absent, and the others seemed less hostile in their absence. There was a new girl there, or rather, she was new to me. Like all the other girls, Margaret or "Bats," had gone to school at Roedean and had known all the boys there since they were children. She had studied at Oxford with Jack too, though they seemed to act more like brother and sister, with none of the over-the-top flirting the other girls employed. Bats was undeniably beautiful in that traditional English rose sort of way. Blond, peaches and cream complexion, and of a build so slim she could have been part elf. She was also very matter-of-fact and swore like a sailor.

"Hello, sluts!" she greeted us. I was so shocked I nearly spilled my drink on the antique rug. She approached me immediately.

"You must be Kate. Jack's told me all about you. Don't worry; I don't think you're a slut. It's funny because, frankly, none of us are getting any at all," she finished in a low voice.

"Oh!" I laughed, liking that she'd explained the joke. "I took you literally, but probably because I have quite a few friends who've lost count of the number of men they've slept with."

"Really?" Her eyebrows moved half way up her forehead. "Great! I need some pointers. Come sit with me." She grabbed my hand and dragged me to the couch with her. I think I spent the night gasping like a fish, amazed by the language coming out of her mouth, but laughing like I hadn't since I'd moved to London.

I think the turning point with my relationship with Jack happened that weekend. I acquitted myself reasonably well during the shoot. I hadn't endangered myself or anyone else, and the only bird I shot died cleanly, so I counted it as a victory, particularly as I did it with my eyes closed. During the formal dinner, Jack was in his usual good form, charming and funny. Maybe it was just that it was a smaller group, or the fact that the men were wearing their smoking jackets and slippers, which made them look a bit Playboy mansion-ish and less intimidating than in their formal black tie, but I found myself relaxing and thinking that one day it might be possible for me to feel like I belonged here.

Bats seemed to make a special effort to talk to me and be friendly, and the other women took their cue from her. I stopped feeling like a complete outsider, floundering to understand the nuances of behavior that everyone else took for granted. Things seemed to click into place, and I got the jokes, and other people got mine too. I looked at Jack and smiled, admitting to myself that I wanted him to be my boyfriend. I had moved him into the right pile, even though it had taken me a while to realize it. There was just one thing that made me hesitate.

"Have you and Bats ever hooked up?" I asked as we went up to our separate rooms.

"No." He laughed. "Though not through lack of trying on my part when we were about fourteen. Mind you, I was so horny I tried any girl standing still long enough. Bats is like the sister I never had."

Jack cornered me as we reached my door and, putting his arms on either side of me, started to kiss me breathless. He broke off only at the sound of voices nearby. Giving me a last lingering kiss, he smiled and walked backward until he reached his room further down the hallway. I laughed as I closed my door.

Chapter Four

Three weeks later, our relationship took an unexpected step forward at the end of one of one of our daily telephone conversations. Not thinking, it just slipped out.

"See you tomorrow night," I said. "Love you, bye."

"You love me?"

Embarrassed, I could feel my face going red. There was silence as I fumbled for something to say. Did I mean it? It hadn't been intentional, but was it true nonetheless?

"Ah, um…" I stammered, unsure.

"That's nice," he said, laughter in his voice. *Nice? Ugh, well, I definitely wasn't going to confirm it now!* I decided to just pretend it didn't happen. Denial was underrated for situations like this.

"Okay, well, see you later!" I said feigning chirpiness and hanging up quickly. I banged my head on my desk with a surprisingly loud thunk. *Oh, God, how mortifying!* I thought.

I saw him the next night, and, thankfully, he didn't bring it up. As we said good night, he asked me to his house again.

"Come and have dinner with my parents. We'll stay, make a weekend of it," he suggested.

"I'm not sure I'm ready to meet your parents," I said doubtfully. Jack hadn't exactly responded in kind to my slip, but yet he seemed keen to fast-forward things. We hadn't even slept together yet, and he wanted to introduce me to his family?

"Come on; it'll be fun," he encouraged, looking at me hopefully before shaking his head and continuing laughingly. "Well, maybe not *fun*. It will probably be a bit of a chore, but still they want to meet you. Plus, my brother is home for the weekend so you'll get to meet him too. Two-for-one!"

"Why would your parents want to meet me?" I asked, puzzled that his parents even knew of my existence.

"Because I've had to tell them why I'm spending so much time in London. My mother's started to drop hints that you don't exist and that I'm making you up."

"I'm not so sure. I'm hardly the type of girl they'd approve of," I said, bearing in mind the sort of girl Jack told me they had been trying to set him up with, mostly Caroline and her ilk. His mother seemed to be fairly fixed in ideas of the attributes of anyone Jack should be dating, and I'm not sure I fulfilled even one, except maybe the gender. "Why are you so keen for me to meet them? It makes me think that you're just seeing me to annoy them." I watched him closely to see if he reacted.

"You're a tall, beautiful, and smart Australian. What's not to hate?" he joked, giving nothing away.

Unfortunately, he was right. His mother detested me on sight.

Jack's parents were out when we arrived, so we decided to wait in the informal sitting room and were playing cards when they came back. We heard them come in the front door, but it was almost an hour later before Jack's brother came to join us. We looked up at the sound of the door opening, and a gangly body followed.

"Crispin!" Jack rose from his chair with a smile and approached his brother. He went to hug him but awkwardly stopped when Crispin stuck out a hand. They then reversed actions in a weirdly amusing dance. Finally, they seemed to settle on a "man-hug" where they sort of thumped each other across the back.

"Crispin, come and meet Kate." He drew Crispin back across the room, and I stood as they approached. Crispin was around my height with unruly blond hair and spots. I tried to see some resemblance between the two brothers but failed. Jack was taller and broader, though Crispin was likely still growing. Beneath the pimples, Crispin's face was rounder, and he would probably always be baby-faced, while Jack was more angular.

"Nice to meet you," I said as I smiled at Crispin. He looked at me through his hair and mumbled something. I just assumed it was a similar greeting.

"How is school?" Jack asked.

"Okay…boring," Crispin answered with a grimace.

"What are you going to do next year?"

"Don't know…whatever…same as you, I guess. It will keep Mummy happy." He shrugged.

"Hmm…yes."

"Is there something else you'd rather do?" I blurted out.

"Umm…yeah, but *she* wouldn't go for it, so there's no point." Crispin and Jack shared a look. I didn't really understand why they couldn't just do what they wanted, but they didn't volunteer anything else. Luckily, I didn't open my mouth to question them further because, at that moment, their mother finally swept in, and I started to understand.

Jack's mother wasn't a tall woman, but what she lacked in height she made up for in barely controlled ferocity. Her graying brown hair was waved and set into a Margaret Thatcher-like coiffeur, her plump body swathed in a blue and green tartan kilt and matching green wool jumper with a white round lace-collared shirt underneath. Stockings and navy court shoes completed the ensemble. Her whole demeanor was reminiscent of the Queen, if one could imagine the Queen as a not-so-benevolent dictator.

When she saw me, her brows drew together in displeasure, and I had the sudden image of an angry Persian cat pop into my head. I felt the corners of my mouth turn up and I had to use every bit of willpower I had not to giggle. I knew even then that laughing at Edwina would not be good for my health. In all the years after, I could take some comfort from this first meeting. She disliked me before I had uttered a word, so her later vindictiveness could not have been personal as she knew me not at all. She hated me for what I was, not who I was, and nothing I did would ever have changed that.

"Good afternoon," she said, managing to peer down her nose, even though she had to look up, and made even that simple greeting sound scornful, as if I had soiled the rug at her feet.

"Hello, Lady Preedy," I replied. "Thank you for having me to stay for the weekend." I smiled blandly, not sure how to deal with such instant, overt hostility. Most people at least made an attempt to fake friendliness for a bit first.

"Yes," she said with a sniff. "We do encourage Jack to have people to stay to keep him entertained." Her voice was loaded with disapproval, though I wasn't sure at what. That Jack needed "entertaining"? That she would need to specify what sort of people he brought next time, because clearly I wasn't the "right" type, even for entertainment purposes?

"Hello, I'm Arthur." Jack's father was an older version of Jack, a tall, thin man with a beautiful thatch of gray hair, with a perfectly bald circle at the back. He smiled at me warmly until he caught Edwina's eye. His smile disappeared, and he moved away quickly to the drinks cabinet where he poured himself a large whisky in a crystal tumbler. Those were the only words he spoke all night, though occasionally he would give me an absentminded wink, though that might have been just a facial tick, I couldn't be sure.

After that, I was largely ignored by Edwina. Throughout the formal dinner, most of her comments were addressed to Jack, Crispin, or the staff, and occasionally her husband, though he rarely replied. I think he had tuned her out and simply didn't register that she was speaking to him, as she talked so much and most of it was complete drivel. Minute details of gardening things or long convoluted stories about people I didn't know. Her soliloquies had so many tangents that I was utterly confused.

"You know Helen, of course. She was married to Paul for years, and they lived in the old vicarage near the river. Shoddy builder, though, who did their renovations. He went out of business shortly after, and they couldn't get him to fix the problems. That's the difficulty with thatch rooves. So many of the old places used to have them, and now the blasted heritage people want everyone to put them back as they were. Great business to get into; there's no one around here doing it since old Mr. Smith went into the retirement. His back was gone, though his daughter…"

I think it was actually impossible to follow what she was saying, and as no one else seemed to even be trying, I gave up. Jack, Crispin, and their father appeared to be in a competition as to who could be the most silent while consuming an enormous amount of alcohol. Even Edwina would have drunk the best part of a bottle of wine over dinner, not that it slowed her down or cheered her up.

Rather than drive us apart, as I'm sure was the intention, Edwina's hostility toward me brought us closer together. Jack became protective whenever she came near, shielding me whenever possible. We snuck off, giggling, when we heard her coming, hiding out in spare rooms and cupboards to avoid her. It was childish but surprisingly fun.

Saturday afternoon, Jack was showing me around the beautiful gardens, resplendent in the autumnal colors, when we heard Edwina coming. Jack grabbed my hand and started running past the ornate stone and glass orangery to the more functional greenhouse.

We were hiding inside with Edwina striding around the gardens looking for us. I think she had seen us from a window and come rushing out, but we had managed to escape her before she caught us by slipping through the hedges and circling around. We were crouched low behind the oranges in their large pots, the scent of citrus mingling with the earthier underlying scent of the greenhouse. We heard her calling us, and Jack placed his hand over my mouth to quiet my laugh as she walked by right outside the window.

As her voice faded as she got further away, I looked over at him with laughing eyes, and he was suddenly serious. He slowly removed his hand and, closing his eyes, replaced it with his lips. We kissed slowly, exploring, something more serious than before. Jack was an excellent kisser, just enough passion to be exciting without being overwhelming, but this time he wasn't so tentative.

The build-up was slow enough that I could have objected to anything, if I wanted to. I decided that I didn't. Pulling us up so we were standing, he slowly slid his hand from my back, around the sides to the front of my white cotton shirt to cradle my breast. He ran his fingers lightly over my nipple, which contracted sharply. He played there for a moment before moving up to slowly undo each button. We stopped kissing and paused, looking at each other from only a few centimeters apart.

In answer to his silent question, I reached one hand behind his head, pulled him closer, and started kissing him again. He reached around and put his hands on my bottom, pulling me against him so I could feel the hardness in his pants against my belly. I arched my back to bring our contact closer. Breathing hard, he broke away and unrolled some turf onto the concrete floor before coming back to me and kissing me more urgently.

He guided me to the turf bed, and unbuttoning my shorts, I wiggled them and my underwear down my hips and off over my legs. I lay down and spread my legs for him, and he fumbled off his pants and underwear in his haste to answer my clear invitation. Then he was on me and in me, finally, and I let go, enjoying the sensation of having him inside me. After so long waiting, I was ready and about to combust. I felt the waves of pressure building at the feel of him until it surged suddenly to a peak of pleasure. I surrendered to it, and I felt him throb as he came, which prolonged my orgasm, the added intensity making me let out a short squeal. He groaned and thrust again, my contractions squeezing him. He groaned one last time and collapsed on top of me.

"Good God! That was amazing, woman," he whispered in my ear.

"Thank you," I responded, slightly smugly. "You weren't bad either." I kissed him lightly on the lips.

After that, Jack followed me around everywhere, pulling me into corners of the house to have his way with me, not that I minded. By the end of the weekend, I was slightly sore, and there were many fewer rooms in his parents' house that we had not had sex in. I think we were caught by some of the staff on occasion, but they tactfully withdrew and started knocking on every door before entering. I was a bit shocked, but Jack laughed it off, and none of the staff gave any indication that they were aware of anything. I couldn't help but admire their professionalism.

Jack finally found a job in London, doing something in banking, though I wasn't sure exactly what. Whatever it was, it didn't seem to take up a lot of time or require onerous hours. There was a bit of work he had to do on his own time at home, but he was still able to go out with friends until the early hours of the morning and either go straight to work or just go home for a quick shower and change. My job wasn't particularly hard, but I certainly wouldn't have been able to do it hung over and without sleep. Still, he was seemingly always available and constantly attentive, which was incredibly flattering. Although he nominally had his own place, he spent most of his time at mine as I lived alone now, Megan having moved in with her South African boyfriend.

Our relationship changed too as we became more familiar with each other on a physical level. Jack seemed to be interested in parts of my life that I wasn't used to a boyfriend delving into.

"Let's go shopping today, Katie," he announced one Saturday over breakfast.

"Huh?" I grunted, still not fully awake. He ruffled my sleepy head playfully.

"We go to so many parties for me, and I want to buy you something to say thanks."

"That's okay, really. I have a few black dresses which work for most of them."

"Ah…actually…don't take this the wrong way, but there have been some comments on how you wear the same thing all the time."

"What?" I spluttered, fully awake now. I was taken aback that it mattered what I wore, or that Jack was listening to snipy comments by those bitchy girls in his group. Since when do men care what you wear?

"It's not a big deal!" He waved his hands, backtracking. "I know it's stupid, but people pay attention to those things. Just let me help you out…"

"I don't need help with money," I answered, my tone frosty. "I have a perfectly good job. I just choose not to waste ridiculous sums of money on designer things that don't really suit me anyway."

"I'll help. We'll do it together," he pleaded. God, I really was embarrassing him, which was mortifying. I nodded, unable to speak at that moment.

Jack dragged me to Selfridges, and I submitted to the pressured shopping with as much grace as I could muster. I really didn't think I was a prime candidate for a makeover — it wasn't like anyone had complained about my style before. Admittedly, I was no fashionista, but I had always thought I was reasonably well put together, though I did run toward the simple and conservative. Jack produced outfit after outfit, all of which were the sort of things the other girls wore. I felt worse and worse with every change, as if I was stripping away layers of my personality with my clothes.

I realized I was being melodramatic. After all, they were just bits of material, and they would make me fit in better with Jack's friends, rather than shout my Sydney roots and my otherness. *Suck it up,* I told myself sternly. *How many women would kill to be in my position, shopping with their gorgeous boyfriend who wanted to buy them clothes?*

Jack sat happily on the couch outside the change room, smiling encouragingly when I emerged in a new outfit. I had to admit, the clothes didn't look bad; they just weren't what I would normally wear — velvet blazers with leather elbow patches, floaty silk dresses in pale pinks and creams, knitted vests, and way too many things with checks on them.

"That one is perfect!" he exclaimed as I emerged in a midnight-blue velvet evening gown.

"Really?" I asked skeptically.

"I'm buying it. I won't take no for an answer."

"Okay. Thanks!" I said, mustering a smile. I felt uneasy about this whole situation, but I also wasn't sure what I could do about it. I didn't want to offend Jack, and I wanted him to be happy, but still.

"We'll get that, the jacket and the black tailored pants, and the silk shirty thing. That will do for a start. How about a headband to match the jacket?" he asked.

I checked to see if he was joking. Unfortunately, he wasn't.

"Absolutely not," I said firmly. There were lines that I would never cross.

"Okay. But you need some pearls."

Swearing under my breath, I went back into the change room to put on my jeans.

"I can hear you!" he called out, amused.

We didn't buy the pearls, but they turned up as a gift the following week. I now had a Sloane Ranger uniform, but could I actually wear it out in public without feeling like I was dressed as someone else? That was the thousand-pounds-of-Jack's-money question.

"Have you ever thought about getting blond streaks?" Jack asked over dinner the following Saturday night. I was starting to see a bit of a pattern here.

"No, have you?" I shot back.

Jack laughed. "I thought everyone was getting them now," he replied conversationally.

"Not when you have hair as dark as mine. It would just look strange and skunk-like."

"Hmm," Jack murmured.

"Right," I said, rolling my eyes. Was I a fixer-upper for Jack? With a bit of renovation, could I be a better girlfriend? It's not like he had suggested anything too radical, but I wasn't used to a man who was this concerned with my appearance.

"Are you trying to change me?" I asked, deciding to be upfront about it.

"No!" He looked surprised. "I'm sorry. I think you're perfect. I just want to be interested in the things you're interested in. Don't girls talk about hair and clothes and stuff?"

"Yes, but not like that." I laughed, relieved my fears were unfounded. "It feels like you're trying to change me into a clone of the other girls in your group, and that's not who I am. It makes me question why you're with me when what you seem to want is one of them."

"I don't want one of them!" he shouted. "God, it would make my life easier if I did. I want you."

"Why?" Part of me was terrified to hear the answer, but this conversation was long overdue. "Why are you with someone who makes things difficult, particularly with your mother?"

"That's what's so fantastic about you; you're not with me because of all that. You actually look at me and see the person inside. Everyone else just seems to see the other stuff and my 'potential.'"

I sat there stunned, trying to take in what he said. It wasn't exactly romantic, but it did seem honest. He reached over and grabbed my hand, squeezing it.

"I'm sorry; I probably didn't say that right. But in my defense, I spent most of my formative years in boy's prison, fallaciously referred to as a school, so I don't really know what I'm doing with the whole relationship thing. I really am trying not to fuck things up with you. I love you."

My heart melted. "You're adorable." I kissed him gently, which now quickly led into other things.

We had been seeing each other for just over five months when we had "the talk." We were spending a lazy Sunday morning in my warm bed, reading our books, when he put his down and turned to face me. He pulled my book out of my hands and placed it on the bed and then put his head on the pillow next to mine and looked into my eyes.

"Hey! I was reading that!" I objected, trying to lean over him and retrieve it.

"What do you want out of this?" he asked. Surprised, I lay back down. His hand started stroking my stomach almost absentmindedly.

"What do I want out of what?" I asked, distracted by the movement of his hand and the randomness of the question.

"From us, from me." *Oh!* Now I knew where he was going.

"Um…I don't know. What do you want?" I hedged.

"I asked first."

"Do we need to do this?" There was more than a hint of pleading in my voice. I was still enjoying the lassitude that came from lying around in bed with him and not having to get up for work. I had a strong feeling this conversation would kill it off.

"Maybe I want to know," he said stubbornly.

"Okay. What specifically do you want to know?" I pushed myself up onto one elbow, resting my head on my hand.

"Are you going to leave to go back to Australia?"

"Well, yes," I said slowly, "but I still have a year left on my visa." I watched his face carefully.

"I don't want you to leave." He wrapped an arm around my waist and pulled me in closer so we were skin to skin.

"That's really sweet, but my work isn't sponsoring anyone at the moment and getting a visa on my own isn't easy. Also, I miss home a bit." I kissed him lightly on the lips.

"What about through me? We could move in together," he suggested.

I couldn't help but laugh at the thought of that, even though I was sure he meant it. "Your mother would have a fit! I'm pretty sure living with someone wouldn't be the 'done thing.'" Thinking of Edwina's reaction to my living in sin with her son was hilarious. I wondered if she would actually spontaneously combust. "You might be disinherited," I said teasingly.

"Why don't you marry me then?" he said, eyes sparkling. He had been playing with me before, intending to get to this question all along.

I looked at him closely, trying to see if he was joking. I half-expected him to grin and laugh and say "just kidding," but he didn't.

"We've only known each other for five months. Isn't that a bit soon?" I said carefully.

"I love you. I know you're the right woman for me, and I want to spend the rest of my life with you. You're incredible, and we're perfect for each other." He kissed me enthusiastically. "You make me happier than I've ever been before. Letting you leave would be unbearable." He grimaced playfully.

"I love you too," I said. I thought for a moment, going through the pros and cons. There were lots of pros, and the only cons were our age and the fact that we hadn't known each other for very long. That and we came from different countries and his mother hated me and so did most of the girls in his group of friends…I frowned as the list started getting longer. Despite all the reasons against it, if I listened to my gut, it felt right, strangely enough.

"But are you sure?" I asked, giving him an out if he hadn't really thought this through and had just made a spontaneous offer. This wasn't how I imagined being proposed to, but it was very Jack.

"Absolutely! Well, then, it's settled. Let's go buy a ring!" He jumped out of bed, full of boyish enthusiasm, pulling me laughing with him.

We were so young and in love, our blood full of fire and so incredibly hopeful. We decided to let Jack tell Edwina on his own, that way he could break it to her gently, and if she behaved badly, then at least I didn't have to witness it and she could get the excesses of her reaction out in a private setting, rather than explode in public.

Jack came over that night with a grim smile on his face.

"How did it go?" I asked after quickly kissing him hello.

"Better than expected, but not great." He sighed and flopped onto the couch. He ran both his hands through his hair, tugging the strands, which was a sure sign he was upset.

"How did she take it?" I asked carefully, sitting down next to him.

"Well, when I said I had asked you to marry me, she started suggesting alternatives. Like Caroline. And Sarah, the daughter of a friend of hers. When I reminded her that Sarah was gay, she ran through all my ex-girlfriends, pointing out how much more suitable they were. She seemed to have completely forgotten that she hated all of *them* when we were going out." He tried to laugh, but it came out desiccated.

"Oh." It wasn't unexpected, this realization of exactly how unwelcome I was in Edwina's eyes, but I thought she would have made an effort to make it easier for her son. I knew she didn't like me, but somehow I thought she might try to hide it, knowing I would be permanent. Strangely, it hurt.

"They'll come around. It was just a bit of a shock for them. She wants the wedding at the Hall, so if you agree to that, I'm sure you'll become her favorite person in no time!" he said, trying to foster enthusiasm but watching my face closely as he said it. I smiled wanly, not sure I wanted a big wedding organized by Edwina. Jack looked so unhappy at what should have been a joyful time that I just wanted him to be okay.

"Sure. Whatever it takes," I said, wrapping my arms around him in a big hug.

Chapter Five

2008

"Urgh," I groaned as I opened the door. "It can't be that time already!"

Bats smiled indulgently at me as she stepped through the front door. It has been said that to be truly happy, you must have a house in Markham Square in Chelsea. I'm not sure if that's true, but it certainly helps. My house was beautiful and gave me endless pleasure. Even when the heating went or the pipes needed replacing, I forgave it and loved it all the more.

"What's up with you?" She raised an eyebrow at me.

"I have baker's remorse." I looked at her dolefully, hoping she would take pity on me and let me out of our run.

"And what's that?" she asked, eyeing my un-sporty clothes. She was dressed ready for our scheduled jog, unlike me who was still in jeans and an old and comfy T-shirt.

"It's where you've forced loved ones and yourself to eat so much fat and sugar that you feel bad about it. I think I have a sugar hangover too," I said over my shoulder as we headed back into the kitchen.

"Are you serious?" She laughed.

"Absolutely. It feels just like a normal hangover, except you haven't drunk anything and have eaten your bodyweight in cake."

"Oh!" she said, still laughing. "Doesn't that rather go with the territory?" She looked around my house, which was in a bit of a state, or should I say more of a state than usual. I had never quite mastered the immaculate look and told myself it's because I actually preferred a "lived-in" aesthetic. "What happened here? Is your daily on holiday?"

"A woman shouldn't have to be responsible for a spotless house and her own orgasms. It's a question of available energy," I answered loftily. Bats merely quirked an eyebrow. "The boys were home, and I smothered them with food because I miss them so much." I made another sad face at her.

The twins had just started at Harrow after a long drawn out battle between Jack and myself. He had wanted them to start when they were eight, as he had done, but coming from an upbringing where that would only occur in the most unusual circumstances, I was firmly against it. Consequently, they had gone to Eton House after St. Luke's, and I reluctantly agreed to let them go to Harrow at thirteen, which was a much more complicated affair. It involved sitting for tests and interviews at the school to get them in on the last round. Jack was so happy, and the boys seemed excited, so I hid my unhappiness at losing them so soon.

There were still some weekends and school holidays with them, but they grew up so much in between each time I saw them that it felt like they were on fast-forward. I missed them more than I could express, and the house seemed too quiet without them. I even missed their vast quantities of laundry, but mostly I missed the boundless energy that flowed in their wake. I know it's stupid, but once I cleaned up their mess, it felt like I would be like erasing all traces of their visit. I just wanted to hold on a bit longer. I was having a Miss Haversham from *Great Expectations* moment. I completely got her perspective now.

"Isn't that why we're exercising?" Bats asked, bringing me back to the present.

"Yes, doesn't stop me feeling guilty about it, though. Nutritionists everywhere would be alarmed if they knew and would report me to the government as a health hazard."

"I can't speak for the children, but everyone else is a consenting adult, and they know the risks before they accept an invitation to sample your cooking. You know we all wait with baited breath, hoping to be chosen as guinea pigs."

"But you said no!"

Bats was always so disciplined with what she ate and couldn't have been more than a size six the entire time I had known her, except during her pregnancies when she gained less than ten kilos. She would literally only eat a single bite of anything vaguely unhealthy. There was a certain amount of pressure in our social group to remain thin. It was such a double standard, as most of the men were becoming rather portly while their wives struggled against slowing metabolisms to remain model-thin.

I had always been outside the game, so to speak, not being a size six except while I was a teenager and yet to fill out. I'd have to be dead for a couple of months before my bones would be able to fit into the expected proportions. My height may have excluded me, but I still heard the snide comments from the stuffy women in our social circle, so they would never let it go entirely.

Bats was so old money and titled as well, but she'd been the most welcoming of anyone. We were just women to each other, rather than a rung in a complicated ladder that I still didn't really understand. I guess when you *were* rather than *aspired* to be something, you could relax a lot more. People would still invite you to things, and you didn't have to worry about all the rules, either because they were bred into you and you just did them without thinking, or because you understood which ones you could get away with breaking. Bats never wore the "right" gear on the shoots and could make a rag look like designer chic. It wouldn't occur to her to say "toilet" or "dessert," but if she did, people would just think she was being droll. No mother would have objected to her; quite the contrary. Edwina would have been a quivering puddle of ecstasy if Jack had brought her home instead of me.

"We're having photos taken next week for *Vogue*. I need to be careful, just until the photographs are taken, then I can eat again. I'm hoping you still have some you need to perfect?"

"You're in luck. The strawberry champagne cake needs some work."

"Great, but get into your running gear!" she ordered, pushing me toward the stairs. I could feel bits wobbling as I moved and had a moment where I felt like Homer Simpson, where everything kept moving even after I stopped. I reluctantly hauled on my exercise gear, fearing to look in the mirror before I left, in case I retreated into my wardrobe, too scared of going out looking like an overweight walrus next to Bats.

I felt better after we started our run, which was in truth part-exercise, part-therapy session.

"How are things with Rupert?" I puffed. Things hadn't been going that well for her and Rupert lately. Rupert was the male version of Bats: handsome and very well bred. Socially, they were the perfect couple, though I had always found him…uninteresting, for want of a better word. He was charming, but he lacked Bats' irreverence, or any other quirk for that matter.

"Fabulous! He's fucking his personal assistant, and I spend his money to get back at him. He feels so guilty, he doesn't dare ask me about it. I have to show you my new Hermes bag."

"I'm sorry." I stopped running, trying to imagine Rupert doing the nasty. The picture in my mind was a Ken doll bending repeatedly in the middle.

"Don't be. I'm not." She kept jogging, so I had to speed up to catch her again. "I'm not that interested in sex anyway, and we work better together when we don't have that—" she paused, searching for the right word "—*obligation* hanging over us."

"So, Rupert knows you know?" I asked, puzzled.

She shrugged. "We're all very good at pretending that everything's fine, and after a while, you know, it *is* fine."

"I can understand that," I said thoughtfully. "Truthfully, that's how Jack and I deal with any unpleasantness. We just ignore it until it goes away. I'm not sure how healthy it is, but it seems to work. Who needs to hash out every small detail anyway?" This sounded like a bit of a cop out, even to me, but it was how we managed. Bats nodded, and we kept jogging.

She did seem fine with it, but she must have been concerned because I'd never seen her face move this much. In the last few years, she had grown fond of Botox and the outward serenity it provided. She once told me she could never yell at her kids because her face simply couldn't express anger; it looked weird with an angry voice and a pleasant face and was very confusing for the children. As a friend, I found it did make it a bit difficult sometimes to gauge her emotional state. I had to pry a bit further, to be sure that she wasn't just unable to express her pain and maybe did want to talk about it. Also I was curious. Her marriage was so different from mine, and I struggled to understand it sometimes.

"But this isn't just leaving dirty clothes on the floor; it's having sex with someone else. Don't you feel betrayed?"

"Yes and no. It doesn't feel great, I'll be honest with you, but it's not a deal-breaker for me. I can understand it from Rupe's perspective. I don't want to have sex with him like we used to, so I've changed too. It's like tennis; just because I don't want to play doesn't mean that he can't play with someone else." She said it flippantly, but I could tell she was serious.

"So, you don't want to see someone else too?" I asked after a few minutes.

"God, no, I don't have time. I'm far too busy," she said. "How about you and Jack?"

"Opposite problem. I want sex but he doesn't."

"Really? You still want to sleep with Jack?"

"Yes. I *like* sex, just like I like food. It's my weakness." I sighed. "Sex isn't a priority for Jack, and it's not like you can just get a man to 'lie back and think of England.'"

"I don't mind it when I'm doing it, but the urge to get there is missing for me. Maybe we should swap husbands." Her face darkened almost imperceptibly. "When did we change so much?"

I looked at her questioningly, not sure where she was going with this.

"I mean, we used to all *feel* things so much more. I remember in my late teens and early twenties being so overwhelmed by my reactions to things. You know, horribly embarrassed or almost giddy with excitement. I used to struggle to control my impulses and emotions, and I would have found Rupert sleeping with someone else unbearable then. Most of the time now, I just feel placid and slightly bovine."

I nodded, understanding. "I feel the same, almost like I'm numb a lot of the time. But I don't think it's that we're necessarily feeling less; it's just that we have more perspective. Once a few truly awful things happen, then you realize how little most of it matters. Very few things are really life and death." I looked away, taking in the view of the river, which was steel gray on this overcast day.

"I guess," she agreed. "But part of me thinks I should care more about Rupert fucking his PA. I'd like to think he'd care if I was doing someone else, but I really think he'd just fall over in surprise."

I reached for her arm and gave her a quick squeeze. She smiled a bit sadly in response. It made me think: when did we all stop being compatible? Did sex really not matter that much in a relationship anymore that we could get by without it or source it from outside the main relationship with no ill-effects? I tried to picture Jack or myself having an affair, but right then it seemed unimaginable.

Chapter Six

"So, how did you get your start in writing cookbooks?" the journalist from the *Sydney Morning Herald* asked. They were doing a feature article on me for their Saturday magazine. I think because I was Australian and living the "fairy-tale dream" — married into the aristocracy and living a glamorous life in London — there was a ready-made market for my books, and I was selling only slightly behind Jamie Oliver.

For a second, I considered giving the real reason. I could just imagine his face if I said, "My first cookbook was a way of coping with a tragedy that was more painful than I could possibly express. I lay on the floor and cried every day after I had managed to get the children to school. Then, once I could move again, I wrote to fill in any empty time in the day or night when I couldn't sleep. My theory was that if I didn't have time to think, I couldn't fall apart. I'd always enjoyed baking, but it had become an obsession: weighing, measuring, searching for subtle improvements. Absolute control, when it felt like there was none in my life. Too many people knew, and shutting myself off to write the book gave me the space to grieve in my own way and let the grapevine do the rest. Eighteen months later, I sold it to a publisher, and over the next couple of years, it sold increasingly well and became a genuine bestseller. No one could have been more surprised than me, except maybe Jack."

The temptation for honesty passed, and I stuck to the well-rehearsed standard response to this question.

"I'd always loved cooking, and we entertain a lot, so when my publisher came to me with the idea of sharing that enjoyment and, I guess, also a piece of my life, I jumped at the chance. Nothing is too complicated, but simple things can still give pleasure to your loved ones, or people you need to impress," I said, with a wink.

The party line was that Jack's family had been wowed by my "breath of fresh air" and loved me whole-heartedly, after I had amazed them with my brilliant cooking and stylish presentation. It couldn't have been further from the truth. They saw professional cooking the same way as if I had become a professional plumber and had my hand in a toilet all day.

"It took some time for *Saint Kate of the Cupcake* to gain momentum, but then it took on a life of its own. What exactly set it apart from the hundreds of others in the market?" he asked.

In truth? Nothing really, just smoke and mirrors and the curiosity that sells Hello! *magazine,* I thought sardonically. I had enjoyed a brief time around my wedding as an almost "It" girl, having the cleverness to snag one of England's more eligible bachelors, rather than anything in my own right. After producing two future eligible bachelors to continue the tradition, I thought that would be it. But enough of the population was still interested in my life and bought the book.

"I think the recipes are good, but with a bit of a twist that is actually my own and how I cook myself. Also, the spectacular styling and photography make it beautiful, and it's always a pleasure to look at something beautiful." Which had less to do with me than one would think. "I work with some of the most talented people in the business who can make my food look amazing." *God, could I get any more perky? If only honesty sold as well…*

"You're a celebrity in your own right now. How does it feel?" he asked politely. I wondered if he could sense my inner dialogue and how it in no way matched my upbeat answers. I wasn't a fabulous actress, so it was possible. I had to try harder.

I gave the question some thought. Fame was interesting. Once the first cookbook came out, people started recognizing me more in the street. I appeared in interviews in magazines and on television, and then more people again recognized me. People I knew from the neighborhood on a first-name basis suddenly treated me differently—I was "famous."

The strangest part of my new fame was the way my life seemed to take on a split personality. One day, the most difficult decision I made all day would be whether to cut sandwiches into triangles or squares and what I could possibly make for dinner from spinach, fish, and corn that could be presented in such a way as to bypass the super-critical palates of my progeny (tomato ketchup was usually key). Other days, I would be meeting with lawyers, agents, and publishers, with large sums being thrown around in the industry created by what I now referred to in my head as "the Book" and workshopping ideas for turning by-products into even more large sums.

Sometimes I would be interviewed by someone, and read what they wrote later, alternating between amusement and horror at the vast inaccuracies in their stories. Though I grew up in Australia, I don't think I'd ever actually been on a sheep farm, let alone run one, and I would never describe myself as a "surfer," nor to my recollection was it ever mentioned in the interview. It was completely bizarre how these things were simply concocted.

I was flattered when someone called me a "classic" beauty and that I had excellent manners, which was nice though strange that they were surprised enough to allude to it. I think it was just that I wrote about baking and dressed conservatively. I was no Stepford wife, but my looks were an old-fashioned kind of pretty, rather than a modern look. I would love to wear avant-garde fashion, but I just looked ridiculous in it. Oddly-shaped clothing, aviators, messy hair all did nothing for me, as much as I would have liked to be stylish enough to carry it off. My hips and breasts were too full for fashion and, without a reasonable amount of control being exercised, could easily get out of hand.

I was often compared to Nigella, and my most recent interviewer said that I looked like a taller Charlotte from *Sex in the City*, or would if she lived in London and was married to an Englishman and was less immaculately groomed. I wasn't sure how complementary that one was. It was never nice to have one's personal hygiene called into question. *Sex in the City* wasn't reality; no one was that perfectly groomed without a team of hairdressers and makeup artists. The comparison wasn't exactly fair.

Gradually things had settled down again, but in the last few months, I had been doing an ungodly amount of publicity to build up the next book, *The Gospel According to Saint Kate*, which had just been released in time for Christmas. It was always difficult for me to do media promotion as it set Jack's friends and relatives' teeth on edge. I had to walk a very fine line: talk to the press so they would promote my book but reveal as little about my life as possible.

The first rule of the English aristocracy that I'd married into was "don't ever talk to the media." Given my chosen career, it wasn't really possible, and unfortunately, it was that family side of my life that gained me the publishing deal in the first place and that people wanted to hear about. Not being naturally reticent, in my naivety, I'd let a few humorous anecdotes about myself slip which the media pounced upon and tried to attribute parts to people in my circle. It didn't seem to matter that it wasn't true; it still was repeated until it might as well have been. It made for some very awkward social events and permanently alienated some people. I think they were looking for an excuse, because it wasn't actually my fault, and I could prove that it wasn't, but they didn't want to hear it. I also received a stern lecture from Jack.

"You can't say anything negative, ever," he explained, slapping the magazine on the table.

"Why not?" I asked, puzzled.

"You are part of a very privileged group of people who have money, beautiful houses, and titles. People run around and do whatever you want for you. If you complain, you look like an ungrateful arsehole."

"But—"

"But nothing. Complain all you want to me or your friends, but not out in public and especially not to the media," he grated out through clenched teeth.

"Sorry." Thoroughly chastised, I got it, but seriously, I had to be upbeat and perky *all the time?* There wasn't enough coffee in the universe for that.

Mentally dragging myself back from my train of thought, I realized I had probably taken too much time answering, so I grasped for the first coherent thing I could manage.

"Well, I'm still the same as I ever was. The only thing that's different is people's reaction to me," I answered truthfully. "It's the same for anyone in the public domain: you do tend to become more cautious with new people, and you try to work out if they like you for yourself or because of what you are." Finally, my first bit of honesty. He nodded agreeably but seemed a bit disappointed I hadn't said anything particularly controversial.

After the interview, they took some photos and, after a bit of messing around packing up, left fairly smartly, leaving me to the rest of my day, which at the moment involved looking at mounds of old cookbooks, searching for inspiration for the next cookbook and doing the Christmas shopping.

This was the best part of writing, where anything was possible and the creative excitement of new ideas whirled around my head in an invigorating and thrilling way. The third book was still untitled. There was less pressure on this one, given the good reception of the previous two and the kitchenware selling well. I'd even been approached for a television show, which would send my mother-in-law into new heights of displeasure. But all that had to be put on the backburner for the next few weeks, as I waited to see if I would survive the festive season.

Chapter Seven

Hell is different things to different people, and my own personal hell was my mother-in-law's place at Christmas. The fact that Clouston Hall was exceptionally beautiful just seemed to make the whole ordeal worse. The dread started around November, and by the time we drove in through the front gates, four days before Christmas, I was usually in such a state, imagining the fresh horrors my mother-in-law would have cooked up for the festive season.

This year, on Bats' advice, I surreptitiously swallowed a Valium in the car half an hour before we arrived so it would be at full effect when we got there. My edges were lovely and soft, and I enjoyed the last five minutes of the drive exceptionally. Jack, I think through growing up with her, or through sheer bloody-mindedness, refused to acknowledge anything other than that his mother was a bit eccentric. If she was eccentric, fish were slightly damp. As far as I was concerned, Edwina was completely bitch-bonkers, with a strong dose of paranoia and hypochondria thrown in.

In summer, tourists swarmed rapturously over the gardens, but now, in the depths of winter, the house and gardens were silent, the flat-topped hedges covered in white, and the formal gardens softened by the snow. It was so beautiful that looking at it sometimes stopped my breath, and I forgot temporarily the social ghastliness that lay within.

Escaping to wandering the grounds, I could picture myself as a Jane Austen heroine, though none of her heroines had to deal with such an awful mother-in-law. Mr. Darcy's and Mr. Tilney's had kindly passed on, though you could imagine Elinor Dashwood having it a bit tough at family events. Fanny Price's mother-in-law was effectively her own mother, which is a bit odd when you think about it, but at least there were no surprises in store there. She knew what she was getting into.

I'd had a few hints that there was something strange going on under the surface of their family, but apart from Edwina being a complete bitch, they'd managed to hold it together until after the wedding. Not that it would have stopped me marrying Jack, whom I loved passionately, but at least I would have had a better idea of what I was agreeing to when I said "for better or for worse." The only sign of how wrong things were came via Crispin, Jack's brother. He had the golden blond curls and pouty red lips of a Renaissance angel, but he'd never had much to say to me, so I couldn't say I really knew anything about him apart from what Jack had told me.

My first real interaction with Crispin was in the lead up to the wedding. Seeking a moment's reprieve from the endless planning, I had slipped off briefly to draw breath in the library. Closing the door softly behind me, I almost hadn't caught the sobbed intake of breath. Following the sound, I'd found Crispin on the floor behind a wood cabinet, his arms tightly wrapped around his knees as he tried to hold himself together. A large raised red welt marked his cheek, and I could see more on his neck and forearms where his sleeves were pushed back.

I'd sat down in the chair next to him, silent and not touching him as he shook.

"Why does she do this to us?" he had asked eventually, when his shudders had decreased.

"I don't know. It's not you. She has some serious issues." There had been no need to ask who had struck him with what looked to be a riding crop. Nor had it seemed to be the first time, from Crispin's resigned look.

"I didn't do *anything*." He'd rubbed the fresh tears out of his eyes. "It's because of you. *This* is supposed to be a reminder that I shouldn't repeat Jack's mistake." His eyes had turned on me, becoming hardened and angry. I was so stunned I couldn't think of anything to say. How was this my fault?

"I see you for what you are—a gold-digging whore who trapped my brother into marriage with your pregnancy. You'll never be one of us," he'd spat and, jumping up, run out of the room. Why did he think I was pregnant? Why would someone be saying that when it wasn't true? I had still been sitting there, shocked and dumbfounded, trying to understand what that had been all about, when someone found me and dragged me back to the wedding planning, not that I'd been needed.

Later, I'd raised what had happened with Jack.

"Did your mother do that to you?" I asked.

"Look, she used to 'discipline' us a lot when we were younger. Crispin never copped much of it and so was just upset."

"Understandably! You know that's not normal," I pressed.

"Yes, I know. Mother has a temper and is stressed about the wedding, so she probably lashed out."

"We are not going to beat our children." There was no way I would be okay with him replicating his mother's parenting. This had not been a discussion I ever thought I would have, but this was a deal breaker for me.

"No, of course not. I know you wouldn't be like that, and it's one of the reasons I want you for the mother of my children. You'll do a much better job." He'd smiled sadly.

"Crispin was really upset. He thinks I'm after your money and trapped you by getting pregnant."

"I'll talk to him tomorrow," he'd said, placating.

Troubled, but realizing there was little I could do, I'd let it drop.

I drifted out of my reverie, aware of the car tires crunching over the cold stones of the front driveway, as we came to a stop directly outside the front door. The drawing room curtains twitched; Edwina had obviously been watching for us. In my pleasantly drugged state, I was completely unbothered by it. Maybe I could take these lovely pills the whole time, I thought, before realizing that not only was it bad for me, but I didn't have nearly enough. *Maybe next year*, I consoled myself.

Willing myself to open the car door, it still took a few seconds. It was the moment after the wax strip had been applied, that peaceful, non-painful moment, just before the pain of lots of small hairs being ripped out. You were committed to the pain—there was only one way out of the situation. I closed my eyes, took a deep breath, and got out of the car.

I arranged my face into a smile and greeted Bellham, the Preedys' most recent butler/handyman, who had opened the door to meet us. Edwina was so diabolical that staff never lasted that long. She was ridiculously exacting, micromanaging every aspect of their jobs, usually with more conviction of her own superiority than understanding of the job. She genuinely believed that birth was more important than character, or rather that birth determined that you were a worthy character. If you were not born into a wealthy and influential family, well, that was your own fault. She had swallowed the theory behind the "Divine Right of Kings" in its entirety.

With a "madam" and a "sir" and a nod to the boys, he escorted us through the grandly tiled entrance hall, with its massive stone staircase rising to the upper levels and the gleaming darkly polished wood railing showing through under the wreathes that decorated the stairs. As it was Christmas, the stately rooms were being used, and we were shown into the vast sitting room with an enormous tree taking up one end, mockingly perfuming the air with the smell of festive family fun.

The decor was perfectly maintained original. Even the imperfections were not corrected, in order to enhance the character of the whole. It was beautiful and, more importantly, appropriate. The sitting room was apple green, with tonal shades echoing in the furniture, which should have been relaxing but wasn't, at least when it was occupied. Edwina rose from one of the wing chairs to greet us.

"You are late!" she thundered, her eyes bulging out of her reddened face.

"Sorry, Mother. Traffic was bad out of the city," Jack said mildly, not even trying to remind her that we deliberately hadn't specified a time for our arrival, saying it would be after dinner. She had no doubt thought up a time for herself and decided that that was when we should arrive, despite us having no knowledge of it. Logic held no sway with Edwina, so there was no point in arguing. My time would be better spent beating my head against a wall. At least then I might be unconscious and blissfully removed from having to deal with her.

"Well, I'm sure dinner is ruined, but we'll all just have to suffer through it, particularly your poor father. You know how his digestion plays up," she huffed ominously and fixed me with a baleful eye, as if the traffic had been my personal doing. Jack didn't bother correcting her or telling her that we'd already had dinner. It simply wasn't worth the effort. We would eat again. Edwina turned away to speak to Bellham quietly. I looked at Jack and raised an eyebrow. He just shrugged, confirming that there was nothing wrong with his father.

Edwina finished her instructions to the butler and gave him a sickly sweet smile. *Condescending cow,* I thought.

"Hello, dear." Arthur had moved up to us quietly, kissing me gently on the cheek and shaking Jack's hand.

"Help yourself to drinks," Edwina said stiffly. "Now, where are my grandsons?" Finally a genuine smile, though slightly too bright, which made her look more than a little crazy. The boys were largely oblivious to her moods as they knew they were rarely directed at them, so they came up to give her a kiss without fear for their safety. I poured myself and Jack large Tomatin Whiskys, and we settled on the lounge, relaxed now that her attention was with the children.

Looking around, I realized Arthur had quietly left the room again. For as long as I'd known Jack, his father had been noted for his ability leave unobtrusively. Sometimes I speculated that he must be able to walk through walls, because the doors never squeaked for him like they did for the rest of us. I used to joke with Jack that his father was actually Bruce Wayne and that he was in reality disappearing to his bat-cave to go out fighting evil as Batman. Though the question of why he didn't battle his wife remained unuttered. Maybe she was his nemesis and every superhero needs one of those to survive. If the nemesis were defeated, then all the fun and excitement would be over. It was the only reason I could think of for him not offing her years ago.

I was just starting to relax when Crispin walked in. He smirked annoyingly at us like the leprous toad he was and gave his mother a kiss hello. Something about the way his lips lingered on her skin was more than slightly unsettling.

"Hello, Crispin, darling." She smiled at him dotingly and stroked his cheek. *Urgh,* I grumbled internally, *love is truly blind.*

"Mummy. You are looking sublime this evening."

She simpered in response; there was no other word for it. I wanted to throw up. How Crispin could act like nothing was wrong was beyond me, given the criminal nature of the things he was being accused of these days. At the moment, it was just rumors, but there was talk of the police being involved. I doubted that would happen, though. Despite, or maybe because of, the fact that the girl was so young, the whole thing would be hushed up. Edwina would pay for it to go away, and Crispin would move on, his depravity unchecked. Sure, he would be unwelcome in certain circles, but he didn't care what they thought. There were always more innocents with stars in their eyes for him to move on to. He made me sick. The poor girl had been barely seventeen, and from the sounds of it was completely fucked up now.

"Jack, Katie, good to see you. Merry Christmas!" he said insincerely. I threw him a weak smile, and Jack just glowered. He tried to come in for a kiss, but Jack leaned forward to block him. Crispin straightened, and his lip curled in annoyance.

We made our excuses shortly after and went up to our room. An hour later and dressed appropriately, we entered the stately dining room for the obligatory four-course formal dinner. It was delicious, though ridiculously fattening with lashings of cream and butter ladled over everything. A haze of fat like lip gloss covered my lips, and only an after-dinner whisky could cut through it. Diet was not something that Edwina believed in, or rather, she had no idea what constituted healthy food, so she just assumed that the food she had grown up eating and liked was therefore good for her.

"I have been remarkably unwell," she announced to the table in general. "I have gained so much weight because of my thyroid problem that I just feel awful and bloated all the time." It was hard not to laugh at her self-delusion.

"Do you have a diagnosis yet?" I asked innocently.

"It's so rare that they are still running tests. They've put me on a meat- and dairy-free diet."

"But, my dear, you're eating meat now," Arthur suggested meekly.

"It's just one little piece of lamb!" she exclaimed indignantly and ate it anyway, but you could tell she was put out by the general increase in glaring.

After dinner, we retired to the sitting room again to talk in the warmth of the fire while the staff cleared away our meal. The room was again in an immaculate condition. I found it intimidating, as I could never be completely at ease having servants to do everything. I didn't find it relaxing to have other people cleaning up after me, and I worried about what they would think of me from the mess I left behind.

I also couldn't help feeling responsible for not only the disruption I caused, but also that of two barely adolescent boys. I'm sure I had instructed them on the intricate function of a coaster, but it had yet to sink in. In perfect obliviousness, they put wetly glistening glasses down on a succession of priceless antique surfaces, thereby ruining them forever. The glances of death from their grandmother were reserved for me, along with hissed insults when there was no one else to bear witness, and the kindly façade she tried to cultivate cracked briefly before being quickly repaired so none of the men she favored saw.

Despite the image she tried to present to the world, Edwina had grown up in more modest, though to my understanding still well-to-do, circumstances and had inherited the bulk of her money from an uncle who had become rich from inventing some sort of glue. She would have been considered new money, but she'd leveraged the capital she had into a very good marriage and respectability with Lord Preedy, who came from a very old family whose finances were distinctly threadbare and in need of cash to fund the upkeep of the family home.

Arthur was gentle and softly spoken, and I'm not entirely sure he was *all there,* so to speak. A few sheep may have been missing from the top paddock, to use a distinctly Australian colloquialism. Still, he was perfect for Edwina as he didn't seem to mind being bossed about continuously. There must have been some deep seated insecurity in Edwina to need to control everyone, but she made a particular effort to punish me for the crime of marrying her son. I think she had decided the way to do that was to appear to the manor born by continually implying my inferior status, having come from *the colonies.* I just kept the smile on my face, and focused on being sunnily charming, which unsettled her more than allowing her to see that she bothered me, which I'm sure she would have enjoyed.

Still, she had helped us buy our house when we married; otherwise there was no way we would have been able to afford an admittedly run-down terrace in Chelsea. A ridiculous amount of time, love, and money later, we had something truly beautiful to live in, and it gave me pleasure every time I walked in the door. I just had to remind myself what I was grateful for when she became particularly painful.

Mind you, there were times when I wished we could have just bought what we could have afforded at the time and not had to owe her the money. Any time she came to visit, she would run a proprietary hand over the woodwork and tell me what I needed to change. I had to try not to throw myself in front of her to stop her molesting my house.

It's hard to enjoy Christmas when someone is hissing at you that you are devil spawn at least once a day. I'm not sure exactly what I'd done to become evil incarnate, except marry her son, thereby cutting back the thorny tangle of the umbilical cord. I'd say it was my career, but she was like that from the beginning. At first, I took it to heart, but after being nothing but pleasant and accommodating, I'd had to conclude that it wasn't me. Still, I kept giving in to all but the most ridiculous requests, but her playing the "it is her last Christmas" card was wearing a bit thin, given she looked in the pink of good health and it had been ten years since she'd first tried to convince us she was on death's door.

So, there we all were, sitting around this draughty old pile, pretending to enjoy each other's company and that there was nowhere else we would rather be. Our boys, being teenagers, were masters at wriggling away, and I hadn't the heart to subject them to more of it than absolutely necessary. I would have escaped if I could too. The immaculate house was more museum than comfortable retreat, and it was too cold and miserable to go out. I pretended to be engrossed in my book and drank a lot.

On the morning of Boxing Day, I gently pulled the long floral curtains back so they rested behind the brass circles beside the window, unbarred the wooden shutters, and opened the room to the gray light of a winter morning, relieved that Christmas was over once again and we would be going home today. Jack had already left to go down for breakfast, and I had a few minutes of peace to myself before continuing the happy family farce.

I watched the river flow silently on the far side of the open fields which lay beyond the formal gardens. Sheep grazed in the distance, unaffected by the cold, their black faces impassive. The view was distorted slightly as I turned my head, the glass so old it was pooling slightly at the bottom and creating small ripples in the middle of the panes. I looked at the flocks of gray and black birds wandering the sky, silhouetted against the streaky clouds. I had no idea what they were called, whether they were pests or helpful to the farmers.

I couldn't imagine ever being more than a stranger here, in this house that was built before Australia had even been founded. The foundations the house was built over were even older, the stone floors concave with the passage of feet and time. As beautiful as it was, I had never found Clouston Hall mentally comfortable. There are too many memories here, and they are not mine in any sense. Paintings of angelic blond children hung in hidden corners, no names or dates to identify them to outsiders. They freaked me out a little, not knowing what had happened to them. Were they represented in paintings somewhere else, grown to adulthood? Or were they reminders of tragedies that had befallen my husband's ancestors? Had their mothers stood before these paintings and cried, or had they looked on them with nostalgia and pride at the men and women they had become? I don't think Jack would have understood my discomfort with the paintings, and one crazy lady in the house was more than enough.

When I first came to this house, I thought I was entering the world of Austen, but it only took a few years to recognize that it was more Brontë. The melancholy and madness barely suppressed that came with this ancient, isolated house made me want to run screaming back to the comfort of the city with its perpetually renewing youth and bright lights and availability. The stillness and quiet that I thought I should enjoy was just a little too complete and serious. I was not bred for this. Maybe if I'd been brought up somewhere less sunny, where old didn't mean something from the sixties, I would have loved it unconditionally rather than ambivalently.

Still, there was no certainty I would ever have to live here. Edwina was forever changing who she was leaving the money to, and without the money, there would be no hope of keeping the house. Jack was the elder son and, without a major trip off the rails, could not be prevented from inheriting the house and the title. However, Edwina held the purse strings, savvy enough to have kept control of her money in the marriage. She was just mad enough to not care what happened after she was gone and vindictive enough to make life difficult for Jack, if the mood struck her on her deathbed. Jack was attached to the house, and it would kill him to have to sell it. At least it would be protected and not demolished, but like so many of the stately houses, it would lose something by no longer being a family home if he was forced to give it up.

Unfortunately, Edwina picked this morning to corner me and confide her intentions, almost like she was trying to reassure me — or win me over. God knows why, though. There was no possible way that I would take her side over Jack's.

"I will leave Clouston Hall to you and Jack," Edwina said solemnly, grabbing my hand and giving it a pat as we sat at breakfast. Unfortunately, we were alone as the menfolk had already left to look at a horse or a ewe or something. Edwina's words would have meant more if I hadn't known she had said exactly the same thing to Crispin, who had revealed her intentions when drunk last night.

"Thanks?" I said, not sure exactly how to respond to that. If you were too enthusiastic, surely that implied to the person you would be happy when they were dead. But if you responded in the negative, then you were dismissing their gift. Hmm, tricky. Crispin was her favorite and unmarried as yet, but once he had children, I don't know if she would be able to help herself, whatever she had said before. As long as Crispin didn't marry someone as unsuitable as me. She was even more protective of him than Jack and her reaction likely would be worse. Only an English princess would be good enough for her darling, not that he would even be in the running. Still, we all have our fantasies.

"Jack is my son, so I love him because I have to, but I don't like him very much," she confided in me to my unbridled horror. The inappropriateness of telling me that, as well as the sentiment, was appalling. This was what Jack had grown up with? No wonder he had intimacy issues.

"Excuse me, Edwina. I need to talk to the boys about something." I could barely restrain myself from telling her exactly what I thought, but I knew Jack wouldn't appreciate it. I rose and left as fast as possible, deciding to start packing for an early trip back.

Chapter Eight

It was with a sigh of relief I turned the key in the door of our house and returned to our sanctuary. This Christmas with Edwina had been worse than usual. *Next year, I don't care what happens, I'm taking the boys to Australia,* I swore to myself.

After a good night's sleep in my own bed, I felt restored. The next week flew by in a rush, as I tried to organize two absentminded teenagers to get back to school. I love them dearly, and it is always so quiet when they are gone, though that is when I start breathing again, becoming aware that I stopped while they were home.

"How do you feel about going skiing in France three weeks from now?" Jack asked over breakfast the morning after the boys left. I think he was still trying to make up for our boys no longer living in the house and my loneliness without them here.

"That would be great. I don't think I have any meetings scheduled. Just us, or should we see if anyone else can come too?" I asked.

"I've spoken to Michael and Edward, and they're keen too," he replied. I tamped down on my reaction to the fact that he'd spoken to his friends before he'd thought to mention it to me.

"Great. Just the six of us then?" I answered, trying for cheeriness. It wasn't like I was objecting to the group holiday—Jane and Fiona, their wives, were lovely, and we had been on skiing holidays with them before. Everyone's children were away at school now, but for many years we had gone on skiing holidays with our whole families.

"Yes. I'll make the arrangements." He snapped his paper shut, drained his tea, and, with a quick peck on my cheek, left for work.

With not much else to occupy me, I was able to pack and do the necessary last-minute tasks at a leisurely pace. In seemingly no time, we were touching down in Grenoble and driving to Val d'Isère. A light snow started falling outside Albertville, and by the time we were driving on the road that swept around the lakes of Tigne, it was snowing heavily. Thick flakes played in front of the headlights, seeming to go in almost every direction but down. It was almost mesmerizing, watching chaos in action.

Night was falling when, after two hours, we pulled up outside the chalet to drop off our bags. Jack took the car to the car park across the road where we had reserved a spot for the week, while I waited on the pavement with the bags. I looked around at the village, fairy lights decorating the bare trees, and inhaled the Frenchness of it all: the patisserie across the road and the busy bar next door to it, *après-ski* patrons getting rowdy, still wearing their ski boots. *Possibly Swedes by the look of them*, I deduced.

The village had obviously started in the valley and then spread up the sides of the mountain at the back. The general impression it gave was a gingerbread village, dusted with icing sugar, as even the few concrete bunkers didn't look too bad with a covering of snow. Most of the buildings were a contrast of warm wood and gray stone with sharply pitched rooves, the chairlifts like black webs going up the mountains.

Ladies of a certain age bundled in furs walked past, while children encased in puffy clothing were pulled around on precarious plastic sleds. Skiers tramped in heavy boots along the treacherously icy footpaths and wandered into the path of slow moving vehicles. Quite a few dogs, both large and small, were being walked, and in the true manner of the French, the feces remained on the footpath and slowly froze solid. I looked away quickly to focus on something else.

It was just starting to get uncomfortably cold when Jack returned, and we hauled our bags up to the reception. The chalet was the same one we always stayed at, a typical seventies building recently remodeled into mountain chic, which involved wood with traditional heart shapes cut out in random places like the backs of chairs and doors.

We were the first to arrive, so we were told by the hostess, and dinner was at seven thirty. After a leisurely shower (it is amazing how dirty you can feel after just sitting in a plane and a car for a few hours) and change of clothes, we headed back down for a pre-dinner drink in the lounge area. A fire crackled in the corner, so we headed for the closest armchairs to enjoy its warmth.

"Hello, my name is Antoine. I run the bar. What can I get you?" A polite and well-groomed man in his twenties appeared at my side.

"Vin chaud, sil vous plait," I responded, just being contrary. His English was obviously far superior to my French, but part of me just wanted to try anyway.

"Et monsieur?" he responded politely.

"Moi, aussi," Jack responded. Jack actually spoke flawless French, at a level I envied, though I lacked the natural ability and dedication to emulate it. When we had gone on our first trip to France, I had found it incredibly sexy. That seemed so many years ago now. We sat there in silence looking at the fire after Antoine departed, the trip so far having exhausted all conversation. We remained silent until his return.

"Cheers," Jack said, looking over his glass.

"Cheers," I responded absently.

Within a minute, Jack pulled out his phone and started fiddling with it, and I tried to dampen the instant irritation that sprang up. Instead, I strove to think of pleasant things so I didn't snap at him, but inevitably, they swung back to the times when I was left less than satisfied with my husband.

We were halfway through our largely silent drinks when some of our friends arrived. Immediately, we stood, and smiling hugely, welcoming the interruption and gaiety they provided. The conversation became lively as the drinks flowed. We were all charming and witty and beloved. We were in company that was fun and pleasant, and the distance we held each other at was pushed back, able to be ignored.

Dinner the first night was *raclette*, which involves a huge chuck of cheese being subjected to a small bar heater. As the cheese melts, it is scraped off with a special knife onto various cold meats and bread and served with boiled potatoes and salad. Vast quantities of red wine accompanied the meal, and we were soon well into the slightly ridiculous typical dinner party conversation.

Michael McGuiness, a spry and energetic man with electrified hair, had been friends with Jack for years since working together in London. His Scottish accent made everything he said even funnier, particularly when accompanied by a big belly laugh or his customary loud hoot, making him not only look but sound a lot like Mrs. Doubtfire. His wife, Jane, was lovely, kind, and gentle, and as a couple, they were full of life and seemed to genuinely enjoy each other's company, which was rarer than it should be.

"Charlize Theron," he said. "She's my celebrity out."

"Daniel Craig," Jane countered with a smile, to the nods of agreement from most of the women.

"Megan Fox," said Edward Jones-Smythe, a friend of Jack's from school. I looked at him in surprise. The thought of big, weathered, country squire Edward with such a dainty slip of a starlet was impossible to imagine. He would crush her accidentally with just one of his large paws.

"Claudia Schiffer," Jack said.

"You've been saying that for years!" I teased him. "This is imaginary; you're allowed to be unfaithful to your fantasy and change once in a while." He just smiled and said nothing.

"What about you, Katie?" Jane asked.

"Easy. Anders Larsen. Captain Milton from *Bad Ways*." I shivered with pretend delight and laughed.

"Never heard of him!" Mike hooted.

"He is divine, but I prefer Peter," said Fiona, naming Captain Milton's goody-goody nemesis on the show.

"No way! He's too vanilla."

"Too vanilla?" Fiona laughingly asked.

"You know, vanilla ice cream is nice but a bit boring, like you imagine bedding Prince William would be compared to the naughtier Harry. Captain Milton is like…a sinfully rich, velvety, chocolate ice cream, with something swirled through, maybe a salted butter caramel sauce. I like my men and my ice cream just a little bit wicked," I said with a wink.

"Woo hoo, Jack!" They all looked at him and laughed. He gave a good natured bow but studiously did not look at me.

"Now I feel like ice cream," said Fiona, forlornly gazing into her black coffee.

Chapter Nine

The next morning, I opened the curtains in our room to brilliant sunshine and clear blue skies. The large windows looked out upon the valley and the peaks dappled with sunshine, their sharp corners leaving cubes of shade down the face of the slopes. The tree line ended around half way up, giving way to the bare white of dusted peaks.

After a quick breakfast, Jack and I hit the slopes. The crowds had yet to arrive, and the groomed trails were hard-packed from the overnight chill. We almost flew, we went down them so fast. The exhilaration was incredible. All too soon, despite my workouts with Bats, my thighs were burning. We had a quick rest on the chairlift or gondola, and then were going again. When it started to get busier, we stopped for an early lunch.

Sitting on the deck outside the restaurant in the sun, I leaned back in my chair with a glass of red wine and realized I felt good, happy. The vague sense of disquiet I habitually felt was gone. I looked across at Jack and smiled. He smiled back, making slightly crazy eyes, and I laughed. All was good in my world. The gray that permeated our relationship was pushed back, even if only briefly, but it showed me what things could have been like, which was so disquieting it was almost painful and took away my momentary joy.

I quickly looked away, hardening my eyes to the burn of tears which threatened. The thought of the black darkness of being alone made me shudder. Surely what we had was better than that, and there were parts of my life that I really enjoyed and took pleasure in, and throwing it all away just because my relationship with Jack wasn't perfect wasn't rational. As much as I tried to reason it away, I couldn't quite regain my sunny outlook for the rest of the day, and my mood remained slightly cloudy as I went down to dinner alone.

You never really think you'll meet the object of your fantasies, the one who keeps you company on those quiet nights when you're alone in your bed, when gently stroking fingers help you imagine you are someone else, in some other place or time and something ecstatically pleasurable could happen. So, when Anders Larsen walked into the bar of the ski lodge the next night, it felt surreal.

I knew him intimately as my lover, but of course, not really. I had watched him on television, playing Captain Milton who was clever, funny, and very bad. I knew that it wasn't him, just as in my fantasies I wasn't really me. But that didn't stop my heart rate accelerating and a light-headedness overtaking me, as if I was going to faint. I was mortified by my reaction, which was embarrassingly pubescent and hardly sensible in a grown woman, even though he was superbly built—very tall, muscular, broad-shouldered, and so good-looking.

He was that pure blond that you usually only see in children, with blue eyes showing the same mischievous twinkle as Captain Milton. A full lower lip suggested a sensuality that was incredibly sexy. His nose was slightly bulbous, his forehead large and a bit shiny, and he sported a couple of weeks' worth of rough beard growth, but somehow these flaws enhanced rather than detracted from the over-all package. He would never be called pretty, but he was certainly handsome. He exuded sex appeal and a healthy confidence, though he was slightly less well-groomed than his character, which was, of course, a fiction of TV land.

I made no move to talk to him, as I could not imagine what I would say and would just make a fool of myself, but I kept an eye on his general location anyway in what I hoped was a subtle way. In the end, though, he came over to talk to our group.

"Hello!" he said, his smile bright, friendly, and unaffected.

A small puddle of lust formed in my belly. I smiled back wonkily, silently chastising myself for being so silly. I had to draw heavily from my inner well of social skills, beaten in over the years by stern elderly relatives and private schools. Everyone smiled and returned the greeting.

"I heard you speaking before. Are you English?" he asked generally to the group.

"Yes, and an Australian too. Are you American?" someone answered.

"No, Norwegian. But thanks! I work in America, so I have had to try hard to get an authentic accent."

"So, what do you do?" one of the men asked innocently.

"I'm an actor."

"Oh." This was not a profession encountered a lot in our circle of friends, and they struggled for something interesting to add. If you wanted someone to do your taxes or balance your share portfolio, then it would have been no problem. Thinking about it, though, none of us would be any good in a medical emergency either. If the world went into meltdown, our skill sets would have zero value and we would all be eaten. What the hell, I thought.

"I really enjoy *Bad Ways*. The character you play is very interesting." Okay, not too bad. Not scintillating, but at least I hadn't come across as a totally mad groupie!

"Thank you." The man in between us started up a conversation with the person on the opposite side of Anders so he moved around him to stand nearer, though slightly behind me. I turned around to face him, distancing us slightly from the rest of the group.

"So, what do you do? I have to say you look familiar." He smiled, dazzling me with his white teeth. *He must get that teeth whitening you see on the make-over shows*, I thought distractedly. *I didn't know they could get teeth that white.* Wrenching my mind away from his teeth, I tried to answer his question.

"Hmm…well, I was on a few talk shows about a month ago." I tended to mumble when embarrassed, but I mustn't have done it too badly because he could actually make out what I was saying.

"Really!" He laughed, showing even more of his fabulously white teeth, and his throat moved sexily. How could he make even swallowing look erotic? He was even hotter in person than on television, which I hadn't thought was possible. I thought the reason everyone looked so good was mostly lighting and makeup, but I was clearly mistaken. He looked down at me, his eyes sparkling.

"What were you on for?" he asked. Getting myself together, I smiled back. It wasn't every day I was flirted with by the object of my fantasy, even if it was just him being naturally charming. It would make a great story to tell Bats when we got back, so I should make the most of it.

"I'll give you a multiple choice answer. See if you can guess?" I grinned, the enjoyment of being able to retell this unlikely event overcoming my inhibitions faster than a shot of vodka. "A: I lost half my body weight, B: I survived a natural disaster, C: I wrote a book, or D:…I married my dog."

"Wow, that's quite a choice! Well, the body looks pretty fine." He looked me up and down, his eyes admiring and not trying to hide it. It was flattering, and I had to fight to control how much he turned me on. It wouldn't look good if I threw myself at him in a haze of lust, particularly in front of our friends. "So I don't think weight loss, and you look too relaxed and happy to have been though a natural disaster. What were the next two again?"

"Wrote a book or married my dog."

"Dog's pretty kinky, which is kind of exciting, but I'll have to say no and go with the book."

"Very clever deduction! It is the book. I like my dog, but not that much. To be frank, Boris is kind of smelly." I wrinkled my nose at the thought of our beloved but very large and hairy dog.

"My dog keeps turning me down. I think she's hoping someone better comes along." He pretended to look sad and rejected.

"Ah, that's tough! Have you tried buying her the premium dog food?"

"No, but I'll give it a go. So, what is your book called?"

"I have a couple: *Saint Kate of the Cupcake* and *The Gospel According to Saint Kate*. You probably don't know it. I'm not sure it would be your thing," I said, aiming for modesty.

"I have seen it!" he exclaimed. "I have to say, though, you're not at all how I imagined the author would look." He looked me directly in the eyes, his arctic blue eyes intent and seemingly genuinely interested. "I pictured some grandmotherly type — white-haired, bun, that sort of thing."

"Well, give it enough time, and you'll probably be right." I shrugged and smiled.

"Are you married?" he asked.

"Why do you ask?" I said, surprised. Looking around, I noticed that everyone else had moved further away, leaving us alone.

"You're a beautiful woman, so I'd try to sleep with you."

Well, I almost choked on my mouthful of wine, burning my throat at the same time as my body became a flaming pyre of lust. My, was I tempted to deny it! Captain Milton just propositioned me! I had a new understanding of why some people cheated. But could I do it? I truly did waver for a moment, just one moment.

"Wow, that was direct," I mumbled. "Ah, unfortunately for both of us, then, I have to admit to being married. My husband is not feeling well and is back in our room."

"Damn!" he swore softly, our gaze holding. I could imagine him closing the distance between us and could almost feel his lips on mine, overcoming my scruples like his womanizing character did on the show. Those thoughts must have shown on my face, as I saw an acknowledgment of it in his expression. He knew I was thinking about the possibilities.

"Are you happily married?" he said quietly. His fingers brushed my wrist, almost as if by accident, but my breath caught. I could feel the prickly tingles of excitement under the skin where his fingers had touched me. I felt like a puppy who had seen a ball that was just out of reach. *Nooo!* The possibility was there, but that was it. Everything about him screamed "player." That should have turned me off, but for whatever reason, my psyche and body had decided to go in the opposite direction. If anything, it made him more attractive.

"Most of the time…" My voice squeaked unbecomingly. This was definitely not his first attempt at seduction, and I was out of practice. I had only met him five minutes ago, and I was already thinking of abandoning my marriage vows. He was very, very good, and I obviously wasn't, so I would have to be very, very careful.

"Come back to my room, and we can talk in private." His voice was gravelly and seductive, his gaze hot and intense, promising sexual delights I could only dream of.

Fortunately, dinner was announced then with a loud clang which made me jump and brought me out of the trance I seemed to have fallen into and back to my senses.

"No, I don't think that's a good idea. It was—" I struggled to think of a word to describe our conversation "—interesting meeting you." I said a quick goodbye and re-joined my friends as they were sitting down at the table we had claimed as ours when we arrived the night before. I was just starting to relax and breathe again when a polite voice asked to join us as we had a spare seat. I looked back over my right shoulder to see Anders standing there smiling innocently.

"May I join your table?" he asked.

To choruses of "yes" and hearty entreaties of "of course," they bade him to feel welcome. He sat down in the empty seat beside me that was usually occupied by my husband, Jack.

"Don't get too comfortable, though. Katie's large and bad tempered husband will be back to health tomorrow night and reclaiming his seat," Edward said jokingly. "Still, it's good to have someone attractive to look at. Jack's an ugly bastard." Everyone laughed, except Anders who looked politely confused.

"Katie's husband is very good looking," Fiona explained, taking pity on Anders. "They're just joking."

"Have you got any films coming up?" Michael asked.

"We're on a filming break from the show, and I'm taking a month off to visit family and relax for a bit before starting on other projects."

"Oh! Kate here is a writer. They're talking of making a TV show of her book. Maybe she can put in a good word for you." Edward was completely tactless at the best of times, and Fiona rolled her eyes.

"Edward, you fool, he's very successful and well known. I don't think he needs any help." I looked at Anders apologetically. His eyes had focused on me, and the intensity of his stare made it hard to breathe for a moment.

"That's great. Who's doing the show?"

"It's not finalized yet, so I really shouldn't be talking about it, and I definitely won't be telling Edward anything more!" I looked at him with a mock glower. He held his hands up in surrender and laughingly pretended to hide under the table.

"Anders Larsen? Why do I know that name?" Michael blurted out. "Oh, that's right! Katie nominated you as her 'celebrity out' last night. I believe you thought he was the man equivalent of *saucy* chocolate ice cream?"

"What's a celebrity out?" Anders' mystified expression was not entirely convincing. I, on the other hand, must have looked as mortified as I felt. Like watching a full glass of red wine fall toward a cream carpet and knowing I would never reach it in time, I could only wait for this conversation to happen and clean up afterward. Trying to intervene might only make it worse.

"It's the famous person you nominate, and if you ever get to sleep with them, your partner has to forgive you," Michael continued.

"Really?" he said and looked over at me laughing, eyebrows raised. I could feel myself going red.

"But it's not real!" I threw a vexed look at Michael. "It's just a conversation game. No one really gets to do it consequence-free." With an effort, I smiled like it didn't really bother me and quickly changed the subject. Anders continued to look amused for quite a while afterward.

The conversation flowed well through dinner. Anders didn't renew his earlier suggestion, but occasionally our eyes would meet and that heat would flare. A couple of times our arms brushed, and I had to fight the urge to lean in and increase the contact. It was like he was a block of delicious chocolate and I had to sit there looking at it, not allowed to eat. What's worse was the chocolate *wanted* me to eat it. The only thing stopping me was my own willpower, which was not one of my greatest strengths. I could never eat just one of anything—biscuits, chips, chocolate, cake. If they were there and open, they were eaten. My only defense against them was just not to have them at all and to give away anything I baked so it wasn't there to nibble at.

Then our legs bumped under the table, and we left them touching for longer than was strictly polite. We were turned to talk to people on the other side to each other, but all I could think of for a moment was that only thin fabric separated our skin and that no one would know that we touched, except us. It was like a secret we shared, this contact. The whole situation was dangerous, and I couldn't believe I was playing this game, but it was too exciting to stop just yet. I would stop in a little bit, I told myself, before it went too far. It was just a bit of innocent flirting, and I had no intention of taking it further, so there was nothing really wrong with doing it.

Liar, said my conscience.

By the end of dinner, I wasn't sure how much more I could take. My nerves and libido were stretched to breaking point. After the main course but before dessert, I could stand no more and made my apologies, citing my sick husband as my excuse for leaving early.

Dessert was my favorite part of the meal, but better to sacrifice the chocolate mousse than my marriage. Anders was a chocolate bar that would have to be left wrapped up and avoided for the rest of our holiday because I clearly couldn't trust myself.

I got back to our room, slightly shaken. I hadn't cheated on my husband, but boy, had I thought about it. I'm not sure where that stood on the moral compass, but if thoughts were actions, I'd be guilty as sin. Probably best not to mention it to Jack and try to forget the whole thing. Still, it was nice to be appreciated as a woman, simply and directly, without the complicating factors that even the best long-term relationships had. Sometimes it was hard to remember what attracted you to each other at first as the things that you loved most about each other now were not so easy to define. I loved Jack for being a good father and husband, more than I lusted after his body.

Not that it was a bad body. I watched him sleeping in the large bed, his long arms spread across the white sheets and his head turned into the pillow, mouth slightly ajar and snoring softly. He enjoyed playing sports, and his body was toned and muscled, not soft and pot-bellied like a lot of our male friends. His hair was still a thick and lush chestnut brown with a slight wave, and his nose was long and well-sculpted. His skin was olive, like he always had a tan, and his cheeks slightly ruddy. His lips were straight and thin above a strong jaw.

All in all, he was still a very handsome man, probably more so now than when we met. Looking at him sleeping, I felt slightly sad. I knew I should want to ravish him into wakefulness, but I wouldn't initiate it anymore. I was too wary of the rejections that happened more and more frequently now. Society says that women have the right of refusal, so it is all the more devastating when no one understands the hurt of being a woman rejected. There are no women standing around at parties and pubs, bitching that their husbands no longer put out. My mouth twisted into a slightly bitter smile.

I loved our children, but I also missed who Jack and I used to be — that fun-loving couple who laughed a lot and went on great adventures, traveling the world. A younger, freer, and more spontaneous us. I sighed and went to the bathroom to take off my makeup and brush my teeth before climbing into bed. The lights went off with a click, flooding the room with darkness and causing Jack to stir and roll over, putting his arm over me and spooning in. I felt his warm breath on my neck as I drifted off to sleep, to dream slightly disturbed dreams about circuses.

The next morning dawned clear, cold, and crisp—another perfect day for skiing. We rose and half-dressed in our ski gear to grab breakfast, which was set up smorgasbord-style in the common room. It would be too hot to get all the way dressed, but easier than having to change completely again before heading to the slopes. I was just making toast while Jack poured the coffee when Anders walked in. His blond hair was still damp from the shower, his cheeks pink and scrubbed. He looked like a sexy grown-up cherub.

"Hello!" he said cheerily. "You must be Katie's husband, Jack. Anders." They shook hands. Seeing them standing together, I was struck by how physically similar they were in build, at least, though one light and the other dark. Jack was the more slender of the two, but I could see that I clearly had a type.

"Anders joined us for dinner last night," I explained as briefly as I could. "He's just arrived from Oslo."

"Are you here on your own?" Jack asked.

"Yes, unfortunately the friend I was coming with had to pull out at the last minute. His wife was sick."

"I'm sorry. Will she be okay?" I asked.

"Yes, I think so. I'll have to go and hire a guide this morning, though. The Alps are a bit dangerous to ski on your own."

"Why don't you come along with us?" Jack asked, and I could have kicked him.

"Sure," Anders said with a happy grin, eyes flashing in pleasure. "That would be great!"

I plastered a smile on my face and went to get my gloves and goggles which I had forgotten back in our room. Grateful for a moment of privacy, I gathered myself together. I just had to not make a fool of myself for a couple of hours, which I should be able to manage.

I cared about my husband enough to not cause him pain by making eyes at another man in front of him, even if he *was* Anders Larsen. Did "celebrity out" clauses really exist? Could I possibly call this one? Somehow I doubted that the real world would let me off on such a flimsy excuse, and I knew Jack would hardly accept that as a justification. *Get yourself together, woman!* I told myself. *It's not like you haven't had sex recently.* I scanned my memory for our most recent encounter, but then I realized I couldn't actually remember the last time we'd had sex. More than a month? Less than six, sometime in the last few months, anyway, though it hadn't been exactly memorable, just functional. It had really gotten away from us. I would blow the dust off my lady parts and seduce Jack tonight to get whatever excess hormones were in my system out. Otherwise, Anders could be a serious danger, or rather, I might become a danger to him in my obviously sexually frustrated state. Unable to put it off any longer, I went down to the ski locker and put on my boots, hefted the skis onto my shoulder, and met them at the door, standing side by side waiting for me.

Jack and I were good skiers, but Anders was a whole other level. His skis were like an extension of his large feet, and not once did I see a moment of indecision or loss of balance. Jack's ski technique was more aggressive and slightly less elegant, founded on confidence and natural athleticism rather than finesse. I lay somewhere between the two. Unfortunately, unlike me, Jack had no compunction about following straight behind Anders, which is when he got into trouble.

Moguls were never his strong point, and the uneven small mounds of snow were trickier than usual. The conditions had turned, and the warm weather had softened the top snow, making skiing down the lower part of the run like sliding through porridge. Jack was going too fast and clipped the edge of one of his skis, losing his balance and falling awkwardly and, at that speed, twisting his knee.

He lay grimacing in the snow, moaning slightly, for he was a true Englishman and would never cry, even in intense physical pain. We hurried over to help him, discarding our own skis at the side of the run where they wouldn't be in anyone's way. Anders and I got Jack's skis off, and I carried his equipment while Anders put his arm around him and helped him hobble to the medical center, which was fortunately not too far from the end of the run.

"Are you right with him now?" Anders asked after getting Jack seated in a chair in the waiting room.

"Yes, thanks for your help. I don't know how I would have gotten him here by myself."

"Are you going back out skiing? I can take your skis back to the chalet," Anders offered.

"No, I'll stay and look after Jack. I'll take them; you don't have to go all the way back to the chalet." I felt guilty putting him to so much trouble, as well as feeling like I was a bit in his debt.

"It's no problem. Besides, you'll have your hands full helping Jack." He had a point there, so I nodded.

"Well, I'll see you later," he said and turned to go.

"Thank you again for your help."

"You are welcome." He smiled, then turned and strode out the door. Damn, he had a great walk. He even looked good walking away.

After a bit of a wait, the doctor pronounced, much to our combined relief, that there was no significant damage and Jack just needed to rest it for a day. Knee bandaged and armed with painkillers, Jack was released from the medical center. I helped him back to the lodge, where he went to bed, slightly woozy from the drugs.

With Jack crashed out in bed, I was otherwise alone in the chalet. I tried to read a particularly trashy novel I'd bought at the airport but was feeling restless and unable to concentrate enough to get into it. For lack of a better option, I decided to make use of the sauna. It smelled like a pine forest, and the heat was bliss.

It was close to the intense heat of my childhood summers, though the smell was not quite the same. I missed the scent of eucalyptus sometimes, and days so hot the air had texture. Plants that were gray-blues and shades of brown, none of the extravagant greens of England, or only in the well-tended lawns of the urban elite. During dry summers of water restrictions, even those went dry and crispy and would crunch delicately underfoot.

After we got engaged, it was never really considered that we would live anywhere but England. Jack would never move to Australia, but even if he had considered it, I'm sure he would have hated it. He didn't even like it for a holiday; it just made him tense. He thought it was too far and had too many dangerous spiders, snakes, and sharks. I think he'd watched too many of those sensationalist nature programs where Australia seemed to have the most venomous everything, despite the fact that my parents' house was in the middle of a densely populated area with little discernible wildlife. He was simply English to his core, and to imagine him living anywhere else was impossible.

I should take the boys back for a holiday soon, I mused as I lay down, relaxing into it with a sigh of pleasure. I had the primal need to recreate some of my childhood for them, and they seemed to enjoy it whenever we went. Traveling along these thoughts, I had drifted off into a daydream when a noise from outside the door filtered into my consciousness. I sat up quickly and grabbed the towel from the bench beside me.

"I'm in here!" I called out, slightly panicked as I hurriedly wrapped the towel around me. I thought Jack and I were the only ones in the lodge. Certainly no one had been there when I'd come into the sauna what felt like only a few minutes ago. It was a bit after midday, and I counted on everyone still being out enjoying the fine day's skiing. Feeling a bit naughty, but secure that there was no one to see me, I'd decided to throw caution to the wind and go naked—an impulse I was now regretting.

I stayed sitting against the wall, my legs out in front of me along the bench, not sure if there was a less-revealing position. At least the towel covered me from chest to mid-thigh, which was more than a swimming costume did, though it felt far less secure.

Instead of whoever it was leaving me in peace, the door creaked open, letting in a gust of cold air and Anders. I pulled the towel tighter and tried not to look at his perfectly muscled chest, revealed in all its naked glory. Only a small white towel covered him from his hips to mid-thigh, his long legs showing like a gladiator's under the short skirt of the towel. The blond hair on his legs glistened, wet from the shower he took before coming in.

"Hello," he said, his Nordic accent slightly more in evidence than last night.

"Hi! I thought everyone was out." I tried to not look as uncomfortable as I felt. If there was anyone I shouldn't be naked and sweaty in a sauna with, it was Anders.

"I came in early," he said, stretching out with a yawn as he took a seat on the wall opposite. I swear if I looked I'd be able to see everything, as he sat with his legs apart. My eyes started to do laps of the ceiling to stop me looking, though it was ridiculously tempting. I was curious to see what he looked like, but I was better off not knowing the truth or my fantasies might take on an uncomfortably life-like quality.

"What are you doing?" he asked, sounding puzzled. I glanced at him and realized that it may have looked like I was having a fit of some sort.

"Just trying to preserve your modesty and not look up your skirt. I don't know if you realize, but if you sit like that, I can see everything."

"That's okay, then," he said, unwrapping the towel. "If you've seen me already then I don't have to worry about this." I swear my jaw hit the floor before I jerked my gaze skyward again. "It's so Anglo to worry about nudity," he continued. "In Norway, no one worries about it. I have no problem with being naked. You can take your towel off again if you like." His voice was all innocence, but he was clearly laughing at me, which fired up my backbone. I lowered my gaze to look directly at him and then up and down, examining him thoroughly. After I had studied him, I returned to his eyes and raised an eyebrow questioningly.

"Your turn," he said, eyeing me challengingly, daring me to do it.

"Fine," I said, feigning nonchalance and leaning back against the opposite wall. My legs firmly crossed at the ankle, I let the towel drop to the sides. I wasn't uncomfortable with my body — Bats' influence had paid off, and our hard work running and at the gym had more than offset my indulgences — but even though I'd gotten off fairly lightly from being pregnant, things were definitely softer and more rounded, as well as further south, than they had been. I felt his warm gaze like a featherlight caress and watched him watch me. His eyes became slightly hooded, and I could see him stir.

"You are beautiful; you should not be ashamed to show your body," he said, his blue eyes intense.

"I'm pretty sure that even in Nordic countries you aren't supposed to openly look. Isn't that a huge faux pas?" I said, nodding toward his lap.

"You're not supposed to notice either, but I find you attractive, and we are alone…" He shrugged. "It is only a mistake if it is unwelcomed." He looked at me questioningly. "Is it unwelcomed?"

I should have said yes, but I was a bad liar at the best of times.

"Are you suggesting…?" I started.

"Yes," he said softly. "I would very much like to sleep with you."

Oh…dear…Lord. For a second I almost had to pinch myself. While none of my fantasies with Anders were set in a sauna, maybe this was a new, very vivid one. In my fantasy, though, he would now be moving over toward me and taking my nipple in his mouth. Instead, he was still sitting against the wall, his eyes like blue fire. I had the chance to make my fantasy a reality, something few people ever get to do. If you ever fantasized about someone in the movies or on TV, the odds of ever even meeting them one-on-one were slight. The likelihood that they would want to sleep with you, even if you wanted to, was almost non-existent.

"So…" he said, and I realized I still hadn't responded.

"I'm still thinking," I said, running through the pros and cons in my head. It should have been an easy answer: "No, I'm married." But somehow the easy answer was still not coming out of my mouth. Here was the offer of exciting, potentially amazing sex, and it sent a shiver down my spine, in a good way. He wasn't after anything else—an introduction, a leg-up socially or career-wise, money—he just saw me as desirable and fuckable, and I really wanted someone who wanted me. It had been a long time since I'd been intimate with Jack on anything but a perfunctory basis, and I missed being touched.

Anders laughed. "Take your time," he said, waving his arm. I looked at him, gorgeous, desirable, and surprisingly attracted to me. I knew I should say no, but I didn't want to, even though it was also impossible to say yes.

"I like that you have hair. It's kind of unusual."

I did a double take. "Sorry?"

"It's just that it's been a while since I've seen pubic hair on a woman," he said conversationally.

"You're kidding, right?" I looked at him skeptically.

"No, really. Everyone seems to get it removed now." That finally snapped me out of it. What was I thinking? He was clearly someone who could and did sleep with anyone they liked, and I couldn't compete with younger women whose job it was to be beautiful and hairless, and he was clearly going to compare me to them.

"Okay, well, enough of this pre-school 'show me yours and I'll show you mine' thing," I said briskly, folding my towel back up around me before I stood up. Anders stood up too, touching my arm to stay my exit.

"What did I say?" he asked perplexed.

"It's not what you said per se; it's that you live in a world that is largely separate from reality, especially in the looks department. I don't want to be a slightly perverted deviation from the mini-hairless people you usually sleep with," I explained, quite reasonably I thought.

"That wasn't what I meant."

"But true, nonetheless. Besides, you may have already insulted the *saunatonttu*," I said archly.

"You've heard about the *sauna elf?*" he asked with a laugh as he smiled down at me. "That's in Finland, though."

"Maybe there's one here on holiday. You'd better leave an offering for him to atone for your immorality or you might have an imaginary gnome after you for violating the sanctity of the sauna," I said as I left him, still chuckling.

Chapter Ten

At dinner, Jack sat with his knee propped up on a spare chair and regaled our friends with an increasingly dramatic retelling of the accident. He was now airborne and somersaulting through the air before landing. I just rolled my eyes and smiled when anyone looked at me for confirmation, no sense in spoiling his fun and the ensuing game of one-upmanship as the men vied for the "worst fall" title with great enjoyment.

Anders kept his distance until after dinner. Jack was stationed on the couch, and I went into the kitchen to make tea, and Anders followed, ostensibly to help.

"Come skiing with me tomorrow," he urged, moving to stand so close we were almost touching, completely invading my personal space. His large body made me feel small in comparison, which didn't happen a great deal, given I was five foot ten and not exactly of fragile build.

"I don't think that's a good idea." I took a step backward.

"You keep saying that to me when I suggest the most interesting things," he responded, standing up straight before flicking back a section of shiny blond hair that had fallen on his forehead. He was clearly amused. "We're outside in the open, and it's pretty cold, so what exactly do you think is going to happen? It's one of the safest places to keep your virtue intact."

"My virtue is hardly intact. I'm a woman in her thirties with two children."

"Really? Then what are you worried about?" he asked teasingly with a smile. He had a point; outside in the snow was hardly a place you were going to get your gear off and succumb to the advances of a rogue, charming though he may be.

"Sure, why not?" I said, figuring it would be more fun with Anders than stuck to the bunny slopes with the others. "I'll see you down here in the morning."

"Let's get an early start. I'll meet you at eight thirty. We'll get the first lift up."

The weather the next morning was perfect: cold, dry, and sunny. The snow sparkled in the sunlight, and as I stood in the small secluded clearing with a view down to another quaint French ski village, the scene was so beautiful it took my breath away. Anders stood by my side, quietly looking at the trees. I have to admit I was having fun. Anders knew the mountain well and had taken me on some great off-trail runs, our skis squeaking through untouched virgin snow.

He was good company. The fresh air and exercise was as intoxicating as the bottle of wine we shared at lunch, and I was floating on a sea of well-being. He flirted outrageously, making me laugh. It had been a while since anyone but the local butcher had flirted with me, and he flirted with everyone. The woman I used to be, young and desirable, peeked out from the box I had stored her away in years ago when the changes brought about by age and motherhood had rendered me virtually invisible as an object of desire.

This was crazy and dangerous but so much fun, as long as it didn't get out of hand, and by that, I meant myself. Anders was too handsome and smooth and obviously up for a bit of fun with someone who wouldn't be an emotional entanglement, being already married. I wasn't exactly immune to his charms, but I hoped that seeing it for what it was would stop my head being turned by it.

"Beautiful, isn't it?" Anders said in my ear.

I jumped, not realizing he had moved so close. My skis tangled, and I lost my balance, falling sideways. I flailed wildly, trying to regain my feet, and grabbed Anders, who should have been solid enough to hold me up. I must have caught him by surprise too, though, because my weight overbalanced him, and we both went crashing into the snow. I landed flat on my back with a thud, winding myself.

Anders tried not to land on me and threw himself sideways, landing on his side in the snow beside me with a loud "Oomph." I lay there, trying to get my breath back and pretend it didn't hurt that much.

"I'm sorry. Are you okay?" I asked finally, when I could. He bent down and unclipped our skis, freeing our legs before turning back.

"I'm fine," he said with his incredibly sexy smile. "Are you hurt?"

Uh oh! I thought. He was way too close.

"No, just a bit stuck at the moment." I looked pointedly down at his body which was still half lying on top of me.

"Let me just check for injuries before you move. I did a first aid course as part of my national service." He pretended to look, running his hand lightly down my arm and my side. The touch was muffled through the layers of clothing, but as his hand rose closer to my breast, my breath caught. He looked up and deliberately ran his hand over the raised area of my parka, and I felt my nipple tighten. He moved closer until our faces were centimeters apart. He moved his head sideways, readying for the kiss. His lips stayed there; only a small movement on my part and we would be kissing.

"Tell me you don't want this." His breath was warm against my mouth. My lips were parted, taking shallow breaths. My head was clouded, unable to think with him this close, wanting to kiss him but having the distant thought that I shouldn't, even though I couldn't remember why right now with him so close.

"Say it." His lips brushed mine, featherlight, barely touching. All rational thought was swept away on a wave of need and desire.

"Kiss me," I breathed, willpower broken. He cupped my face in his hands and brought our lips together, slowly moving his mouth against mine. I moaned, wanting more, and he deepened the kiss, his warm tongue entering my mouth to gently touch mine. We explored the wet heat of each other's mouths, and my hand snaked up into his hair, twining in the thick blond strands. He drew himself up over me, resting his weight on his forearms, his large shoulders dwarfing my hands, his hips moving instinctively toward my pelvis.

Our kissing became more passionate and heated, and the small part of my brain that was still working wondered at the likelihood of anyone stumbling upon us. Given we hadn't seen anyone for hours and we were well away from the main trails, it was probably safe. Distracted, I hadn't noticed his hands opening the zip on my jacket as he started kissing my neck, and it wasn't until I felt the cold air hit my chest that I became aware that he had lifted my undershirt and thermals to reveal my breast, virtually naked though the thin lace of my bra.

I gasped in shock, but then his hot mouth closed around my cold nipple, and all thought left, except the glorious sensation of his warm tongue moving over it and the gentle tugging as he sucked. There seemed to be a direct connection down to my sex, which started to throb, and I felt a wet bubbling warmth between my thighs. His hand slid down my stomach and under my pants to dance over my clit and dip inside me until I was groaning, completely lost.

The desire was unreasonable and irrational, but my body wanted to be possessed by his, and it wanted it now. I didn't want to agonize about it, or think it through, weighing the outcomes. I wanted to have sex with Anders, and that was that. Consequences be damned; I'd think about it later.

Anders stripped his parka off and raised my hips to slide it under my legs. Then he quickly slid my pants down past my knees, taking my underwear with them. He fumbled in the pocket of his pants, pulling out a condom before opening his zip and pushing his ski pants down far enough to free his erection. I only got a quick glance at him as he rolled the rubber over himself, and I had a moment of slight panic at seeing him fully erect, which was more than sizable, before he was kissing me and lowering his body to press against mine.

He used his hand between us to guide his hard shaft until I felt it nudge the lips of my sex apart, and then he was sliding inside me, stretching me to the point of pain, heavy, thick, and hot. I shifted my hips a little to accommodate his size and moaned softly, urging him on as he surged up inside me, my hands on his smooth and tight buttocks, pressing him closer. Using his hard cock, he stabbed deeply into me, making me shiver with pleasure.

He then slid his hands down and under my hips, lifting slightly to change the angle so he went even deeper and harder, hitting a spot no one had reached in a long time, bringing a wildness to the pleasure enveloping me. I was swallowing the masculinity of him, even as he was piercing me, drinking him down with a need I hadn't known was within me. I could feel the excitement building with the feeling of him as he started pounding faster inside me and a tingling in my clit before I exploded with a short scream and felt my bones melt as tides of pleasure rippled outward through my body. Anders threw his head back as he buried himself inside me again and again until, with a strangled cry, he collapsed on top of me. It had been quick and straightforward, no bells or whistles, but easily the best sex I'd had in years.

"Oh…holy…fuck," I breathed softly when the power of speech returned. Anders raised himself up on his elbows to look at me.

"Is that good or bad?"

"Yes, no…both." I was making no sense.

"Regrets already?" He seemed to tense.

"Not yet, but I'm still flooded by endorphins. It will probably come later, but right now I'm freezing my butt off." It was true; I had the urgent physical need to get back into the warmth of my clothing. His jacket had certainly helped, but lying on snow, all the bare skin exposed was going numb.

"Right, yes." He withdrew from me and climbed to his feet. He offered me a hand to help me up, hamstrung as I was by my pants around my ankles. As I refastened my pants, he picked up his jacket from the snow and shook it out. I took my time adjusting my clothing, until I couldn't put off conversation any further. It hadn't taken long for the guilt to swamp whatever other feelings I might have had, with the exception of the toe-curling shame and embarrassment at my own wanton behavior, which seemed able to co-exist alongside the guilt. I felt the need to escape and be alone for a while to work out what I was going to do now.

"I'm going to go back," I mumbled, barely able to look at him. "I'll see you later."

"Wait," he said. "Can we talk about this?"

"Um…I'm not sure what there is to say."

"I thought you enjoyed it."

"Yes, very much, but I'm married." There was no point in denying it.

"Haven't you ever cheated before?" He looked surprised.

My eyes flashed to his face as blood flooded my cheeks. "No!"

"So, why did you?"

"I…Let's just call it a lapse in concentration." I clicked my boots into my skis. "I'm sorry; I should probably be more gracious about it, but I just need some space to think things through right now. I'll see you later at the lodge." I finished more quietly and skied away.

I couldn't sleep that night, and rather than keep Jack awake with my tossing and turning, I went down to the common room to make myself a hot chocolate and read for a while. My time alone that afternoon hadn't exactly been productive, and I was squirming uncomfortably internally. Jack, as usual, noticed nothing, which made me unreasonably angry at him. I had the uncharitable thought that if he paid me more attention and satisfied me sexually that it wouldn't have happened, so it was actually his fault. While that would have been comforting to believe, any deficits in my relationship with Jack were equally my fault, and he would hardly be tacitly encouraging me into an affair with another man.

I quashed the impulse to behave badly toward him and compound the problem, which was simply immature. Anders was fortunately absent from dinner, so at least I didn't have to face him too, but then I spent the night wondering where he was. Probably out trying to seduce someone else now, I thought unkindly, then berated myself for such a mean thought. It's not like he owed me anything, especially after my poor manners afterward, scampering away as soon as the deed was done.

I was waiting for the kettle to boil, tapping the spoon impatiently on the bench, when I heard a sound behind me and jumped a foot. Anders stood there in all his masculine glory, wearing only low riding pajama pants. He scratched the back of his head lazily, intentionally showing off his biceps and chest to their full advantage. My mouth hung open as my gaze traveled down his smooth and hairless chest, past the defined abs to the sexy V-shaped muscles just above his groin. I had no idea what they were called, but they were like an arrow pointing to what lay below. His grin showed that he knew exactly the effect he was having. He sauntered closer, and my mouth went dry. The kettle began to whistle, and for a moment I thought it was me. I turned quickly to switch it off, and I kept my back to him as I tried to regain my composure, which was more easily done if I wasn't looking at him.

"I'm just making a hot chocolate. Would you like one?" My voice was slightly too high, but under the circumstances, I thought I was doing quite well.

"Hmm...I do feel like something sweet." He had moved closer and was standing directly behind me. *His skin smells like sunshine,* I thought dazedly. I felt him move the thick curtain of my hair to the side to expose my neck before his lips started slowly kissing up toward my ear, sending goose bumps of pleasure straight down to my toes.

"What are you doing?" I breathed, gripping the bench for support as my knees went weak.

"Distracting you. Maybe you'll have another 'lapse.'" His large hands went around my waist, pulling me against him and breathing in deeply. His hands wandered up to cup my breasts through the thin fabric of my T-shirt, tweaking the nipples slightly when they hardened into points. My wanton body arched out to increase the contact, and my head fell back against his chest.

One of his hands left my breast and slipped inside the waistband of my pajama pants and down between my legs, and my eyes rolled back in my head. My hands gripped his thighs, and I was carried away by the waves of pleasure rolling over me from the effects of his long and very talented fingers. I felt him grow hard against my back, and I reached around to find him and easily slipped a hand inside his loose pants to stroke his impressive length firmly. He groaned in response and started thrusting into my hand.

"I want to be inside you," he said raggedly, undoing the drawstring on my pants, which fell into a puddle on the floor. He turned me to face him, and we started kissing voraciously as he lifted me up onto the bench, moved in between my thighs, and slid smoothly inside of me; I was wet and ready.

"Wait! We need a condom." I had no thoughts about stopping him. What few thoughts I'd had since he walked into the room had led to the conclusion that I had already been unfaithful and might as well be hung for a sheep as a lamb, as the saying went. It was pure sex, uncomplicated by baggage, simply pleasure. Why not, now that I'd already crossed that line? More than crossed it, really; I'd galloped crazily over it with barely a passing glance to mark my passage.

"God, you feel so good." He moved his hips in a circular motion. "Are you sure?"

"Yes, I'm sure," I gasped.

"Okay, hold on." He grabbed me around the waist with one hand, and the other supported my bottom, and while still inside me, he shuffled us over to his room on the far side of the common room. With a slight jerk that sent him further inside me, he opened the door and, closing it with one foot, fell with me underneath him onto the bed.

"That was pretty impressive," I whispered as he leaned over to the bedside table and retrieved a condom. Not many men would have been able to carry me.

A slight smile made the corners of his mouth turn up. "I thought you may not let me back in, so I had to make the most of it." He began to thrust gently as he kissed me until my head spun.

"Condom!" I gasped.

"Yes, okay. You sure?" He grinned cheekily.

"Absolutely," I said as firmly as I could. He ripped the condom packed with his teeth to open it and withdrew.

"Shall I do it?" I offered.

"I'm not sure I could hold on with you touching me. Next time." He rolled it quickly onto himself and slid back up inside me.

"There may not be a next time," I said breathily, my eyes closing.

"I'll have to make sure there is, then."

"You're very cocky."

"I've been told I'm pretty well-endowed, so I guess you could say that." His smile widened into a grin.

"Hmm…" I couldn't find the words to carry on the conversation, so I wrapped my arms around his neck to pull his face toward mine and started kissing him. He responded enthusiastically, and we were carried away again with the delights of each other's bodies and the thrill of illicit sex.

Chapter Eleven

I woke bolt upright at the sounds of people making breakfast in the common room next door.

"Fuck, fuck, *fuck!*" I said under my breath, completely panicked. Jack would be wondering where I was and why I hadn't gone back to bed last night. I reached for my clothes and started to get dressed, but my pajama bottoms were missing. Shit! They were still on the floor in the kitchen! There was no way out and it was going to be ugly and very public and I would have to do it with no pants on. I sat on the bed chewing my lip, wondering what to do and how on earth I was going to get up off the bed, knowing what awaited beyond that door was utter humiliation, for Jack and myself.

Anders' huge arm wrapped around my waist and pulled me back to him.

"Good morning." He smiled lazily, his eyes still half closed.

"Oh, God, Anders!" I wailed quietly. "It's a disaster! I fell asleep, and now everyone is awake and having breakfast. If I walk out of your room, everyone is going to know. Jack is probably already looking for me!"

"Don't worry," he said soothingly. "I'll tell him you went out."

"My coat is still hanging near the door. He'll know I didn't. And my pants are still on the kitchen floor!"

"No problem. Leave it to me." He hoisted himself off the bed, threw on a T-shirt over his naked chest, and pulled on his pajama pants that were lying on the floor. He opened the door and quickly walked out, closing it behind him. I waited anxiously but couldn't hear anything for several minutes until I heard Jack's voice asking whoever was in the common room if they'd seen me. Several voices answered "no," and then I heard Anders say, "I saw her earlier this morning. She was on her way out to the village. She said to tell you she wanted to let you sleep but wasn't feeling like skiing this morning and you should go without her."

"Why was she going to the village?" He sounded puzzled.

"I think she said she was going for a walk then getting a massage and doing some shopping."

"Oh." I could hear the relaxation in Jack's voice, clearly mollified by the explanation. It was something I would do, and Jack would be happy to avoid having to go shopping with me. The conversation continued on, Jack arranging to ski with some of the others who were there, saying his knee felt better. After a few minutes, I could hear them collecting their things and heading for the door.

"Not skiing today?" someone asked.

"I've got some scripts I have to read, but I'll go out later. Have a good day!" Anders answered cheerily, his voice getting closer to the door. He opened it and slipped inside, handing me my pajama bottoms that he had rolled into a small ball and concealed under his loose T-shirt. We waited silently, looking at each other until the front door slammed for the last time and the lodge was quiet.

"What did you do about my coat?"

"I put it underneath mine. It is completely covered."

"Oh…good thinking. You are really quite adept at this."

He was completely calm and professional, and I didn't want to think about how many times he had done this before. Clearly, potentially jealous husbands didn't faze him.

"I'm motivated by the proximity of your luscious body." He flopped down onto the bed and pulled me over on top of him, his hands running up and down the curve of my back. "And now we have all morning with no interruptions and a nice warm bed to get better acquainted." He pulled my mouth down to his and kissed me thoroughly until my toes tingled and my anxiety melted away. I gave in to the liquid desire pulsing through my veins and his enthusiastic and inventive lovemaking. By the time the morning was over, there was no part of either of us that hadn't been kissed or licked, and I left him sated and sleepy in his bed. On rubbery legs, I climbed the stairs to my room and had a long shower to wash away the external traces of my unfaithfulness.

I slept for a while and was reading on the bed when Jack returned in the afternoon. He suggested we go out for dinner, and I quickly agreed. I had deliberately not gone down into the common room for the rest of the day, and not seeing Anders at dinner would give me some much needed space. It had been a close call this morning, and throwing away my marriage for a holiday fling was really stupid. Jack deserved better than that. He shouldn't have to suffer public humiliation because I was weak and horny.

I fought the urge to seek out Anders, though he occupied my thoughts as if he were a narcotic. Like a glutton, I wanted to wallow in the intoxicating allure of him and the way he made me feel: like a woman able to revel in her sexuality, confident that she was made to give and receive pleasure. But as I had to keep reminding myself, the reality was that I wasn't free and my life had other guises I was expected to dress in: mother and wife, sexuality firmly in check. Part of me railed against it, but what was the point? So, my partner no longer saw me as a sexual being, but I didn't generally see myself as such either. There was no longer the time or the inclination for the abandon that it required, should the desire have been there in the first place. I had cheerfully killed off that part of myself after our children were born, with what I think was a quiet sigh of relief from Jack.

Anders, on the other hand, had resurrected the lusty beast, who was now loath to be leashed again. With only two more days left, I could manage this, I told myself. A return to domesticity would surely anesthetize whatever remained alive after the holiday was over, and then I could decide with a cool head what to do about my marriage.

I dressed with greater care than usual to go out that night, clothing immaculate and makeup perfect. I blow-dried my hair until it fell in a glossy dark brown sheet around my shoulders. I stared at myself in the mirror, surprised that I looked the same as always, light golden brown eyes staring back at me, unchanged. I examined my face carefully, sure that some evidence of my infidelity would show there like a brand for everyone to see. Apparently not, though. Just the usual face looking quizzically back at me. Jack, oblivious as always, simply asked if I was ready. I nodded, applying a last coat of rose-colored gloss, hoping and not hoping to see Anders on the way out.

Our friends were relaxing on the lounges, reading, talking, and drinking large glasses of red wine when we walked out. Anders was sitting with them, with his back to us. I didn't look directly at him, but I could see him in my peripheral vision turning around. Involuntarily, I looked down at him. His face twisted back to look at us, his head big and leonine, blue eyes admiring, but with a telltale look that was far more intimate than should be there. Heat flowed through me, and I had the foolhardy urge to go to him and fulfill the promise in his eyes. Disturbed by the ease at which I might be discovered by something as simple as our looking at each other, I hurried us out the door before Jack noticed.

As usual, dinner was nice and uniformly pleasant. We had been together as a couple since our early twenties, so it was easy to slip into our default interaction: polite, courteous, and non-controversial. Jack said little, but I was used to our companionable silence. As long as I didn't think about Anders and flashes of his naked body pressed to mine, the feel of him moving inside me, I was fine and the blood didn't rush inappropriately to heat my cheeks.

But the lack of obligation to make conversation left me time to think about Jack. Was I happy? The conventional wisdom is that something has to be broken in a relationship in order for someone to cheat, but nothing had happened in recent history to fundamentally change my feelings toward Jack, and I had never been tempted to cheat before. Our relationship had its issues, but it wasn't bad, just not that exciting. Our primary interaction was as parents, rather than lovers, something that seemed fairly average and to be expected.

I thought we would find each other again later when the kids had left or work no longer required so much of our attention. Had we let it go too far? Had our connection slipped away and neither of us cared enough to notice? I had no answer. Did I still desire him? I looked at Jack, carefully evaluating him. He was tall and good looking, slightly weathered by the years but still handsome in a more distinguished way. Though by no means perfect looking, he had become better looking with age and graying hair.

He looked up from his food and met my eyes, and instantly I hit on the problem. His gaze was impersonal, unemotional, and it was the way he had come to look more and more in recent years. I couldn't actually recall the last time he looked at me with any sort of emotion in his eyes. I had mistaken it for an evenness of temper and far preferable to the disdain I sometimes caught in the eyes of my friends' partners, but maybe it was worse. Love and hate were at least in the same ball park. Indifference was something else altogether.

Even happy or exciting events in my life failed to raise anything but the barest traces of interest. Jack had read snatches of the original book when I insisted, but he always looked like I was trying to torture him by making him read a book about cake, which he had little interest in, apart from eating it on occasion. When I discussed the publishing deal, he smiled absently, in his mind already making the journey to his desk and the call of his most serious relationship: work. Though he never said it, I knew he thought his working was more important than being physically present in family life. It was his way of providing for us, showing that he loved us by allowing us to be comfortable, in a way he could no longer express verbally. Slowly, so slowly, I hadn't really noticed it; he was turning into his father. How long before he started slipping silently from rooms?

What about my feelings? It wasn't that I didn't desire him; it was that I was afraid to be open with my desire because I was pretty sure he didn't desire me. I loved him, but it was tinged with nausea, that slightly queasy feeling in the bottom of my stomach that was the awareness that it wasn't returned equally. Not that he was looking for something else; I really think he just didn't want anyone with any passion. Sports provided a safe outlet for any of his more uncomfortable emotions, allowing the rest of his life safe passage.

This was the way of life I'd willingly conformed to, and in exchange, I received a comfortable existence, protected from any hardship that money could avert, and the freedom to pursue my own interests. With any relationship, there is a trade-off: you can marry a prince and live in a castle, but don't count on keeping your kids if your marriage ends. I married into old money, and in exchange, I had to put up with Edwina and the necessity of sending my children off to boarding school when I'd rather have kept them home. I understood, but it made me sad to be loved from a distance now. The man I married had become a stranger.

But at the same time, I knew myself, and even though I craved intimacy, I could recognize another part of me that was terrified of the vulnerability it demanded. That part needed the space an emotionally absent husband could provide. If things went wrong, which I had always been slightly afraid was going to happen, I would lose any place I might have had in this world. Now I was actively courting it, which was madness, but in a way, it would almost be a relief. I'd been waiting so long for something to disrupt our marriage that it would almost be a blessing to be able to stop anticipating it.

I was lucky in so many ways with my lot in life. It was a deal that almost everyone would make, and I had no right to feel dissatisfied now. Sex was great, but you spent far more time doing other things after the first few years, so it couldn't be that important. Maybe I needed this fling to get it out of my system so I could return and keep going without breaking down into a screaming heap when I hit forty. *This was an early mid-life crisis*, I decided. *Was there really a need to break up our family over it? If I was careful, could I get away with it?* It was an interesting thought. I felt an excruciating amount of guilt, but intellectually, I knew that I was doing it to myself. If I gave myself this one free pass, maybe I could ride this guilt until the end, trading it off against the irritations of married life, thereby assuaging any of the self-destructive impulses I occasionally felt to end my marriage, a desire that sometimes called to me like a siren-song.

By dessert, I had concluded my internal negotiation and given myself a free pass, just this once. It was unlikely that there was any further chance to sleep with Anders, given that there was only one night after tonight. After this, we would go back to London and our lives as they were and carry on until we were dead. A ripple of despair lapped at my heart. It was a depressing thought, that this week would be my farewell to sex and intimacy for the rest of my life.

I was making coffee in the kitchen the next morning when Anders came in behind me.

"This reminds me of two nights ago. If only there weren't so many people here…" he said. Just hearing his voice, low, gravelly and slightly accented, created a lick of lust in my stomach.

"I'm pretty sure we could clear the room if we tried a re-enactment," I said jokingly.

"Did you have a nice dinner last night?" His words were unexceptional, but there was more behind them. I snuck a glance at him, and his face was more intense than the situation required.

"Yes, thank you."

"Am I going to get to see you alone again?"

"No, I can't. We leave tomorrow morning. It's just not possible," I said with regret. I had already given it some thought.

"We may never get to see each other again. Let's say goodbye properly," he urged. "Pretend you feel sick and come in after lunch. I'll wait for you in my room."

"I'm not sure that's a good idea. Jack may come in with me."

"Please."

"Okay, I'll try. If he comes with me, then I won't be able to."

"All right, but try to get away."

"Anders, can you hurry Katie up with the coffee?" Michael called from the common room.

"Coming!" I sang out, hurrying away. The sick nervous feeling churning my stomach from the fear of getting caught might not make a lie out of my claiming to be sick, and I started setting the groundwork for my excuse right then.

I hated pretending to be selfless by encouraging Jack to keep skiing without me, claiming I was just going to lie down for a while. In case he came back early, I told him that if I felt a bit better I might go for a hot chocolate later, which would explain my absence if he came looking. The only thing I had to worry about was someone seeing me coming out of Anders' room, but I could get him to check the coast was clear first. This was the last time, so if I didn't get caught now, then I would get away with it.

Anders must have heard the front door open because when I came through the common room, he was leaning against the door to his room, wearing jeans and an old T-shirt that draped softly over his chest, hinting at the muscles underneath. He looked behind me to check I was alone before opening up his arms.

I walked slowly over to him, wanting to savor every moment of what would be our last time together. Our eyes locked together, and I started undoing my parka and then unzipping my ski top. There was nothing underneath, and I heard his intake of breath and saw the desire fire up in his eyes. I reached him, and he silently bent and, sweeping one hand under my knees, lifted me into his arms and carried me into his room, kicking the door closed behind us.

Chapter Twelve

We left early the next morning, in the usual rush of departure. I didn't see Anders again, for which I was half-happy, half-sad. Happy to avoid the awkwardness of having Jack there and disappointed that I didn't see him one last time, brief and unsatisfying though it would have been. We made our plane in plenty of time, and only a couple of hours later, we were in the back of a black car, driving through the gray bleakness of London, heading back to our house and the real world.

The holiday break was now officially over, and I recommenced the promotional trail for my second cookbook, *The Gospel According to Saint Kate*, in the lead up to Valentine's Day, which was fun but exhausting. I had now been deemed successful enough to have been upgraded to a more senior publicist, who accompanied me to all the events. I was not the easiest of clients, having such an ambiguous relationship with the media, but Lindsay took it all in stride. She was a tall, lanky American with wide green eyes and long, deep ruby-red hair, which she tossed around and played with like a small pet. The cost of maintaining her quite astonishing mane probably cost the same as a pet too. We got on well, even though she scared me a little. She was spectacularly efficient at her job, which involved setting up publicity events, not only the usual appearances at premieres, ballet, opera, and movies, cooking demonstrations, and book signings, but also spreads in magazines and media interviews.

Today's event was a morning show interview and "cooking" demonstration, though most of the actual cooking had been taken care of beforehand. Though I'd done them before, there was more pressure with this one, given it was on the same network I was currently in negotiations with. Interviews could become quite boring after a while as I'm not one of those people who find themselves endlessly fascinating, and it just feels like you're repeating yourself constantly. It's really hard to keep it fresh and interesting when you've already been asked the same question, albeit worded slightly differently, twenty times before.

It's part of the job, though, and I did it willingly, which didn't stop it being a bit like the movie *Groundhog Day*. I did the cooking demonstration, smiling in all the right places, chatting with the hosts in heavily scripted exchanges, until it felt like the pancake makeup on my face was going to crack or melt from the heat of the lights and my tension. I tried not to think about how heavily my performance today was going to be scrutinized, but it was hard. After the show wrapped, they gave us a recording, and we went back to Lindsay's office to review it. Miraculously, I looked relaxed and happy, a far cry from the automated robot I felt like underneath the heavy makeup. It was amazing how something that felt so unnatural in the flesh looked normal on the television.

Bats and I recommenced our exercise sessions.

"How are things?" she asked as we cut through the path at the back of St. Luke's Gardens. Bats wasn't even puffing, unlike me who sounded like an asthmatic pug.

"Hmm…Career-wise, everything is going amazeballs. The second book is selling well, and the talks for the television show are slowly progressing, though nothing is signed yet." It would be a lot more work, but with the boys away at boarding school, there was nothing preventing me from taking on a bigger workload.

"How are things with Jack?"

"Not as good." My relationship with my husband was going nowhere. As the weeks passed since our ski trip, the subtle attempts I'd been making to revive our intimacy had failed. "I try cooking nice meals at home with candles, which we eat in silence. I ask him questions, and he gives me one word answers. I can't even have a conversation with him about the weather at the moment! I've arranged dinners out at restaurants, which he comes to, but it's the same. He never says no, but he doesn't participate. If only he said no, then it would bring the matter to a head, but instead, he agrees to any suggestion, leaving me nothing to work with. At night, we rarely go to bed at the same time. If I am in bed, he'll stay up until I fall asleep; if he goes in before me, he'll be sleeping no matter how quickly I get in there after him. I'm beyond frustrated."

Bats nodded sympathetically.

"Have you tried talking to him directly?" she asked.

"That never works too well for us. If I try to confront stuff head on, he runs for the hills. I have to approach things gently, or he just shuts down."

"It sounds like you don't have many other options."

"I know. I could leave it and sweep it under the rug with the other stuff, but I think we're starting to run out of room under there. I think I need this to get worked out."

"You can do it!" she yelled, raising imaginary pompoms. "Yes, you can!"

"Why are you shouting slogans at me?" I looked around, but the park was fortunately empty.

"I'm your cheerleader, and you are my relationship guinea pig. If you can't do it, no one can. Go, Katie!" She winked and picked up speed.

"You're an idiot!" I laughed, racing after her. "You know I only hang out with you because you make me look sane."

She poked her tongue out at me and ran faster, the skinny bitch.

After a week of mulling it over, I finally tried a direct conversation with Jack.

"Have you noticed that we don't talk much anymore?" I tried to make my voice even and non-confrontational. It was after dinner, and we were sitting in the casual sitting room, reading our books, so I thought it would be the best time to have a potentially difficult conversation.

"No," he said shortly. "We're talking now." He didn't take his eyes off the page, but I could see his body tense.

"I mean that we don't talk about anything more than the basics, and I can't remember the last time we had sex."

He huffed and looked pained.

"Look, I'm really tired and work is stressful. With the credit crunch, I'm not even sure I'll have a job in the morning. Five thousand people are getting laid off worldwide, with two thousand going from London alone. My team is barely meeting targets, so there's a good chance some of us are going to go. I just want to relax when I get home and not have to deal with this rubbish. You're just being needy. We're fine; there's no need to get worked up about it. I don't feel like having sex when I'm stressed and tired." Thoroughly put out, he got up and walked off.

I got up to follow him, to make him listen, but forced myself to stop. The more I confronted him, the more tightly closed off he would become. I shut the door and let out a frustrated growl. I stalked about the room, trying to control the impulse to smash something. When my cell phone rang, I snatched it up, hoping for a distraction that would stop me from doing something I would regret.

Ironic, really.

Chapter Thirteen

"Hello!" I barked, not caring for a moment how it would make the person on the other end feel. I was almost hoping it was a telemarketer on whom I could anonymously vent some of my frustration.

"Hi! It's Anders."

The unexpectedness of his calling stopped me instantly, and I struggled to respond with the conventional greetings. We had exchanged numbers but had made no plans to actually speak again. After a pause, he went on.

"How are you?" His deep and slightly accented voice took me straight back to the ski lodge, lying on his bed, one hand clutching the sheets, the other in my mouth to stop from screaming my orgasm, his head moving between my thighs.

"Fine, good." I finally found my voice. "How are you?"

"Great! Uh, I'm going to be in London in two weeks. Are you free for lunch?"

"Oh!" I breathed, strongly ambivalent. Part of me leaped in anticipation, delighted at the possibility, but another equally strong part that dealt with survival felt fear at his coming. If I met up with him in my home city, it wasn't just a holiday fling—it was an affair. This was where I lived and people knew me, and the risks of being discovered skyrocketed. I had escaped detection once, but this was reckless.

"Sure," I said, seemingly on automatic. I hadn't finished thinking it through! *Why had I said that?* I mentally slapped myself on the head.

"I'm staying at the Mayfair. Come up to the Amarillo suite. There's a dining room in the suite so we can order some lunch and eat in privacy."

"That sounds nice," I said noncommittally.

"I'll leave a key with the concierge for you so you can get up to the suite without having to show ID. I'll make up a name and text it to you. I'm booked in under a different name myself."

"That is very…sensible." The media in this country were nuts, and it made sense not to use our real names, just in case. "What day?"

"Whenever you're free." Damn that meant I couldn't say I was busy, but I didn't really want to say no, even though I definitely should. Still, lunch in his room was unlikely to be seen by anyone I knew and was the safest possible option.

"How about Tuesday?"

"Tuesday is perfect. See you then." He hung up after we said goodbye. The conversation was far from romantic, so either he did just want to catch up for lunch on a purely platonic basis or he was simply after sex. I wasn't sure how I felt about either of those options.

Without thinking it through too much, I started preparing for seeing him like I would for a major event. I ate more oily fish for a good complexion, cut out treats, and worked out a little harder at the gym and with Bats. Two days out, I went to the beautician for some waxing, even going a bit further than I usually did on the intimate areas. I gave way too much thought, though, to what I was going to wear, wanting to look spectacular without, of course, looking as if I had tried. I had a facial and got my nails done.

By the time I left the house in a red and cream printed Celine shift dress with pale leather heels, matching belt, and my cream Chanel jacket, I was as buffed and polished as I got. Hopefully the statement the outfit made was dressy but not overdone. Considering I was going to lunch with a man who probably wouldn't notice anyway, I should just have worn jeans, but fashion was like armor, and it gave me the confidence, knowing I looked good, to meet him with the minimum of nerves. Great plan, but the nerves grew the closer I got to the hotel, and the further up my esophagus the butterflies flew until I felt I was about to vomit winged insects. Sheer determination that I wouldn't damage the Chanel kept everything down. *You don't have to do this,* I reminded myself. *Walk away and tell him you don't want to see him again.* I couldn't imagine him being too upset. Or I could just have lunch and decline anything further. There was no pressure on me to do anything. It was just lunch with an acquaintance. I really wanted to see him, so I took a deep breath, blew it out, and then walked into the lobby and looked around for the concierge.

"Hello, I think there is a key here for me. Ursula Andress?" I felt silly just saying it and looked around to see if anyone had heard to compound my embarrassment. No one was paying me the slightest attention until I started staring at them, so I concentrated on the concierge. I realized, then, how suspicious I was looking and tried to relax and look less like I was about to rob a bank or engage in some other nefarious activity, like start an affair. The concierge looked completely unruffled and ignored my discomfort. This must be an everyday thing for him. How odd.

"Certainly, madam. Here is your key."

I took it and scampered for the privacy of the lift.

Anders opened the door and kissed me on the cheek in greeting, waving me inside. His hair was shorter and neatly combed flat, which made it look darker. He wore a white T-shirt with blue horizontal stripes, dark blue fitted jeans, and no shoes, the warmer weather clothing changing him into someone younger, trendier, and faintly nautical. He looked like something out of a Ralph Lauren catalog. More than just clothing, it was selling a lifestyle. *Was Anders the lifestyle choice I wanted to make now?* I wondered.

The suite was tastefully opulent. Anders stood behind me as I looked around for a moment, not sure where to go. He moved out from behind me and placed his hand on the small of my back, intending to guide me toward the sofa. Wound up as tightly as I was, I started involuntarily. He dropped his hand, and awkwardness descended. He went and sat on the large three-seater couch at one end, and I took the other, folding my knees to the side, feeling prim and overdressed.

"I have some menus. Shall we order now? It will take a little while for the food to arrive."

"That would be lovely," I said as he handed me the menu. I could pick up no intimation from him that he expected anything. Maybe I had been too speedy in my assumption that he wanted to take up from where we were before. Even in my head, I couldn't call it an affair. It was possible that it really was just catching up for lunch. I felt some chagrin that I hadn't seriously entertained the possibility that I was just someone he knew in town and I was saving him from eating alone. How strange to try to be "friends" with him now! I really didn't know him at all, even though I'd licked the most intimate parts of him.

Years ago, I was living in a flat in a row of apartment buildings, and a neighbor had caught sight of me naked through a bathroom window accidentally left open. There was only a gap of a few meters between our apartment buildings, so as I stood in the shower, I looked over to see him watching me as he did the washing up. Somehow, it was rather funny, more than a little uncomfortable, but less so after I caught him vacuuming and dancing in his boxer shorts shortly afterward. Bumping into him at the local shops or on the street, we nodded to each other in greeting, never actually speaking to each other beyond a casual hello. We had seen each other in unguarded and intimate moments that probably even our close friends would never see, and it led to a weird sort of intimacy, though we never knew each other's name. The situation — "affair?" I wasn't sure of the taste of that word — with Anders was like that, only much more.

I ordered a chicken salad, having the ridiculous notion that if I didn't ruin my diet, then all else would be forgivable. Anders chose fish and a bottle of Australian white wine.

"To make you feel at home," he said with a smile, and I was touched by the thoughtful gesture. It had been many years since Jack would have thought of something like that, if ever. He wasn't exactly the sentimental type, so it would probably not have even occurred to him. Making a conscious decision then not to think of Jack, I looked over at Anders on the other end of couch. It felt odd to be sitting here alone with him again, but in completely different circumstances. He was so familiar, but not. Like an ex-boyfriend from years ago, but without the angst from breaking up lurking in the background. I felt nervous but excited too, a slight quivering in the stomach.

"So, how have you been?" I asked inquiringly.

"Good," he said, his eyes focused on my face. "You?"

"Really well. My second book is selling well, and the TV show looks like it might be going ahead," I said brightly. To stop myself from babbling on, I glanced around the room. It was hard to keep looking at him. He was staring at me so intently, but I didn't know what exactly we were doing here. Did he want to be friends? Lovers? I just couldn't tell, and it was starting to drive me nuts.

"What brings you to London?" I asked politely.

"Work, doing some publicity for the show," he said dismissively. "Boring stuff. How is Jack?" he asked, his voice deepening slightly.

"Fine," I said slowly, not sure where this was leading.

"So, you're still together?"

"As much as ever," I answered somewhat cryptically, though it was the best possible description. I was starting to feel a bit warm and stood up to take off my jacket and hang it over a chair. It was also a convenient excuse to move away from the couch and have some space to think. I was puzzled. His look was intimate, too intense for a "just friends" lunch, but asking me about my husband was surely not going to be the start of anything. Reminding someone about their spouse was the last thing you'd do if you wanted to sleep with them.

"Why did you call me?" I asked softly, searching his face, just wanting the truth out there. I didn't know how I was supposed to act, and it would be easier if I just knew what he wanted.

"Truly?" He stood, walked over to me, and reached down to pick up my hand. "I kept thinking about France. It was distracting." Looking into my eyes, he brought my palm to his lips and kissed it gently. It sent a shock of desire down to my toes, and my lips parted in a soft exhalation. Such a simple thing and already I wanted to sleep with him again. But who was I kidding? I'd wanted to sleep with him again the moment I walked in the door. Or was it the moment I'd heard his voice on the phone?

"Oh?" I asked a little breathlessly. "What about it?"

"You. Naked. Me inside you."

"Ohh…" It came out as a sigh. He was still only holding my hand, and I was already melting into a puddle of lust and need.

"I wanted to see you again to see if it was still the same…" He paused, seeming to drink me in with his eyes. "Yes, I am still on fire for you." He raised his eyebrow questioningly and moved closer. "Have you thought about me?"

"Yes," I whispered, feeling unaccountably exposed with that admission. Then there were no more words as we almost collided in our rush to each other. When our lips met, it wasn't tentative, neither of us holding back. We kissed like teenagers, as if we were desperate and drowning. We were in bed again long before lunch arrived.

Afterward, we were facing each other, our legs entwined, my head on his shoulder as he gently stroked my back. The sex with Anders was simply mind-boggling, and this latest time was even better than before, if possible. We seemed to fit together; there was no other way of explaining it. My body was still thrumming as we lay there.

"Can I ask you a question?" he said.

"Sure." I nuzzled his neck lazily. He smelled so good, clean and masculine with just a hint of aftershave.

"You said you'd never slept with anyone other than your husband."

"Umm, well, yes, I have. I wasn't a virgin when we married."

"No, I mean after you were married." He rolled his eyes, looking adorable.

"Okay, no, not since I met Jack." I wondered why we were talking about this.

"So, why now?"

"What do you mean?"

"Why with me?"

I sat up and looked at him, his eyes showed his concern about this. "I don't know. I was attracted to you, and it just kind of happened. Thinking isn't my strong suit around you."

"You're not some mad fan or anything?" he asked, anxiety tightening his eyes.

"Err, no. I like the show, and I admit that I did have a few fantasies about you." He raised his eyebrows, and his smile was a little self-satisfied as I continued. "But I can distinguish reality from fiction. I'm not here because you're some actor on TV. That's awful of you to say." I playfully whacked him on the arm.

"So, I'm not your screensaver or anything," he said, pulling me on top of him and laughing up at me, looking relieved.

"No, that would be my children!" I said in mock indignation.

"I'm glad," he said, serious again. He reached out and pulled me down for a deep kiss.

It gave me a moment to think about it, and there was an explanation of sorts. "They say you have to be looking to have an affair, and to be honest, if you hadn't been someone I was aware of and fantasized about a bit before, I wouldn't have *seen* you, if you know what I mean. But that wasn't the reason I gave in to your roguish advances." I gently pushed the hair back from his forehead.

"Then, why did you?"

"Because I found you interesting and funny, as well as gorgeous. Something seemed to click. It wasn't a surface thing; it was more fundamental than that. It felt right, even though it was wrong."

He nodded in agreement. "This is too good to have ignored."

"Okay, well, what about you? Why me?"

"Are you fishing for compliments?" He tucked my hair back behind my ears.

"Absolutely!" I laughed. "But seriously, you're so good looking and have all these *women* who follow your every move and comment about it on the Internet, as well as the screaming fans at those events. How can I possibly compete with that adulation, let alone the amazingly beautiful women you meet every day for work?"

"First of all, I don't consider how I look to be particularly important. Women find anyone on television attractive and a sex symbol. I don't think I'm particularly good looking, and I find the whole thing slightly baffling. It's not like girls found me irresistible before I was famous. Quite the opposite, really." He laughed self-depreciatively. "I had to work pretty hard to get a girlfriend then, so I don't think of it as being real now. It's just something that's part of the job. I liked that you obviously wanted me but tried to deny it. You saw the man, not just the man on television."

"Oh. That makes sense on one level, but I can't imagine anyone not thinking you were incredibly sexy. Every time I see you, I just want to rip your clothes off."

"Even now?" he asked as his lips found my neck and started kissing in a downward direction.

"Ah…Really? Well, I would, but we're both still naked." I had the feeling I was being side-tracked, but I couldn't remember what we were talking about when he looked at me with that hot, hooded look in his eyes.

"So we are…" His smile turned slightly predatory, and his gaze fixed on my breasts. "How could I not want you? You are all woman, so soft and responsive." Lust lit his eyes. "I love your breasts." And then he showed me how much.

Chapter Fourteen

And so it started. We met as often as we could whenever he was in London. Every few weeks, he'd fly in for a day or two, and we would meet. It was exciting, and I was inexpressibly happy to see him. It felt like the sun had come out again after a long winter. I thought everyone would be able to see my joy. I started to miss him when I didn't see him for a few weeks, but the anticipation and the time we had together made it worthwhile.

I loved that it was uncomplicated, just the two of us enjoying each other, laughing, having sex. There were no everyday irritations to dampen it, or familiarity to dim the excitement of seeing each other. I felt free to be myself, the self I had been years ago, and I realized I liked the version of me that Anders saw: someone who wasn't needy and resentful and a little bit angry.

The sex was great because I could just let myself go — I wasn't holding back, on guard and protecting myself from being hurt. I wasn't worried that he would reject me, turning away with a thin excuse about being tired. He made me feel like I was the most desirable woman in the world and that he couldn't get enough of me. It was a miracle cure for my self-esteem as a woman, which had been running low for an impossibly long time. We're surrounded by so many images of teenagers who are held up as the paragons of beauty, and any woman over the age of twenty-five is past her use-by date. By her late-thirties, forget it. Bring on the wise old crone.

"You're supposed to be this amazing cook. When do I get to taste something that you've made?" We hadn't made it to the bed and were lying side by side on the carpet in the lounge room of the hotel suite, catching our breath.

"That's a fairly random request!" I said, laughing. "I can't even think yet."

"Well, one appetite is sated, so I can start thinking about the others. For a little while anyway." He smiled as he started running his hands over my bottom.

"Well, if I keep all your appetites satisfied, you'll keep me satisfied?" I grinned at him.

"Deal," he said, giving me a light smack.

"Cheeky," I muttered at him.

I started baking for Anders. Every time we would meet, I would bring something, and we would eat it together, usually still naked in bed. The first time I brought him a chocolate brownie. It was a beautiful recipe, simple and easy, all the ingredients together in a bowl, a rich mixture of butter, chocolate, and eggs, still soft and luscious in the middle but crispy and caramelized on the outside.

Anders sat up against the headboard in the white-sheeted bed, eating and groaning in delight. Dark crumbs dotted his abs and thighs, and I leaned over and licked them off. He held the brownie over the curve of my hip and sprinkled the last of the cake on me. He then pounced, tickling me with his lips as he enthusiastically cleaned me off, pinning me down until I was nearly crying with laughter.

"More," he laughed. "That was nowhere near enough. How could you torture me by only bringing one?"

Next I brought a small raspberry and white chocolate cheesecake. Anders wolfed it down, laughingly refusing me any but the smallest bite and licking his fingers with relish.

"Amazing," was all he said before kissing me deeply, the smooth taste of sweet vanilla-laced cheese still in his mouth.

"You are amazing. Lie back," I said.

Raising one eyebrow, he complied, lacing his hands behind his head, making his biceps bulge. I climbed on top of him, resting back on his thighs. My gaze roamed hungrily over his spectacular body, laid out like a gift in front of me. I ran my hands down the muscles of his chest with its umbrella of springy dark blond hair, tracing its path down. His stomach muscles jerked as I moved closer, his cock starting to swell again. I ran my fingers lightly down his length and lower, testing a weight of his balls, making him groan.

"Don't move," I cautioned before lowering myself between his legs. He watched me with hungry eyes as I reached out with my tongue to lick him. I started at the wide base of him, holding him firmly as he grew larger. He had to be nine magnificent solid inches, his cock completely in proportion with the rest of him. He was so hard under the surface of soft skin, the engorged purple head as soft as velvet.

I swirled my tongue over the top, keeping eye contact with him until his head rolled back as I lowered my mouth to take as much of him in as I could. I could only get half way before I had to come back up. I licked both my palms to lubricate them and wrapped them around the lower half as one hand was not enough to encase him and used my hands, together with my mouth, to pleasure him. I reached a rhythm of sucking and massaging until he quivered with the need to move.

Breaking finally, his hands dove into my hair, wrapping his fingers in the strands as he rolled us sideways so he could use his hips to thrust into my mouth. His wild groans and incoherent words turned me on, and I sucked harder and opened my mouth wider to take more of him in. Just when he reached the point where it was almost too much, he was too big and his movements too forceful, he started shaking and came hard with a loud yell, the cream of his come bursting into my mouth. I swallowed hurriedly as more came pouring out, taking all of him and licking him to the finish. He fell back onto the bed, still moaning. I moved up beside him on the pillow, grinning at the boneless mass I had turned him into. He reached over and pulled me to him in a tight hug, still panting. I gave him a few moments.

"Fuck me," he swore.

"Yes, I think I did." I laughed quietly at him.

"Thank you." His mouth found mine and, through his lips and tongue, showed me his gratitude.

"I assure you, it was my pleasure." I smiled.

I started planning the food with more thought than my outfit. After all, it's not like I was wearing clothes for very long. As soon as the door closed, we started fumbling for buttons and zippers in our haste to be together. It is only surprising that I never gave in to the temptation to just wear elasticized clothing. Anders, being already in the room, was often already naked, just wrapped in a towel like a big gorgeous present. I loved the way he became aroused so quickly at the mere sight of me. There is nothing better for the female libido than being desired so openly. So many months and our appetite for each other was still as strong as when we met. After sating ourselves, we would eat whatever treat I'd brought with me: tiny vanilla cakes topped with sweet decorations, brown ale chocolate cake with tangy cream cheese icing, spiced biscuits with zesty lemon filling, yeasty cinnamon buns still warm from the oven, creamy vanilla tarts with light flaky pastry topped with luscious berries, chocolate truffles boozy with whisky.

"Come here." He beckoned me from the bed where he sat naked, legs outstretched, polishing off a cinnamon-sugar-coated baked doughnut. I sauntered over, intrigued by the twinkle in his eye. He rose to attention as I climbed up the bed toward him.

"I want to eat you then the last bun as I fuck you."

"Really?" I laughed, raising an eyebrow. "Multitasking?"

"Two sins for the price of one." He licked the sugar crystals off his fingers and, grasping my hips, pulled me up as he slid under and between my thighs. His tongue connected with my clit and danced enticingly around it. Working his hands underneath me, he held my lips apart so he could torment me more easily. Floods of pleasure flowed through me, peaking again and again until I was unable to stand it. I tried to get away, but he held me there easily, fingers digging firmly into my electrified flesh as the pleasure and pain combined to make me scream my final orgasm. He let me go, and exhausted, I went to climb off him, but before I could collapse in a heap, he moved up the bed. Gripping the base of his erection with one hand, he held it straight up.

"Come and sit on my cock." His smile was wicked. I swung my leg over to straddle him again. Pulling me down remorselessly onto his straining erection, I could barely endure the sensation of him stretching my overly sensitized flesh, and I sat there, waiting for my body to adjust to the sudden invasion. Through slitted eyelids, I watched him reach for another doughnut before he started to grind his hips upward. My hand reached down to steady myself on his hard stomach as we started to move faster into each other.

"Fuck, it doesn't get better than this." Taking one last bite, he pulled me down to him, and I licked the sugar coating off his lips before he took me hard, body and soul.

I felt reinvigorated by Anders. I baked from a place of joy, new recipes flowing with an ease I hadn't experienced before. Even when they didn't work out, it didn't bother me as much, and solutions and new ideas popped into my head almost immediately, as if once an idea was out, it made room for another to take its place. I was just so happy whenever I saw him and wanted to share my elation, but there was no one I could tell without destroying the source of my happiness. I decided to call my new book *The Temptations of Saint Kate*. It seemed fitting. The only downside was that my muse could never be acknowledged or thanked for his huge part in it.

Anders could easily have taken over my every waking minute, except for the constraints of distance. In a good month, there were only a few days we could actually be together, and I think that is why I was able to maintain a normal façade with Jack. It also helped that the kids came home some weekends, which provided a distraction and reminded me why I wanted to be a family with Jack. It wasn't as if we ever fought, or life was unpleasant with him, but there was a fundamental piece that was lacking. I'm sure Jack knew something was going on with me, but he never asked or said anything to intimate that he knew. He wasn't blind, though, and I'm sure it was obvious that something in my manner toward him had changed. But, still, at those moments we were together as a family, I was happy, just in a different way.

We were at Rupert and Bats' place for a party, all our children together, sitting down for an informal dinner. I looked around as I sipped a glass of wine, seeing everyone content and happy. I felt a welling up of contentment; it wasn't the exuberance I had with Anders, but still a quiet happy that was calm and nurturing, and almost as satisfying.

But just as I acknowledged the worth of what I had with Jack, a dark pit of guilt opened in my soul, and the stupidity of the risk I was taking having an affair, however happy it made me, could easily cost me my family and friends. I tried to hide the sudden anguish I felt at the possibility of losing this. Unable to help myself, I rose and, with the pretense of checking on my boys, gave them a quick hug.

"Hey, Mums. What was that for?" Edward asked.

"No reason. It's just good to see you."

"Uh huh," he said, looking at me strangely. I ruffled his hair and went to find Bats in case she needed help.

On Sunday night, the children left again, and it was back to the two of us, and the happy feeling came less frequently. If it had gone entirely, then I would have known my marriage was over and the decision to leave would have been easier, but that wasn't the case. I still loved Jack, though the passion had abated and was covered by a hardened shell of unresolved issues. At times, it got so bad that I was one word away from ending it. I felt so overwhelmed by anger and frustration that I was poised, just waiting for one more thing to push me over that brink. But it was as if he knew subconsciously and never crossed that line.

Summer came, and everyone was a bit more joyful in the heat. With the long days of sunshine that beautiful summer, I didn't even stand out as being more cheerful than most. As the days lost their heat, I was still warmed by the glow of my secret lover and the delight of stolen moments together, though they were harder to come by. Anders' filming schedule had also picked up pace, and he was unable to get away as often. Also, the shooting season had started, and we were away so many weekends. With a more casual dinner on the Friday night and the formal dinner on the Saturday night, after the shooting, we didn't get back to London until Sunday lunch at the earliest.

"Corridor creep" was not uncommon at these house parties, but while Jack's parents' generation talked about it quite openly, it was done more quietly by ours. Still, mistakes were made, particularly after several bottles of wine had been consumed at dinner, along with lots of whisky or gin before and afterward.

We were staying at Rupert and Bats', and Jack and I had gone to bed relatively early. We were sound asleep when I was woken by someone softly moving into the room, closing the door with a soft click. Whoever it was, they were trying to be very stealthy. I nudged Jack, who quickly reached over to turn on the bedroom light. The man quickly averted his eyes, but not before we both recognized him.

"Crispin, what the fuck are you doing?" Jack boomed, not finding it in the least funny. I, on the other hand, was trying not to howl with laughter at the embarrassment on his face.

"Ugh…argh…" he stammered, gathering the cords of his dressing gown around his nudity, trying to work out an exit strategy. "Sorry…

wrong room. Good night." He turned and fled. I couldn't help myself and burst out laughing. Jack looked at me a bit puzzled, but then he saw the funny side and started laughing too. He turned out the light and spooned against my back as my laugh subsided into giggles.

"I hope I didn't spoil your night with Crispin." He chuckled, his breath brushing my ear.

"Frankly, I'd rather set my eyeballs on fire," I said, disgusted at the thought of anything even vaguely intimate with Crispin. I wondered at the identity of the poor unfortunate who was the focus of Crispin's attentions. The only bedrooms near ours were married couples and the children's rooms, which were empty tonight. While in the back of my mind, I hoped that whoever it was had invited him for the tryst, with Crispin, nothing could be assumed. I was tempted to get out of bed and make sure he went back to his own room, but there was no way of ensuring he would stay there.

"Really? I don't think that is actually possible," he said with a laugh.

"Hmm…I'd give it a go." There is something seriously wrong with Crispin, not that I'd say that to Jack. He was his brother, after all. The irony of joking about having a fling also made me feel slightly queasy.

Chapter Fifteen

I did wonder how long I would last, living this double life, but after six months, everything was still together and functioning. I started to hope that maybe I could have it all: a stable life with Jack and a thrilling affair with Anders. Jack couldn't give me everything I needed, and Anders more than filled the void. We were both happy with what we had, and I felt fulfilled.

I still experienced a thrill every time I saw Anders. He was amazing—clever, intuitive, funny, as well as so damn masculinely beautiful that he took my breath away in those first moments when I saw him after a break of a few weeks. I couldn't believe sometimes that he was there, waiting for me, wanting me still. Like he was a really, *really* good dream, the kind that you are disappointed when you wake up and try futilely to get back to sleep so you can go back there. Only Anders was real. So, I had to tempt fate by relaxing, thinking I might just be able to have it all.

"Would you ever leave Jack?" he asked, stroking my stomach lazily as I lay in a daze in the aftermath of almost frenzied sex, endorphins pumping around my body.

"I'm not sure," I said slowly. "It's far from perfect, but we have the kids and a lot of history. Are you asking me to leave him?" I watched his face carefully. Why had I jinxed it by thinking that everything was perfect, and everyone was happy with what they had?

"Maybe."

"Maybe? That's a pretty loaded word." My heart sank. I knew that this was the conversation where everything changed. He was going to break up with me.

"Maybe this won't be enough forever. I'm thirty-four and I'm starting to think about the future. I don't feel so comfortable being your bit on the side. I'd rather be the main meal."

"You knew I was married from the beginning," I pointed out.

"I know, and maybe it should have mattered, but it didn't bother me then. It bothers me now," he admitted.

"Why does it bother you?" I asked, curious.

"I want more."

"What happened to the 'player' thing you were doing?"

"What do you mean?" he retorted, eyebrows coming together in an almost straight line.

"You were so smooth and very practiced at seduction, I never stood a chance against that kind of charm assault." I smiled at him to take away the sting of the accusation.

"Well, I'm no virgin, and I know what I want. Does that make me a player?" he said gruffly.

"It does if all you are looking for is sex, which you were."

"I love sex with you, but that's not all I want. You don't really think that I need to be here every few weeks for work or just to have sex?"

"No, I guess not." I had deliberately tried to not read too much into it.

"Are you still sleeping with Jack?"

"No. We haven't had sex in a long time, since before I met you."

"Really?" he said, looking happy. "Great."

"So, if what you want is me sleeping just with you, you already have that."

"It's not the same thing. We have to hide the fact that we're seeing each other. I'm tired of sneaking around." He sighed, no longer looking so happy. "Don't you wish we could just be together?"

"Of course!" I exclaimed. "You were my fantasy guy before I even met you, and you turned out to be even better than I could have imagined." I kissed him lightly on the lips.

"Why not then?"

"If people found out about us being together, it's not just my marriage I'd be risking. It would be devastating for my children. Also my career depends on my lifestyle to a great extent. Unless we were really serious about each other, it makes no sense to risk it all, even though I would love to not have to hide where I'm going all the time."

"I'm not after a friends-with-benefits arrangement."

"What exactly are you looking for?" I asked.

"A wife…maybe children."

"Really? Oh…I…" I lay back and thought for a moment before responding. "I've done that already. I'm not sure I could have another child, physically or emotionally," I said quietly.

"Right." He looked down so I couldn't see his eyes.

"So, this is it? Do you want to stop seeing me?" I felt a pang at the thought of not seeing him again. I ducked my head so I could catch his eyes. I was surprised to see the same pain echoed there.

"We don't want the same things. Would you ever change your mind?" he asked directly.

I hesitated before answering. "That's a big decision and probably something I should think about before I answer definitively. I don't want to lose you, but if I decide that it's absolutely not something I would do, then I won't leave you hanging. It wouldn't be fair."

"I guess that's as much as I should ask for, but much less than I want."

"What do you want?"

"You, every day. In my bed, in my house instead of these impersonal hotels." He huffed in frustration. "You've never seen where I live nor have I seen your place. I don't get to see you enough, and its driving me crazy, thinking of you with him, when I want it to be me there sharing your day, telling you what happened in mine. I can't even call you to tell you in case he gets suspicious."

"So, how would it work exactly? We live on different continents, and you're away working so much." It seemed like a fantasy, having Anders on a daily basis. I don't think we'd ever leave the bedroom.

"I figured that if we decided to do it, then we'd work it out. You haven't actually said that you'd leave Jack yet."

"Until today I didn't know you even wanted that. I thought you were after a fairly casual thing."

"I don't feel very casual about you."

"How do you feel?" I asked teasingly, not really thinking he would answer with anything other than a joke.

"I love you, of course," he said, exasperated, like I should have known that already. "Sorry," he apologized. "That didn't come out how I meant it to. *Jeg elsker deg.* I love you." He stared into my eyes and then kissed me gently but thoroughly, and I was breathless when we broke apart.

I wasn't expecting that. At most, I thought he was going to say "I really like you." I had to put some thought into how I would respond. I liked him, *more* than liked him, but I hadn't let my guard down, not expecting this to ever become serious. It made me see him in a new light, and I had never felt the differences in our stages of life before, but now it had become a gulf.

Despite his beauty and glamour, life had been largely kind and easy for him, a few skirmishes here and there, but nothing too serious that would shake his optimism about love. But he was the green recruit to my scarred and cynical veteran, who had seen pain and grief and been wounded to the point where I didn't think I would survive. I couldn't tell him that I loved him back. I was about to become a painful memory for him, and it would hurt me to do it, but I couldn't lie to him. He was the one place where I was being honest in my life at the moment, and lying to him would pollute what we had. If this was the beginning of the end, I would at least be honorable about it. I owed him that for offering me his love.

"I've been careful not to think about you like that because I was sure you weren't serious about me," I answered carefully. "I really like you. I adore you, but…"

"I can wait. I'll wait for you because we belong together and I know you know it too, even if you can't admit it right now." His gaze was clear and focused, showing his sincerity. This shocked me.

"Umm…" It was so unsettling, his confidence. I had no such faith, and I knew from experience that no matter if you wanted something so much you would give anything, literally anything, to have or keep someone, there were no guarantees that you could influence the outcome at all. Or that what you wanted wasn't actually more painful than letting go.

"Shhh. Don't look like that." He hugged me closer, and I clung to him, my head on his chest, trying not to cry at the dark turn my thoughts had taken. His hand stroking my back brought me back to the present.

"I'm so sorry," I mumbled into the valley of his chest.

"Do you think there is a chance you ever might love me?" he asked. I couldn't believe he was so calm and understanding. It's a hard thing to put yourself out there and not get a reciprocal declaration. Most people would be having a meltdown and walking out around now.

"There are so many amazing things about you; it would be strange if I didn't. I just never let myself think about where we were going in case I ruined it."

"Hmm…" he said, considering it. "Maybe there's something I can do to hurry you up."

His hands became more determined in their movements, and I sighed in pleasure. I turned my head to watch us in the mirror on the wall as he entered me, still wet and open from our previous lovemaking, my skin white to his golden hue, my thighs wrapped around his hips as he moved rhythmically back and forth, his beautiful rounded buttocks squeezing tightly as he reached the apex of his thrust. I looked up at him above me and twined my hand in his blond hair. His eyes were shut in concentration but opened at my touch.

"My beautiful Viking," I whispered. His bright blue eyes were intense as he stared down at me. He suddenly stopped moving and, rolling us over, pulled himself back up the bed until he was leaning against the headboard and I was in his lap, with him still hard up inside me. He put his hands on my hips and started rotating me on him, rubbing me back and forth to work my clit too. My head lolled back, only his large hands keeping me upright, moving me back and forth as the tension built. Just when I was about to come, he would stop, slowing down before starting again. By the fourth time, I was aching for it so badly I was about to scream or weep with his delicious torture.

"Do you love me?" he asked.

"Oh, God, yes! Don't stop!" I gasped, my body wrapped in incandescent pleasure.

"Say it!"

"What?" I breathed, barely cognizant. I was so close.

"Tell me you love me," he urged, moving faster.

"I love you!" I panted as I exploded and the waves of pleasure wiped out all coherent thought and I collapsed on top of him, shuddering with the aftershocks from the huge orgasm. I was so wrapped in my own pleasure, I barely felt his climax, only the after-pulses and pooling warmth as he came inside me with a loud groan.

"Oh, God, we forgot to put on a condom." I had been so distract-ed by our conversation that I had completely forgotten to think of it.

"I got tested a couple of weeks ago for insurance stuff. I don't have anything. I can show you the results if you like."

"Are you sleeping with anyone else?"

"No. You've got me so tied up, I haven't been able to look at anyone else. Are you?"

"No, not even Jack."

"What about pregnancy? Are you on the pill?"

"No, but it's not possible for me to fall pregnant naturally."

"Why?"

"I think things got a little screwed up when I had the boys. Twins sometimes do that."

"I'm sorry."

"Don't be. It's just one of those things. Let's talk about something else." I moved to roll off him, but he held me there.

"I love you." He pulled me down for a kiss. His words caused a flow of pleasure inside, it felt so good to hear the words and feel the sincerity behind them.

"I love you too," I said, as I sank into him, not sure whether it was the endorphins talking or whether I just might mean it.

Chapter Sixteen

One can't hold reality at bay forever, and the fact that Anders and I were both recognizable meant that eventually rumors would get out. I think it took so long because not many American programs are shown on television here, so not everyone would recognize him, and not everyone is interested in food, so they may not have known me.

It started out on the Internet, of course. There were always rumors about Anders hooking up with some starlet or other. Rather than give in to the unsettling doubts, I decided to just ask him about it, but he brushed it off.

"They need something to fill their pages; that's all. Some of it is true, but it's old stuff from years ago that they're recycling. That one there?" He pointed to the picture of a tiny blond girl. "We went on exactly one date three years ago. This one," he said as he pointed to another, "we were in a movie together, and those are stills from when we were filming. I never saw her outside the set." I looked at them all and couldn't help but notice that they were all small, perfectly formed blondes and couldn't have looked less like me.

The next time Anders visited, he rented a serviced apartment with a full kitchen. For the first time, we had a whole weekend together, as Jack was in the US for a conference for a week. He let me in the door, kissing me breathless up against the closed door.

"Hello, honey. How was your day?" he asked with a smile against my mouth. He slid his fingers into mine and led me into the kitchen. He'd been shopping, and the groceries were still on the bench.

"What's all this?" I asked.

"Let's see if we can do the domestic thing together. We can pretend we're doing it for real."

"Oh." The thought of living with Anders was so tempting and scary at the same time, and it felt like the stakes had just been raised.

"I'll cook for you tonight, and you do tomorrow night?" he asked.

"Sounds fabulous." I pulled him to me for a kiss and ran my fingers in his hair. He groaned and grabbed my hips, pulling me tightly against him. I could feel his arousal against my thigh.

"You're so hot, woman. I want to take you now, from behind, over the bench," he growled.

"Okay." I smiled in delicious anticipation.

It was one of the best weekends of my life—cooking and sex with Anders with no time limit or need to rush off. We lazed around naked in bed, talking while the Norwegian cinnamon buns I was making rose, the beautiful yeasty aroma mingling with the scent of our coffees. The freshly baked buns proved an aphrodisiac as we ate them hot in bed, the laughing lust in Anders' eyes turning me on.

"My God, you can cook!" He licked his lips, cleaning off the buttery cinnamon crumbs. "Guess what I'm good at."

"I don't know. What?" I smiled at him.

"Making you come." He jumped on top of me, pinning my arms to the bed.

"But I haven't finished my bun yet!" I protested, still holding part of the pastry in my restrained hand.

"You can finish it later." He kneed my legs apart and, with a single thrust, drove up inside me, still wet and swollen from our last session. The intense pleasure of it made my eyes roll back. He stroked hard and slow until I was gasping for more.

"Anders. Please," I groaned. He withdrew suddenly, and I made a mewling noise, wanting him back. He flipped me over, raised my ass into the air, and plunged into me again, his fingers finding my clit. I came almost instantly, shaking and throbbing as he kept going. He removed his fingers from my sensitive folds to grab my hips with both hands.

"You feel so good. So warm and wet. I could stay inside you forever." He buried himself over and over, and I could feel myself building again at his hot words. He started moving even faster, the slap of his body into mine moving me up the bed until I braced my arms against the headboard. The feel of him was intense but so good.

One of his hands slipped backward and traced the line between my buttocks. As his fingers found the bud of my ass and pressed lightly, I squealed.

"Stop that!"

"What? This?" He did it again.

"Yes, that!"

"Don't you like it? I thought it enhanced a woman's pleasure."

"It just feels weird." I squirmed a bit, trying to get away from his finger. It didn't hurt, but I wasn't so keen on the idea.

"Hasn't anyone taken your ass before?"

"No!"

"So, I could be your first?"

"What? No, I don't do that."

"It can be good. Let me just show you with my finger."

"Just your finger?"

"Yes." He leaned over me and nipped my ear, sending shivers down my spine. "For now. I promise you'll enjoy it."

"Okay," I breathed out, apprehensive.

He straightened up and, still moving in and out of me, used some of my lubrication to coat his finger. He moved it upward and circled my ass, making it pucker.

"Relax," he said, stroking my back. I tried. He moved his finger slowly in and out in time with his thrusts. The sensation was different but surprisingly erotic. I relaxed a bit more, and his finger moved deeper. The orgasm seemed to come out of nowhere, hitting me hard, overtaking all my senses in an incredible release until I was a quivering bundle of shuddering nerves, unable to move other than to twitch.

"Oh, fuck, yeah!" Anders groaned as my internal muscles clenched around him, and he came pumping furiously before collapsing on top of me. We lay that way for a few minutes, catching our breath.

"Wow," I said.

"Yes," he agreed, kissing my hair before rolling off me and pulling me to spoon against him. "If you moved in with me, we could do this all the time."

"Remind me to make you buns again." I leaned back and kissed him too, avoiding an answer.

The gossipy pieces about us started to get more frequent and detailed. Then, a week after it happened, an item came out on one of the gossip sites about our weekend at the apartment. The fact that the information they had was correct was even more startling. I was used to the trashier papers just printing what they liked. No one ever tried to correct them or take them on; it just made it worse. But the information they had was too close to be an accident. I would have thought I'd been phone tapped, except some of it had never been in a phone call. I then thought about the apartment being bugged, but how did they know we were going to be there?

I had no real fears that Jack would see it, as he would never look at that sort of thing, but the danger was that someone else would and tell him about it. When Lindsay arrived at my front door at eight in the morning, I knew I was in for a bullocking. Part of me was just surprised it had taken so long.

"Are you having an affair with Anders Larsen?" she demanded, walking in and closing the door behind her. Fortunately, Jack had already left for work and it wasn't school holidays so the boys were away. Her scrutiny was fierce and unflinching, and despite myself, I wilted slightly and could only nod. I led the way back into the kitchen and started making us both a coffee.

"You are supposed to let me know what's going on! I was completely unprepared when I got a call from a reporter this morning asking for a comment. Do you know how bad that looks?" she railed.

"Sorry," I mumbled, feeling chastised.

"Just because you're doing something like that doesn't make you a bad person. I'm not here to judge you," Lindsay drawled, flicking back her dark red hair, a frequent action when she was annoyed or unsettled. I looked closely at "my" publicist, though she was actually employed by my publisher to look after me as well as several other less troublesome authors. I could only watch her blearily in the weak early morning light. I hadn't slept well and was feeling a bit under the weather. I was still in my pajamas, though at least they were nice ones.

"We can work around this, but you have to tell me everything," she announced in a strident voice. "The only thing I can't handle is a surprise in tomorrow's papers. It's bad enough that it's on the Internet before I heard it from you."

I realized that it did make a publicist's job difficult to be blind-sided about a client's activities, but from the client's perspective, it's not always your first thought when you do something nefarious to ring your publicist and brag about it, not if you're a woman and aren't the star of a popular TV show anyway. Very few people would try to argue that there wasn't a double standard still firmly in place.

"I want you to tell me everything, now!" she demanded, completely in my face.

"I met Anders on holiday in France, and it started there, but we've been meeting up in hotels when he's here too."

"How long has it been going on?"

"Since March. I last saw him a week ago."

"Does Jack know? About the affair?" Lindsay lit a cigarette and started smoking absently. Seeing as she was here to save my ass, I didn't think I could object. I grabbed a small soy sauce dish from the cupboard and slid it over for her to use as an ashtray.

"No, I don't think so. We haven't spoken about the rumors. I'm not sure he even knows. They're not the kind of thing he ever pays attention to."

"I'm not going to tell you to stop; that's not my place." She waved her cigarette at me. "But you have to take appropriate steps to hide it. Which hotels have you been meeting at?"

"Mostly the Mayfair. Sometimes Browns or the Berkeley." I couldn't tell her about the apartment; somehow it seemed too private.

"That's good. Change around a bit and make sure you stay at the big ones with more than one exit. Whatever you do, avoid the small boutique ones. There aren't enough guests to hide amongst. Also, try to make sure you have a back-up reason to be there if possible. You know, visiting a friend, doing some writing, consulting with the chef, whatever floats your boat. Just make it vaguely plausible."

I just nodded, amazed that this happened enough that she had this kind of information at the ready.

"You have to figure out what you want in the future too, particularly if things are going to get serious with him. Leaving Jack for Anders would be an appalling career move for you."

"He's not that bad," I said a bit churlishly. "It's not like I violated Daniel Radcliffe and released a sex tape of it." It was slightly willful to refuse to see what she was referring to, but a masochistic part of me *wanted* to hear her say it. Refusing to be side-tracked, despite being a huge Harry Potter fan, she went on in an accusatory tone.

"Your image suits an affair like a pit bull suits a tiara. There is just no way you can make it work. Do you really need me to tell you why he is not great for you?" She paused for a moment, looking at me deliberately. I stubbornly looked at the floor, feeling like a belligerent teenager being given an unwanted lecture. She sighed and continued. "He's not great because he has a reputation for seducing woman and moving on quickly, bored once the chase is gone. That's his image. Whether it's actually true or not is irrelevant; it's the image he's willingly created and developed over a substantial period of time, and I can't see that he would let all that effort go to waste now. To salvage both your reputations if you were to go public, there would need to be coordinated groundwork—you, on your husband being unable to keep up with your career and having to go it alone to events, and him, telling people how he's looking to settle down. Otherwise, you're going to look like the loser who left her husband and then got dumped if it doesn't work out, on top of the hit you'll take from the loss of your marriage."

I winced, but I obviously needed to hear the brutal truth. I hadn't thought through the consequences nearly enough, and it was sobering to hear that I might lose everything I'd worked for, which had kept my sanity for the last decade. Work wasn't everything, but it was valuable to me, and I wasn't willing to throw it away.

"People will forgive a lot of things you do for love," Lindsay continued. "The only exceptions are where money or fame is involved. Then they become a lot more cynical, and the latitude you might otherwise get evaporates. The more money or fame, the less latitude. Unfortunately for you, you symbolize both money and fame, and you are going to be crucified if you leave Jack for Anders. The only way around it is to impose a buffer between the two of them, sufficient enough that people forget the rumors were around before the breakdown of your marriage. With the Internet, it's unlikely, but the lines can be blurred, as long as there aren't photographs. Nothing is more sordid than grainy images of people cheating in alleyways. You would be better off with a heroin addiction. People will forgive that a *lot* more easily."

Ouch.

"Really? Heroin is less harmful for your image than sex?" I asked quizzically.

Lindsay nodded sagely. I wasn't unaware that it would be far more sensible and less likely to be career suicide to stay in my marriage, stop seeing Anders, and try to salvage whatever was left. But easier was not what I wanted. What I wanted was Anders and my career, and to not hurt Jack or the kids in the process. I wanted my cake and to eat it too, and to not gain any weight in the process. The likelihood of keeping things as they were now for the long-term was almost non-existent. It might have worked for a while, but the rational side of me knew that eventually I'd find myself in a world of trouble. It looked like that time was fast approaching. Lindsay was right; I was going to have to figure out what I wanted, but right now, I really didn't know who I would be willing to give up.

"How serious are things with Anders?" Lindsay asked insistently. I understood that she was just doing her job, but I couldn't open up to her about things I barely wanted to admit to myself.

"It's not going to become anything serious. It's just good old-fashioned lust with an immensely hot man who happens to be on TV," I lied. Anders was more than that, but as a long-term partner, I just wasn't sure.

"So, you're going to stay with Jack?"

"I don't know." I rubbed my eyes tiredly. "We hardly speak and never sleep together anymore. I'm not sure what's left, if anything. I think the main reason we stay together is inertia."

"Inertia can be a powerful force." She ground out her cigarette and picked up her burgundy Mulberry bag. *It almost tones in with her hair*, I thought absently.

"I'll leave you with some homework. The first thing you need to work out is whether you want to make things work with Jack or if you're going to move on. We need to prepare our strategy now to minimize the impact of these rumors. The more coherent we make our statements, the easier they are to sell. If you do decide to leave

Jack, we need to give it some time before going public with Anders, if he's going to be your new boyfriend. Given the investment he's made in his playboy image, you'll have to make sure he's on board with it, or it could all blow up in our faces."

"I don't know about Anders in the long-term. He lives on another continent, and the odds aren't good that it will work out anyway." I knew it was a realistic assessment of the situation, but it was hard to think about, particularly as we were still in that stage of being so happy together, where you can't imagine you'll ever feel differently about each other.

"I can't tell you what to do; I can only make things easier with the media and the public and minimize the impact on your career. Unfortunately for you, what you're selling is yourself and your lifestyle, so if you make big changes to that, it's going to affect sales. There's no guarantee that if you leave Jack you won't lose everything. I'll do my best, and staying with Jack would make that much easier. If you decide you want to stay with him, I'll arrange invitations to some touchy-feely premieres where you can be photographed looking happy together. If you decide that you want to leave him, I'll change the invites to you on your own and start dropping hints to the paps about him not being there to support you, etcetera. They will pass it on 'anonymously' to the gossip writers, and then we can ease into a separation. Maybe I can arrange a professional shoot in a magazine to get you out there as a single woman. If lover-boy is going to be around, we can move him into a supportive, new partner role in a little bit. Jack just wasn't able to keep up, etcetera."

God, it sounded so clever and sensible, but horridly cold and heartless. This was Jack we were talking about, and she was treating him like he was a bug infestation.

"In the meantime," she continued, "if you are followed by photographers, *be nice*. Stop, let them get the photo. Be polite. If you cover yourself and run, they'll think you have something to hide, and they'll chase you. If you're an asshole, they'll sell the worst photos they take, and you'll be out there forever looking appalling and drug-fucked or whatever headline they choose to come out with. Trust me, there are always bad photographs with your eyes half-closed or while you're talking, and only through their goodwill will those photos not see the light of day. No matter what they say or do, you need to keep a smile on your face."

My stomach went into free-fall, and I barely recall showing Lindsay out. I could no longer stay with my head in the sand; I needed to make a choice. My thoughts just kept going around in circles. I couldn't make a decision. The thought of leaving Jack scared the bejesus out of me. The upheaval to our lives would be huge, and it wasn't like I hated him or didn't want to be around him. He was a good, if distant, husband and a great father to our boys.

Then there were the financial and social implications. We'd have to sell the house, and with the extra costs, we might struggle to pay the boys' school fees and support two households. My income would likely drop substantially, further eroding our already shaky financial position. If Jack lost his job due to the credit crunch, we could potentially be in real trouble. But if you took away the money side of the decision, I would probably leave him. Unfortunately, the money side of things wasn't going to resolve itself. Taking a risk, I decided to tell Bats. I thought she would be supportive of any decision I made, but it turned out, strangely enough, she was still cheering for Team Marriage.

"Family life is an investment. You put a whole lot of time and effort and money into it, and I'm not just talking about the children, but also into your marriage. Without your marriage, there is no family."

"Family is what you make it," I shot back. "Should I be unhappy? It's not like the boys are little anymore. They're barely at home now anyway and will be there less and less when they're off at university. How much difference will it make?"

"I think you'd be surprised. Are you unhappy with Jack? I've never heard you complain of anything but the lack of sex."

"There is that, and the fact that we're so distant from each other, but you're right. There are some good things there too. We've just hit a wall."

"Everyone hits a wall. What you do about it is entirely in your hands. Does Jack know?"

"No, I don't think so. He's not very observant, and he doesn't listen to gossip."

"Have you talked to him about your sex life?"

"I've tried, but he shuts me down. He doesn't want to acknowledge there's a problem."

"Could he be having an affair?"

"No. I'd know about it. He's too absent-minded to get away with it. I really think that he's just not that interested in sex."

"Do you still love him? Underneath it all, do you still like him as a person?"

I had to think about that one. I hesitated before answering. "Yes, I think so, but I have no idea what to do. I love Jack, but I think I might love Anders too. With Jack, I know what's missing, and I'm not sure it can be fixed without both of us really trying, and I don't think he'd be willing to acknowledge there is even a problem, let alone do anything about it. With Anders, anything is still possible because what we have is incomplete. We lack that everyday thing, the familiarity with each other. He might have annoying habits, but I don't know of any."

"So, Anders looks good because, at this stage, he could still be the perfect man."

"Yes, but the unknown is also scary. What if I give everything up for him and it doesn't work out? I would lose my husband, my work, everything."

"If we were in one of those trippy feel-good movies, I'd urge you to trust your instincts, take a leap of faith." She rolled her eyes.

"But we're not," I said doubtfully, wondering where she was going.

"No, that's just stupid. Real life doesn't work like that. You take a leap, and then you land on your face and everyone laughs at you. It's called comedy." She opened her arms. "Come here. Let me give you a hug."

I put my head on her shoulder and breathed out heavily as her arms settled down around me.

"Stay with Jack. I'll put out for you."

I laughed despite myself when she gave me a kiss on the forehead.

"You're a good friend. I know you're right, but the problem is how to give up Anders when I really don't want to."

"Be sensible. I know you have it in you. You can't give up everything you've spent years building on the off-chance it might work with this guy. If not for Jack and your kids, do it for yourself. You've just got everything taking off with your cookbooks and other ventures. Don't throw it away on something as risky as this."

They were wise words, and I knew what I had to do. I just really, really didn't want to. I was like a pack-a-day smoker who was going to go cold-turkey with no nicotine patches to help me through it. I would just see him one last time. I couldn't tell him over the phone. I was so nervous; I was shaking as I dialed his number.

"Hello?" he answered sleepily. God, in my anxiety I'd forgotten to check the time difference.

"I'm so sorry to wake you Anders. It's Kate."

"Katie!" he exclaimed, obviously not expecting me to call.

"I need to see you. Are you coming this way anytime soon?"

"Ah…no, but you sound upset. Is anything wrong?"

"I need to talk to you, face to face."

"We're not shooting this Friday. I could take the red-eye Thursday night and be there Friday morning. I'll have to leave again Saturday morning."

I nodded and then realized he couldn't see that.

"That would be great. How about I meet you at the Mayfair?" It seemed fitting to end it where it had begun.

"Sure. How long can you stay? Shall I book the suite or just a room?"

"No, let me. I'll arrange it all. It's the least I can do after making you fly all the way here. See you Friday morning." I hung up before he could say anything else.

Chapter Seventeen

I waited nervously on the couch for the sound of his key swiping the door. He finally opened it, and I fought not to run to him. He shrugged off his overnight bag and let it drop on the floor. He looked a bit puzzled and concerned as he saw me sitting on the couch.

"Sweetheart, what's wrong?" He came and sat beside me.

"I'm so sorry, Anders," I said, trying not to cry.

"What?"

"I can't see you anymore."

"You're breaking up with me?" His voice rose, sounding strangled.

"The rumors are out there, and sooner or later Jack is going to find out. I love you, but I can't give up everything—my family, my career, my home. What if we don't work out?"

"We both want to be with each other. Why wouldn't it work?" he insisted.

"We're not risking the same things here. If our relationship doesn't work, you just walk away. I will have lost everything."

"I'll have lost you." He trailed his fingers down my face to catch the tears I hadn't even noticed I'd shed. "Fuck," he swore, "I love you, but I'm not going to force anyone to be with me. If you want to leave, then fine." His voice broke, and he shook his head, his eyes hard and glassy. My heart broke to see him so upset and know that

I caused it. Before I knew it, I was holding him in my arms, both of us crying uncontrollably. Then we started kissing. I tried to break away, but he pulled me back.

"No, if this is goodbye, I need to fuck you one last time. You owe me that," he said harshly before crashing his mouth and body into mine, pinning me back down on the couch.

My body strained into his, just as eager for the contact. I had no idea how I was going to survive without this, without him. We tore at each other's clothes, fumbling to remove the barriers between us, the desperate knowledge that this would be the last time, making it bittersweet. He pulled me onto his lap, slamming me down hard, piercing me until we were connected as completely as a man and a woman can be. I expected him to take me roughly, but instead he held me tightly, breathing hard into my neck, not moving at all. Puzzled I waited, but he stayed completely still, one arm around my hips, the other straight up my back with his fingers gripping my hair.

"Anders, are you okay?" I whispered.

"No," he gasped. "Just give me a moment." His body shuddered, and his cock jerked inside me. After long moments of just holding me with his whole body, he began to move gently, almost unwillingly. When we came together eventually, it was sad, beautiful, and an end in more ways than one.

I kissed him chastely goodbye as he held the door open, and he pulled me back against his chest to kiss me desperately, holding me tightly against him.

"Stay, Katie," he ground out. "We could make it work; I know it. Just think about it for a week or so. I will wait for you, however long you need, if you just give me hope."

I nodded, knowing I would do nothing but think about it and second-guess my decision. I smiled weakly at him, trying not to cry at the thought of him with someone else. I trailed my fingers along his chest as I moved away, keeping contact as long as possible. My smile faded as I looked down the corridor at a group of suited men who had obviously left a meeting in another suite.

I froze as one of them detached himself from the group to stare at me with hard, mocking, and all too familiar eyes. Crispin approached me slowly, his smile widening into a predatory grin. I glanced back to see Anders still standing in the doorway, a worried expression on his face as he watched Crispin approach.

"Go!" I mouthed silently to him. He looked like he would argue for a moment, but, mercifully, he shut the door.

Everything seemed to be moving in slow motion as my life as I knew it was sucked into a black hole of my own creation. There was no mistaking what Crispin had seen. I couldn't lie my way out of this, even if I wanted to. A small part of me was stupidly glad, relieved that the issue was going to be decided finally, but the larger part was devastated and bracing for the painful events about to create a wreckage of our home.

"Well, hello there, Kate!" he drawled and started to circle me. "Tell me that wasn't what I thought it was."

"No, it was exactly that." There was little point in denying it.

"Does Jack know?" he asked with a wide grin.

"Of course not," I said shortly, trying to keep track of him as he moved around.

"Well, I'm not going to keep your filthy little secret," he breathed too close to my ear. "Unless…"

"Unless what?" I wasn't hoping for anything, not from Crispin.

"Hmm…Turns out you *are* a dirty little slut, and that's something that appeals to me. You know, I had a bet years ago that I'd do you. Better late than never…" He laughed and I flinched. "I'll call you," he said in a mocking voice while waggling his fingers to mime a phone. Then he walked off, chuckling to himself.

That was Crispin to a T and why I had despised him since a hunting weekend at Clouston Hall, shortly after Jack and I had become engaged. Everyone was drinking a lot on the Saturday night, me included. We were still sitting at the dining table, drinking red wine. The conversation had turned a bit bawdy, everyone talking about their sexual fantasies.

"So, what's yours Katie?" someone had asked.

"A pool of melted chocolate and a sexy man to take a dip in it with me," I'd said, making it up on the spot. Crispin was next.

"I'd like to tie someone up and have them any way I like," he'd said, grinning darkly.

"That's definitely in the BDSM spectrum!" I'd laughed at him, in my inebriation, making a mental connection I should never have voiced out loud. "You must have some serious mummy issues." Everyone had laughed, seeing as it was actually true. Crispin had just glowered, and the conversation had moved on. I'd thought nothing more of it.

Jack had gone up to bed, and I'd stayed up talking to Bats and Rupert. Everyone else had drifted off, and I'd been last to leave, turning the lights off as I went. I'd been walking along the underground corridor that connected the kitchen to the north wing where our bedrooms were located when I was grabbed from behind. One hand covered my mouth, and the other arm clenched painfully around my waist. The unmistakably male body had forced me up against the wall, the skin of my cheek being grazed by the rough surface.

"You laugh at me, but I know you want it." Crispin had ground his hips against my buttocks. "I will fuck you hard until you scream for more."

I'd bitten his hand as hard as I could, and he'd yelped, his grip loosening. I'd turned and kneed him in the balls. He'd fallen to the ground groaning, cupping himself protectively.

"You are delusional!" I'd hissed at him. "I wouldn't sleep with you *ever*, you freak."

"Bitch!" he'd snarled, and I ran away before he could follow me.

Needless to say, things were a bit strained with Crispin after that, and I made sure I was never alone with him. The brothers had always had a difficult relationship, and after I told Jack what happened, he went after Crispin. I don't know what was said, but Crispin turned up with a black eye and a lame excuse about a cupboard the next morning.

Now he had something over me, and there was no getting around it. Despite giving up Anders, I was going to have to tell Jack anyway. The alternative was unthinkable. There was no way I was leaving myself to the mercy of Crispin. It was only a matter of time before he called.

No moment would be right, but every time I started to tell Jack in the days that followed, we were interrupted or I chickened out. It had been a week since I'd last seen Anders, and I was missing him fiercely. Giving him up was harder than I had imagined, and I was wavering. I was going to hurt Jack anyway when I told him, so why not go the whole way now and tell him that I was leaving him too? Imagining Jack and I fully reconciled was a castle in Spain. The best I could hope for was more of the same. With Anders I could be happy. Would the loss of this life mean more?

I didn't know what to do, so I Googled Anders just so I could see his face. It wasn't like I could carry a picture of him with me, and there were so many to choose from: young Anders, older Anders, sexy Captain Milton Anders. That was when I saw the new paparazzi photographs. They were a bit fuzzy, but even so, it was clearly Anders. He was all over some tiny skinny blonde in designer jeans, his tall and lanky frame bent down, kissing her. The gossip articles gushed about their "hook ups" in the last six weeks accompanied by a gallery of photographs and dates. They also thoughtfully included headshots of them both, so I could see her exquisite and delicately pale beauty in glorious Technicolor. All those Internet articles about the other blondes that he had told me were not true flashed into my mind. I ran to the bathroom and vomited.

Anders had felt too good to be true, and he was. In a way, I had been waiting for something like this, not truly believing that I would be lucky enough to be with Anders fully, in an everyday way. Being caught by Crispin had almost seemed like a sign that the way might be opening up, but it was really just my last door shutting. I had tried to have everything, and I would end up with nothing. Now both my relationships were going down the toilet.

Andres' betrayal had shown me that if my time with him was food, it would be homemade marshmallow: sweet and delicious, light and fluffy, but no substance. It hadn't been real, just wishful thinking. I felt sad and embarrassed that I had been taken in, sold on his professions of love, despite my determination to remain clear headed and see the relationship for what it was. He had seemed so sincere, but then he was an actor. I was angrier at myself because I had known better but had still been so stupid. *I wish I had never met him*, I whispered to myself as I lay on the bathroom floor. Then giving in, I curled into the fetal position, holding a towel over my mouth to muffle the sound of crying.

"Did you see the pictures?" Anders' call came later in the day.

"Yes, I did." I was proud of how emotionless I sounded. In truth, I was just drained and tired after crying for hours already.

"It's not what it looks like," he said uncomfortably.

"Your tongue wasn't down her throat?" I asked caustically.

"Yes, no, not really. It was all staged. It's to get publicity for the movie. Two stars hooking up is big news and raises interest in the film.

They asked us to do it months ago. I didn't know they were going to release the photos yet. It's just a publicity stunt, I swear. I was going to tell you about it last time we met, but I got distracted. I love you."

"Maybe that's true; maybe it isn't." I'd never know, though, and I'd always wonder. What do they say about smoke and fire? Maybe if he'd told me before it happened, it would have made a difference. Now it was too late. "I could handle anything except you lying to me."

"I know I made a mistake not telling you, and part of me wanted to make you jealous. I was stupid. *Please.*"

"So, which is it? You forgot, or you wanted to make me jealous?" I couldn't believe he couldn't even get his story straight. *Amateur.*

"I wanted to make you jealous. I thought it would make you see that you wanted to be with me. I fucked up!" he said miserably. I had a sudden epiphany, and it wasn't a good one. I was nearly choking on the lump in my throat.

"You leaked the stories about us." My voice was low and barely controlled.

"Why would I do that!" he said unconvincingly.

"How did they know all the details, then? Only you and I knew about the food."

There was a long pause.

"You're right," he admitted finally. "Not everything, but some of it. I did it because I knew that you would be forced to choose. I thought you'd choose me," he rasped. "I'm so sorry I fucked this all up."

"I think it is best for both of us if you don't call again," I said stiffly. "If I'm not in the background, you can find someone…" I was trying to be generous, but mostly I wanted to scream. It was too much.

"You were never going to leave him, were you?" Bitterness had crept into his voice. "You're just using this as an excuse."

"It was never going to end well. We both know that." I fought to keep my voice calm. Whatever warped trust we had placed in each other had been completely destroyed.

"Why? Why wouldn't it?" he demanded.

"Because we're both untrustworthy. You because you had no problems seducing a married woman, and me because I chose to sleep with you, even though I was married. We can't trust each other not to do it again."

"That's bullshit! It was a first for both of us."

"We crossed that line. We have to accept that it wouldn't have worked between us out in the open. My career would be over and yours hampered by being labeled a home-wrecker."

"This is fucked."

"I know," I whispered.

"You know we belong together. It's just unfair that he met you first," he said, his voice urgent. "I can make you happy. I know you're unhappy with him."

"I have to try to make it work." I sounded so wooden, but I was holding on by my fingertips. "We have children…a house…history…" It sounded weak, even as I was saying it. "Please just accept it."

"I love you!" he said desperately, as if that could magically make everything better. Maybe if this was a fairy tale it could have.

"I love you too…Goodbye, Anders." I put the phone down softly and only then did I allow myself to crumple.

Chapter Eighteen

I heard Jack come home around two hours later, and I hauled myself off the bed, washed my face in the bathroom, then I went to find Jack and tell him everything. There was no point in putting it off anymore. Although this would probably end it, all I could think about was how it had begun, our marriage at least.

My parents and close relatives had flown over for the wedding. The dinner to introduce them to Jack's parents had been interesting. My parents as usual had been lovely, though slightly emotionally detached. I think that's why I was an only child; they had me because it was the "done thing" for their generation, but they found out that they had little interest in children so didn't bother again.

My father was a doctor who worked long hours, and my mother the curator of an art gallery. They lived their lives consumed by their own passions and interests but with no friction. They were glad for my happiness, but they would have been equally satisfied if I'd been marrying an impoverished goatherd, as long as it was what I wanted. They'd seemed rather startled by Jack's parents but too polite to comment, for which I was grateful.

The wedding was extraordinary, or at least the bits I can remember. It all went by in a blur, and it is like I have only small fragments of it committed to memory. I can remember nothing of what the minister said in the beautiful old stone church, just that he was there,

Jack beaming at me from the front, and that so many of the guests were wearing hats. I'd felt an overwhelming happiness at marrying someone I loved so much and that the world was a beautiful place, particularly the lovely part of Gloucestershire where we had been.

The marquee had been set up on the lawn next to the formal gardens, and inside there'd been a vision of abundant white and green flowers in the soft light of a summer afternoon. I cannot recall the food or the speeches or who exactly had been there, though there had been an unspoken divisive undercurrent of the Australians being "them" while the English were "us."

I'd felt bad that my relatives hadn't been invited to the dinner dance later, despite having traveled so far, but supposedly that's the way it was done. I have flashes of clarity, like at the dinner dance, moving in Jack's arms to our song—Leonard Cohen's darkly beautiful "Dance Me to the End of Love"—and the fireworks later on. But my clearest memory is sneaking off with Jack later in the evening and running away like delinquent children into the hedge maze, giggling from the champagne and sheer joy of it all. We'd gone deeper into the maze, and Jack had led me to the fountain in the middle. We'd sat on the sandstone edge and drank from the bottle of champagne Jack had brought with us.

"Hello, wife," he'd said, smiling his beautiful slow smile.

"Hello, husband." I'd smiled back and leaned over, kissed him gently on the lips, and then snuggled closer to him, his arm around my shoulders. At that moment, I'd known a pure happiness and contentment so perfect, and I had thought the rest of our lives would just be an extension of that feeling. God, we'd been so happy.

"Jack, we need to talk."

"That sounds ominous!" He put down the paper and, smiling, gave me his undivided attention. There was no other way to say it than straight out.

"I had an affair with Anders Larsen. It's over now."

"What does that mean exactly?" He looked confused.

"We slept together, more than a few times." I raised my head to look at him.

"When? Where?" he barked.

I guess he deserved the details, though I'm sure he wasn't going to like it once he had them.

"In the chalet hotel in France, and we met up at his hotel here in London when he was here for business until a bit over a week ago."

He looked at me, shocked.

"Why?" His face crumpled. "Why would you do that to us?" He didn't try to hide his devastation. I had a good clear look at what I had done to him, this man I'd promised to love forever.

"I don't know." I broke down. "There is no good reason that I can give you, and I'm sorry for that. It's never happened before." I hesitated, knowing he deserved something, even though it would only hurt him more. "It's been a while since we were…intimate. I think I wanted someone to pay attention to me, as well as the physical side."

"So, it's my fault because I didn't pay you enough attention or provide enough stud services!" he shouted, roused to immediate anger and bitterness at my criticism.

"Well, maybe I just needed to have sex with someone who wanted to be there, rather than treating it like an odious chore!" I said hotly, my deep-seated hurt and resentment turning on him in a flash.

"Maybe if you didn't ask all the time, we could be more spontaneous and enjoy it more." His voice was sarcastic and angry.

"All the time! We have sex maybe once every few months! Most people have sex at least a couple of times a week!"

"Where did you read that? Some women's magazine?" he said bitingly.

"You bastard!" Tears pricked behind my eyes.

"So, what you're saying is, if we don't have sex based on your imaginary quota system, then it's okay for you to go and sleep with someone else?"

"No!" I wailed. "I was just…"

"I gave you everything," he said furiously, fists clenched. "A house, money, freedom to do whatever you want—work, not work—and this, *this*, is what you do?" He took a deep breath. "I think I need some space to calm down. I'm going to go back to the office, and I might spend the night at the club." He left, slamming the door behind him. I heard the front door shut with force, and I let the grief in. I knew I deserved it, and part of me welcomed the penance of pain.

It was a hard and lonely few days with no sign of Jack. I couldn't call him at his club; I could only leave a message there which he was unlikely to return, and his mobile was switched off. I miserably went about trying to work, but my output was dismal. On the fourth day, I was in my study, trying to distract myself, when I heard his keys in the door. I jumped up and met him in the hall.

"Do you want a divorce?" he asked with no preamble.

"No, I don't think so. Do you?"

"Then, why did you do it?" he asked, his voice full of pain. He ignored my question.

"I don't know. It just happened."

"Once just happens. The rest wasn't an accident."

"I don't know why I did it. Maybe it was trying to reclaim a younger me, maybe I wasn't happy with our sex life, maybe I just did it because it felt good. It could be all of those things! I did it. It's done and over with. I can't undo it. The question now is can we get through this?"

"I need more time to think it through. I'm going to stay at the club for a few more days. I'll call you when I'm ready." He went into our bedroom and packed a bag with more clothes and then left again. For the first time since they left, I was happy the twins were away so they didn't witness this, or us trying to cover it up.

The only bright point was when Crispin called to try to blackmail me.

"Come to room one-twelve of the hotel. I expect you in thirty minutes," he barked.

"Actually, you can go fuck yourself, and I hope your diseased and repellent dick falls off afterward."

"W-What…?" he spluttered.

"I told Jack about Anders, and if you ever call me again, I'll tell him what you tried to do." I slammed the phone down and smiled tightly. That had been more than a little satisfying.

Two days later, Jack came back.

"Are you back for more clothes?" I asked tentatively.

"No," he said shortly. He couldn't even look me in the eye and talked to a point on the wall over my shoulder. "I'll move into the spare room while we figure out what to do."

I nodded, miserable for hurting him so badly, and left him alone, which was what he clearly wanted.

I did everything I could to try to make him happier. I cooked his favorite duck ragu for dinner, bought him some new shirts and ties from his favorite tailor, took his suits to the dry cleaner, and got his car washed and vacuumed. The house was spotless and gleaming, and the silence between us continued. He thanked me, using the smallest words possible, and still didn't look at me. I was determined not to push him into talking and to give him some space, but it was hard.

We were into the fourth week of me killing myself to show him how sorry I was, and there was no thaw in his treatment. He generally ignored me, and we ate in silence, only the loud clicking of cutlery disturbing the silence. Finally, I broke over the lasagna.

"Are you going to talk to me?" My knife landed against my plate with sharp crack.

"No."

"You want to stay like this for the rest of our lives?"

"Frankly, it's an improvement. You should have gone and fucked someone else years ago."

"Stop being an arsehole. It's not like I didn't try to talk to you about our problems—"

"What?" he shouted, interrupting. "When did you tell me you were unhappy?"

"You don't think that not having sex for months on end was a bit of a red flag?"

"Not this again!" He snorted dismissively.

"What more do you want me to do?" I started to cry, despite my efforts not to.

"Nothing. I don't want you to do anything." He pushed away from the table and walked out.

Jack didn't come home for dinner the next night. I tried calling him, but the phone just rang out. After trying five times, I gave up and ate in front of the television in an attempt to distract myself. Unable to sit there waiting any longer, I put on my running shoes and went out for a walk. Jack was still not home an hour later, and I went up to bed, where I tossed and turned until I heard him come in around eleven. I fell into a restless sleep and woke up unrefreshed to find him already gone. It became our new routine.

Jack didn't stay out every night, but he would never call to tell me that he wouldn't be home. He never answered my calls anymore, so I stopped trying to call him. He would either press the end button, hanging up on me mid-ring, or would just let it go to voice mail.

Finding the positive became increasingly hard to do. The hostilities escalated, slowly but steadily. I tried to remember why I wanted to stay in this marriage. Jack was dismissive and cold; I was hurt, guilty, and resentful. What exactly were we trying to save anyway?

I remember talking to a friend years ago who was getting divorced and asking what she thought was the breaking point. She said it wasn't any one thing in particular, but many small things over time wearing away the base of affection that underlies a marriage. All the trivial hassles and stresses of raising children and having jobs and mortgages are temporary blights that will eventually stop attacking your relationship and you will be fine, as long as your base is still there.

But these things stop you from being able to see clearly what lies beneath, and she said she hadn't realized that there was nothing left until it was too late. Their base was gone, and they didn't like or even respect each other anymore. There was nothing to try to save. Not that it didn't hurt, or that the process of breaking up wasn't brutal. Would it be better or worse if you still loved your partner? The love I felt for Jack was still there, despite everything, but this couldn't go on. Whatever feelings for him I had left were slowly dying.

"Jack, I know you're still angry, but if you're never going to forgive me, then there is no point in putting us both through this." I looked over the table at him as he ate his veal scaloppini, too upset to touch my own food, worried about how he'd react to my ultimatum. "I love you, but this is just making us both miserable. We would be better off apart."

"I love you too," he said. "I want to forgive you, but I'm still really angry." His eyes reddened, and he looked away, blinking.

"I understand." I nodded.

"I've been speaking to Mother and Father. They're getting older, and it's getting a bit much for him to run everything. I was thinking that it might be time for us to move up there."

I nearly choked on the mouthful I had finally taken.

"They'll move into the Old Manor, and we'll live in the Hall. A change of scenery might do us a lot of good."

"You want us to go and live with your parents?" I gasped. "Seriously? Are you giving up your job?" To commute from Gloucestershire to London every day was not possible, no matter how keen you were.

"We'll sell the house and buy a flat here, and I'll come up on the weekends."

"So, it will be just me living with your parents?" To say that sounded like a terrible idea was an understatement. "You're doing this to punish me."

"Look at it as a show of faith. I'll know if you agree to this that you do really want our marriage to work."

"What about you? If I agree to this, will you go to marriage counseling? I'll give you time to learn to forgive me; I just needed to know that it won't be like this forever, especially if we're living at the Hall. This can't go on indefinitely."

I knew I was at fault for the major event, but it didn't just come out of the blue. How much hurt has to accumulate before you do something to relieve your pain? Anders had not only made me feel better when I was with him, but he'd forced me to face what my relationship with Jack had become. But that wasn't being entirely fair. It was more than that; it was not only for how he made me feel. It felt wrong, but I missed him. I had to stop thinking about him, though, if there was any hope of putting my marriage back together.

"Absolutely not!" Jack retorted. "It's bad enough that you go off sleeping with other men. Why should I be punished twice?"

I smarted from his unnecessary reminder but showed no reaction.

"This is too much, for both of us, and we're not getting very far on our own. I'm tired of going over and over the same stuff. If you're not willing to go, then we might as well call it quits now." I sounded so calm, but inside I was quivering with panic. I felt a tingling coldness, like I was going to faint, the same dread that happens in that first awareness that you've hurt yourself badly, before the pain even hits, but you know that it's going to get a lot worse.

"Fine, I'll go." He threw down his cutlery and stalked from the room.

The next morning, I rang Bats' therapist and made an appointment. The earliest I could get was the following week. I sent the appointment through to Jack's phone. I wasn't going to rely on him remembering if I told him, not that I felt like chasing him down right now. If it was on his phone calendar, it would sync with his work computer, and he'd have no excuse, or at least not the "I forgot" or "I didn't know" ones. He'd have to put some thought into it, some creativity, and that alone might mean he'd turn up, solely because he couldn't think of a good enough reason not to. God, I was so cynical.

Chapter Nineteen

We barely spoke in the days leading up to our first session. I think we were both honing our opening arguments. We sat in the narrow waiting room on plastic chairs with slightly padded seats, not that they helped much with the comfort level. Maybe the accumulated angst of all the couples who had sat here before had seeped into the furniture. From the industrial gray of the walls to the fluorescent lighting, the whole place had a dismal feel. An attempt had been made to cheer up the look with a framed poster of Monet's *Garden at Vetheuil*, but even the original would have struggled to brighten up these surroundings.

A small thin woman came out and introduced herself as Faye and led us into another room. Closing the door behind her, she indicated that we should take a seat in the group of three chairs provided. I snuck a glance at Jack, who seemed a bit more relaxed, probably because she appeared quite normal. Faye sat down in a chair facing us.

"I'd firstly like to tell you that I'm not here to tell you what to do or to fix your problems. My role is to find out where you both want for your relationship to go and help you get there. I'll work hard with you, but you both need to be committed for this to be successful," she said, and I now picked up a soft Welsh accent.

"Kate, let's start with you. Can you tell me what brought you here?"

"I had an affair." There was no point in trying to avoid it. "I'm here to try to see if we can work things out."

"Jack, why are you here?"

"She made me."

"You walked in here on your own, so there must be a reason for you to come to counseling." She gently pried away at his defensive attempt at humor and left him time to answer.

"I don't want to get divorced," he said after a long pause. "I want to know why she did this to me."

"All right. So, we want to explore why Kate went outside the marriage and the issues that led to this. That is our goal. What about an end point? What do you both want at the end of these sessions?"

Jack and I stared blankly at her, but she squared her shoulders at our lack of self-awareness and plowed on. After a good ten minutes, we came up with our finish line: we would work toward resolving our issues of trust and individual needs in the marriage so that we could achieve our ultimate goal of reconciliation. It sounded impressive. It also sounded exhausting.

"There is a lot of work to do for you to repair your relationship, and you need to both be committed to work at it."

"But I've done nothing! She was the one who had the affair."

"I hear what you are saying, Jack, but something must have been not right before the affair for Kate to want to be intimate with another man," she explained with not even a hint of exasperation. "Are you both committed to working at this?"

"Yes," I said firmly.

Jack paused, and then nodded.

At our next session, the real work commenced.

"Let's start by looking at something positive. What about the relationship is worth saving? Jack, you first."

"Our family being together."

"That's good. What about something relating to just the two of you?"

"Umm…her cooking, I guess."

I snorted with disbelief. He couldn't come up with anything!

"Kate, how about you? What would you like to save?"

"It's easier to think about the things I'd like to change, but I guess I miss jokes we used to share and how comfortable we used to be with each other."

Jack stared at me, finally looking me in the eye, but his expression was unreadable.

We put our beautiful house up for sale. Part of me was hoping that it wouldn't sell and I'd have a legitimate excuse not to move. Unfortunately, the opposite proved true. We had a three-way bidding war and sold it way too quickly and for more than we'd hoped. I cried as I packed away memories of happier times and all the small reminders of moments when our children were growing: the chip in the bookcase where one of the twins had thrown a toy truck, the faint remnants of red crayon behind the door from early artistic endeavors, their bedrooms which still smelled faintly of their warm and wiggly childhood selves. It was like saying goodbye to the best part of us, the part where we had been secure in our happiness. Now we were launching out into the great unknown, the worn vessel that was to carry us already sporting a poorly patched hole in the hull. I couldn't help but be aware that this last-ditch effort to save our marriage was likely to end badly.

It was with a heavy heart that I drove through the gates of Clouston Hall, the moving van behind me, blocking my retreat. Edwina was waiting in the informal drawing room with her usual disapproving scowl. Jack was supposed to be here with me, but as usual when there was a difficult personal matter, something had come up at work and he was coming later.

Forcing my lips into a smile, I greeted her with a kiss on her reluctantly proffered cheek.

"You're here at last."

"Yes." I couldn't think of anything else to add.

"It will be good to have Jack here to help out." She frowned. "It's been terribly hard on his father, you know."

"Hmm," I murmured noncommittally. I ignored the inference that it was only Jack who was required.

"We haven't had a moment spare to move to the Old Manor, so I've told them to put your things in the barn for storage."

I shouldn't have been surprised, but my stomach sank to an all new low. They weren't moving out. I thought it was out of character for Edwina to agree to step back as lady of the house, and I should have known that she would hold on to her position with a death grip.

"Well, now that we're here, it should take some of the burden from you and give you more spare time to yourself," I said sweetly.

Edwina looked at me sharply but managed to twitch her lips into the semblance of a smile.

"Yes, we'll see," she answered stiffly.

I'd have to wait for Jack to work out a strategy to deal with this, because there was no way in hell I was going to live with Edwina, and it was obvious she had no intention of going anywhere. *Game on, bitch*, I thought as we gave each other a hard stare.

Edwina and I spent the next couple of days circling each other, waiting for the opening volley. We were hosting a pheasant shooting weekend in three weeks, which was going to be interesting. While most of the plans for the seven or so hunting weekends this season were already finalized, we had to plan for the next year as well.

"Now you are the lady of the house, it will be your responsibility to make the arrangements," she announced over breakfast. Surprised that she was willingly handing over control, my instincts were telling me that she wouldn't really be stepping back. That or she had an ulterior motive.

"Yes, thank you, Edwina. Of course, I'm sure I'll still need your help and advice, seeing as this is the first weekend I will have hosted." *En garde*. She gave me a false smile but said nothing more. Her strategy was not hard to figure out. She wanted me to fail, spectacularly, so she could step back in and save the day.

First thing I did was corner every staff member I could find, from the house manager, butler, Head Gamekeeper, and functions coordinator to the dailies and gardeners, learn their names and find out what they did. I'd thought I had an idea of what it took to operate what was essentially a business, but the scope was at once much larger and smaller than I had assumed. While the detail was immense, overall it wasn't a particularly diversified operation.

The main task was to maintain the house and grounds in good order so as to maximize the revenue the Hall could bring in through tourists, film crews, and weddings, paying guests on the shooting weekends, and the odd festival. The rest was just support functions, like marketing the Hall as a venue and providing food and merchandise to maximize profits, the bulk of which were plowed back into maintenance, which was ongoing and exorbitantly expensive, given the heritage listing and the age of the building. As a secondary branch, there were the estate farms and village housing, as many of the long-serving staff still lived in houses provided by the estate. These also needed to be administered and maintained.

Once I had a handle on what most people did, I decided to tackle this as I would a work meeting. I called together the staff and Edwina to start planning. Because everything was organized so far in advance, we were working on finalizing repair projects for the winter, when the house was closed, and what would be done the following year. We also needed to cover the final arrangements for the upcoming shooting weekend.

The Head Gamekeeper, Mr. Watkins, had started his preparations long ago, rearing the birds, laying out the drives, and controlling the pests. He would be responsible for coordinating the Beaters, who would drive the birds toward the Guns. They would use sticks to beat the bushes, while others acted as Flankers to direct the birds or Stops to prevent them going in the wrong direction. Some of them would be paid, but most would be the more industrious wives and older children who were happy to help out.

Invitations had been sent and acceptances received weeks ago, so I just had to finalize sleeping arrangements and the menu for the weekend. Edwina sat silently throughout, which I was glad about, though it made me wonder what she was up to. I didn't have to wonder for long.

Every time I spoke to one of the staff and asked them to do something, Edwina went behind my back and changed the order.

"Excuse me, madam," Mr. Watkins said in his quiet gravelly voice. "I hate to bring this up, but I thought you should know that Lady Preedy is changing your arrangements. It is upsetting the staff, who don't know what to do, caught in the middle as we are."

"I'm sorry, Mr. Watkins. I will talk to her. I understand how difficult this transition is for everyone." *Fuck,* I thought, *how do I make Edwina behave?* We were going to have to talk, but how to make a dent? I needed something big to make an impact, but I had no idea what. She was determined to make me look like a fool, and I had little leverage with the staff. They might like me, I hoped they did, but Edwina had been their boss for years. Running to Jack would solve nothing. I needed to sort this out on my own, but how?

The answer came the following week, in a form I could never have imagined, even in my darkest thoughts, during one of our sessions with Faye.

Chapter Twenty

"**J**ack, how is your relationship with your mother? Are your parents still together?"

"Yes, they're not divorced, but they were never that affectionate with each other. I don't really know what their relationship is like."

"You don't think they have sex?"

"They probably do," he said, huffing uncomfortably, "but not with each other."

"Do they have affairs?"

"I don't know about my father, but my mother did."

"How do you know that?"

"She told me." He coughed to clear his throat. "She told me when I was younger that she had been in love with another man and my brother was his."

I gasped, completely shocked, but at the same time not. It explained why she treated Crispin differently and why he didn't look like Jack or his father.

"Why would she tell you that?"

"Because I asked her why she didn't love me as much as she loved Crispin," he said, breaking down, his chest heaving. "She was always touching him and hugging him and telling him how wonderful he was. Nothing I ever did was right."

My heart broke for him and the difficult childhood he had endured.

"One night I saw something." His voice had lowered to a whisper. "I saw my mother touching Crispin…inappropriately."

"Jesus!" I murmured, feeling sick.

Jack wept uncontrollably. *Oh my God! How fucked up was his family!* It explained so much, about him and about Crispin. I broke out in a cold sweat, as an unimaginable possibility occurred to me. I raced through my memories, trying to recall if there was ever a time I had left the boys alone with Edwina. My chest eased slightly with the realization that we had never left them with her for any length of time, and she didn't treat them the same way she did Crispin. They seemed well-adjusted and happy, but I was going to talk to them — carefully, of course.

"Jack, I am so sorry." I put my arms around him tentatively, trying to comfort him. "Why didn't you tell me?"

"I was afraid you would leave. I'm still afraid of that," Jack admitted, and my heart leaped in response. "You and the boys are the best part of my life."

"I moved to Gloucestershire. I wouldn't have done that if I wasn't committed to staying," I explained gently. "But we have to get Crispin some help. What he's been doing…" There was no argument that Crispin was deeply disturbed, and despite the family's denials, there was little doubt in my mind that the rumors were true.

He nodded. I reached over and squeezed his hand. He returned it, gingerly at first and then with great fierceness, as if he were trying to hold me there forever.

I returned to the Hall on my own, still in shock. I didn't see Edwina, for which she should be thankful. I went up to our room and sat down heavily on the window seat, feeling lost, sickened, and out of my depth, not knowing what to do or say that could make this any better or easier.

At that moment, sitting in the enormous, antiquated, cold house, I felt what my life could have been, pressing heavily like a physical pressure on my brain. It was the life I could have had if I'd chosen differently all those years ago. A life that was lighter and sunnier, without the heavy dampness of living in an ancient society. My children would be home with me, tracking in sand and laughter. I could almost see the flash of their bronze skin as they passed through the white house in my mind. A few decisions here and there, and I would have ended up living in Sydney instead of London.

Stopping myself, I hauled my thoughts back to the present. It was too late for regrets. I had a life that so many aspired to, and I should appreciate what I did have. Just because I had never planned it didn't mean that it wasn't where I should be. I couldn't afford to think that my whole marriage was a mistake. My eyes caught on the photographs of the boys taken when they started school at Harrow in a room surrounded by the signatures of so many other boys who had been exactly where they were, a continuity unbroken in centuries. So much history had value and importance, and wishing it away was an insult to half of them, even if it came from Jack's side. Whatever was to happen, I had my children, who would make everything worth it a hundred times over.

The next morning, my shock and disbelief had turned to cold, hard fury. Edwina, knowing nothing of what was coming, was cheerfully ordering the staff around with great huffing and puffing.

"Edwina, we need to talk. Now," I said icily, keeping my voice low.

Her chin rose disdainfully. "I am busy right now. I'll get to whatever it is later."

"I'm happy to do it in front of everyone, but what I have to say I'm fairly sure you don't want the staff to know."

She looked at me, uncertainty fluttering behind her eyes. With poor grace, she agreed, and we went off to the library.

"I want you out of this house today," I said as soon as the door closed behind me. I clenched my fists to hide my shaking, wanting to inflict pain on her, to make her feel some of what she had done to those innocent young boys. I wasn't generally someone for physical violence, but she was the lowest, most despicable version of a mother. I couldn't imagine how she lived with herself.

"Excuse me?" she asked haughtily.

"Did I mumble?" I could barely restrain myself from punching her in the head.

"Who do you think you are to order me out of my own house?" She glared at me.

"Who do you think you are to molest your own son?" I said with utter disgust. Then, I had to ask the question every other mother would ask. "How could you?"

"I…I don't know what you're talking about." She stumbled and sat down heavily.

"Jack told me what you did to Crispin when he was a *child*. You fucked him up so badly, he's hurting people, and you just pay everyone off to protect yourself. You are responsible for this. You will leave here. I don't care where you go. I will give you no opportunity to see my children. If you choose not to leave, I will expose you. I will ring the *Daily Mail* and give them a long and in-depth interview and then every other publication that wants one. I will tell them how you sadistically beat both your children with whips and sexually assaulted Crispin."

"You need me. You need my money," she gasped indignantly.

"We'll manage. This will be your only warning. I expect you gone by the end of the day." I turned and left.

Edwina and, I assume, Arthur too were gone by dinner that night, though only to the Old Manor at the other end of the property. Frankly, I would have liked to see her go to the other end of the world. It grated badly that she wouldn't be punished, but I knew Jack and Crispin would never do anything about it. Going to the police? Refusing all contact? It wasn't going to happen. At least I wouldn't have to see her every day, knowing what she'd done. At least that's what a sane, rational person would assume. I forgot, momentarily, that Edwina was insane, and she topped up with a bowl of crazy for breakfast every morning so she would never run low.

Two days later, I was sitting in the room I had made into my study, as it was one of the few rooms that had working Internet. Wireless wasn't possible in a house where the walls were two feet thick. I was having my morning cup of tea when in waltzed Edwina.

"Good morning." She smiled. "I've come to help you out with the shooting party organization."

"Um…no…" I said, astounded. "What are you doing here? I thought I made it clear that you weren't to come back here." I had, hadn't I? I had a moment of doubting myself in the face of her certainty.

"Don't be silly. You need help."

"No, I don't. Not from you. I would like for you to leave now." I gritted my teeth.

"Aren't you going to offer me a cup of tea?" she asked, seeming genuinely confused that I wasn't pretending nothing had happened.

"No, Edwina, I'm not. You are not to come here again without an invitation from either myself or Jack. Do you not remember our last conversation?"

"No. What?" She cocked her head, looking at me questioningly. Fuck, it was like she had wiped it from her memory.

"Seriously, Edwina. Get out!" I wasn't going to go through the whole thing again. My God!

"Fine! I'll be speaking to Jack about this," she said with a huff, as if I was in the wrong. Fortunately, she left, and I followed to make sure she went out the door. I immediately sought out the head housekeeper and butler to make sure they passed on to the rest of the staff that Edwina was not to be admitted without notifying me first.

It should have been a turning point, Edwina moving out and Jack opening up to me, but it wasn't. As if the admissions had been too much, Jack retreated behind a well-constructed wall, cleverly camouflaged with politeness and courtesy. That was the closest we ever got to genuine sharing of emotion, other than the ever-present anger that was buried uneasily in shallow graves.

"You can't order Mother out of the house," he said on Friday night after returning from seeing his parents at the Old Manor.

"Yes, I can. How can you expect me to just pretend that everything is okay?"

"Just because you want things to be different doesn't mean they are. We need her money for the house. Nothing about that has changed, and we can't afford to upset her too much." He ran his hands through his hair agitatedly.

"She beat you and abused your brother. How can you stand to be in the same room as her?"

"Stop being a child!" he thundered. "I'm the one it happened to, not you. If I can deal with it, you certainly can."

"You're dealing with it?" I scoffed.

"What did you think was going to happen? That she would apologize and hand herself in to the police?"

"No—"

"If you confront her again, she's going to deny it, and we'll be in a worse position because she will strike back. Just pretend I never said anything. God, I wish I'd just kept my mouth shut. *Fuck!*" he swore violently.

"Ignoring something isn't dealing with it. You're suppressing everything, and one day you're going to explode when you can't push it down any more!" I accused him. "By letting her get away with this, you're telling her it's okay! What if she touched the boys? Are you saying that's okay too?"

Jack glared at me, his eyes wild, his breathing heavy and labored behind his tightly clenched jaw. A shiver of fear raced down my spine, causing my heart to beat faster. A zing of adrenaline gave me a burst of mental clarity: He was holding onto his control by a hair, something I had never seen in him before in all the years we'd been together. His hands were clenched in fists by his sides, shaking with effort to remain still.

Subconsciously, I took a step backward, then another, until I reached the bathroom door. I went in and locked the door. I sat on the closed toilet lid for what felt like hours, unsure of the man outside the door. I had pushed too far. He was right; I wasn't the one who suffered. I just couldn't understand the way he was willing to let this go. If our positions were reversed, I would have…But really, what would I have done? Something like this changed you. How could I, someone who had grown up in a completely different environment, say how I would react? Was my desire to make this "better" helping? My head dropped into my hands. I was not equipped to deal with this.

When I finally crept out of the bathroom, Jack had gone. He didn't come back for several days.

The shooting weekend went off without a hitch the following weekend with none of Edwina's interference. Jack was polite but even more distant. Despite his admission that he didn't want me to leave, he kept pushing me away any time I tried to apologize or talk about it, and I was almost ready to admit defeat. Being around him was exhausting, and I eventually gave up trying to talk to Jack anywhere but at the therapist, where I roused myself from my haze of misery to work on our marriage.

I hadn't forgotten about Crispin, though.

"Have you spoken to Crispin yet?" I gently asked Jack every weekend.

"No, it's not just something you can do over the phone. I'm waiting for the right time." He rolled his eyes, exasperated that I kept asking him. Finally, I'd had enough. If he wasn't going to do it, then I would have to. As much as I thought it would accomplish little, my conscience wouldn't give me peace. He was hurting young women, and, for their sake, I had to try.

Amazed that I was voluntarily ringing him, I half-hoped that the call would go through to voice mail. Instead, he answered.

"Well, if it isn't my slutty sister-in-law," he drawled.

"Crispin, I would like to talk to you. Would you be able to come to the Hall sometime this week?"

"You've reconsidered? I thought you said you told Jack?" He sounded unsure. I'd managed to floor him.

"No, he knows. This is about something else."

"What?" he asked suspiciously.

"I'll tell you when you get here."

"Okaaay," he said slowly. "I should be able to come for a few hours on Thursday. I'll be there early afternoon."

"I will see you then." I hung up the phone. I thought the house would be the best place to meet him. There were always people around to hear my scream for help if need be.

I had afternoon tea waiting in the library. Crispin entered with his usual slimy smirk. He sat down on the couch next to me, sitting slightly too close.

"Tea?" I asked, surreptitiously moving a little further away as I poured for both of us. Handing him the cup, I held mine in front like a tiny china shield. "I wanted to talk to you about something that came up in our therapy sessions," I began as gently as I could.

"Jack is going to therapy?" He scoffed.

"It was about you."

"What about me?" He immediately jumped to the defensive.

"It was about seeing your mother doing something…inappropriate," I hedged. Crispin slammed down the teacup onto the table, sending tea splashing.

"That's a lie!" he shouted.

"You're reaction says not. I am so sorry that happened to you. Have you thought about talking to someone about it? It might help."

"What?" He leaped to his feet.

"Crispin, you are hurting young girls. There are too many rumors for it not to have some truth. You need to stop and deal with what happened to you before you go so far that even your family will not be able to cover it up. You will go to jail. If you care about yourself or your family, something needs to change. I have some names…" I stood up and handed him the piece of paper with the contact details of some therapists I had found who specialized in childhood trauma. The look of stunned incredulity on his face changed to something darker. Slowly and deliberately, he tore the paper into small pieces and threw them in my face.

"You bitch," he said slowly. "You know nothing. How dare you, a lying, cheating slapper, tell me that I need help?"

"Because someone needs to, and your family are all too repressed to talk about this sort of thing."

"My family are perfectly fine. Do you know how many people wish they were us? We have wealth and history and can trace our family tree back to the twelfth century!"

"How many of those people would want to be you if they knew the truth? Your mother is an incestuous pedophile, your father is completely absent and so inbred his mental faculties are in question, and you beat up and rape young girls. You and Jack still suck up to your abuser, refusing to force her to acknowledge the damage that she did. Why would anyone want to be you?" I spoke the truth thoughtlessly to punish him, completely losing sight of trying to help him. For a brief moment, his pain showed before he shut down completely.

"Fuck you!" He strode from the room and slammed the door behind him. I sat back down in the chair. That had not gone how I'd hoped it might. I didn't think I had made anything better, and the thought that at least I had tried was a hollow one.

Chapter Twenty-One

The Temptations of Saint Kate was released with mixed feelings on my part. Everyone raved about it, saying it was beautiful, brilliant, etcetera. All I could think about was Anders, in bed, and his enjoyment of the things I had made. Even with how it ended, I found myself wishing I could be back there with him and make that time last forever, stuck on a loop. I had dreams where I would be with him, and on waking I would try to force myself back to sleep to get away from the current hell of my life.

Jack and I turned up at the required events and posed happily for photographers. Reporters asked their questions, and we laughed off the rumors of my affair with Anders as extraordinary and without foundation. Despite the pain in my heart at the mention of his name, nothing showed on my new poker face, honed through having to repeatedly face Edwina and keep my silence. Lindsay nodded approvingly in the background.

Just when I thought the situation couldn't get any worse, a bolt of lightning came out of nowhere. The signs were all there: the tiredness, sore breasts, and the aversion to the smell of meat. I was so emotionally exhausted that I didn't notice until I brushed too close to a door, whacking my breast on the edge, and it exploded in pain.

"What the …?" I gasped, trying to deal with the sudden and unexpected agony. *Why did that hurt so much?* I wondered. I ran through some likely and then not so likely possibilities, like breast cancer or unknown trauma while I slept, before my sluggish mind stumbled upon the most obvious scenario.

I looked at the stick I'd raced out and bought from the store three villages and a forty-five-minute drive away and swore. Then I swore some more. I was still swearing two days later as I drove to meet Lindsay at her office for our weekly meeting.

"How are things going with Jack? The media reports have been largely positive about the two of you. The book, as you already know from the sales reports, is doing very well," she began without preamble as we sat down on her black sofas. Her entire office was super-stylish and entirely monochrome. It was visually stunning and showed a remarkable ability to adhere to a theme. Even the glasses of water she put down on the coffee table were white instead of the usual clear.

"Couldn't actually be much worse. I just found out I'm pregnant," I said with a bitter sigh.

"Interesting." She nodded to herself. "Do you know whose it is?"

"Anders'." There was no doubt; Jack and I had finally tried sleeping together a couple of weeks ago. It had been so tentative and awkward, I don't think either of us had relaxed enough to enjoy it.

"Does Jack know?"

"No, but he's bound to notice eventually. He's pretty unobservant, so I could probably get through the whole pregnancy first, but I'm sure he'd notice a new baby in the house. Mind you, the house is so huge, I could stash the baby somewhere he'd never find it." Bleak humor was my only refuge from despair. Lindsay's eyes had rolled sideways at the new bomb of information. For a second, I thought she was going to allow herself to have a genuine reaction of some sort, but she gathered herself quickly.

"Have you thought about terminating it?" she asked softly.

"Yes, but I couldn't. Not after what we went through."

"Well, you'll have to tell him, then. There's no way it could be his?" she asked, slightly hopeful.

"Not unless it's the next messiah." Somehow that joke didn't seem funny.

"Oh." There was nothing more to be said on that topic. Lindsay went into action, amazing as usual at her job. I felt about two inches high.

I went for an ultrasound and saw my baby for the first time as a smudgy blur on the screen. The only thing I could see clearly was a beautiful and tiny heart beating, and I started to cry. My obstetrician gave me the all clear the following day, though given my age I would still have to have an amniocentesis in a few weeks. It was time to tell Jack. He had just been showing signs of starting to…not exactly thaw, but to be calmer and less angry. This was going to blow it all to hell. I waited until Saturday night, so he hadn't just come in from the long drive down and had had enough fresh air and manual labor to hopefully be in as good a mood as possible.

"Jack?" I called out as I heard him come in. He stopped in the sitting room, a small smile on his face as he looked at something on his phone.

"Yes?"

I looked at him and felt so guilty about the pain I was about to cause him. "I'm pregnant."

His smile faded, and he looked at me with wide eyes.

"How?" He looked stunned. "We were told we had almost no chance of falling pregnant naturally, and now you're nearly forty and your fertility is declining, it happens?"

"I'm more than three months along," I said, trying to hide my exasperation that Jack had taken the time even now to point out to me my lack of fertility. We had no trouble with the boys, who were conceived on our honeymoon. With an heir required, I had to quickly come to grips with the concept that birth control would not be in my future until I had ensured succession. With not one but two *male* babies, I was then allowed to go back on the pill.

When we decided to go again, we both just assumed it would happen as easily as the first time. We were wrong, and after trying for more than two years, went down the expensive and heartbreaking IVF path. Jack reminding me of this put me instantly on edge, and that wasn't the way I meant this to go. I needed to be calm and handle this gently as it would probably be harder than the affair on him.

He looked at me silently for a long moment.

"Right," he said quietly. "So, the baby is his."

"Yes."

With a sharp outtake of breath, he started pacing the room. I watched him doing laps for about five minutes, the only sounds that of his heavy steps and harsh breathing as he fought for control.

"What do you want to do about it?" he asked unevenly, not looking at me.

"After all we went through, could you imagine willingly terminating?" I asked him. It was a while before he answered.

"No. I guess not. So, where does that leave us? Do you expect me to raise it as my own?" he asked angrily.

"If we want to stay together, then, yes, I guess that's what I'm asking. I know this is an extra complication, but you said you could forgive the—" I swallowed hard before I could say it. "Affair." God, it was still hard to say that word.

"You're kidding, right?" he shouted. "This is hardly the same."

"No, but I haven't done anything more than you've already said you would forgive."

"You're still a lawyer. Your talent for twisting logic is exceptional." He breathed out heavily. "So, how far along are you, exactly?"

"Fourteen weeks."

"Have you had the scan?" he asked.

I nodded. "I wanted to be sure before I told you. Everything is fine. The baby looks strong and is a good size."

"Have you told him?"

"No."

"Why not?"

"Because…we aren't in contact anymore, and things are complicated enough."

"Do you intend on telling him?"

"No, I guess not. I don't have to."

"Fuck," Jack said and walked out.

You think I would have learned my lesson about the Internet, but apparently not. Jack had been AWOL for a couple of hours, and to distract myself, I Googled Anders guiltily. I knew I had no right to have any feelings about his life, but I was using him as a fix, to remind myself what I had given up and why.

I found pictures of him looking hip and young at music festivals, inhabiting a galaxy far, far away from my world of a troubled marriage and now pregnancy. The dark jealousy felt bad and good at the same time, finding out which coffee shop he had been to and which super-skinny beautiful starlet was currently keeping his bed warm at night. It was painful but somehow masochistically satisfying, comparing myself to them. They were younger, thinner, more glossily beautiful than I had ever been, their limbs smooth and flawless despite the bad lighting of some of the paparazzi photographs. They looked self-satisfied at the interest being shown in them, being on his arm. He just looked amused and slightly distant, or perhaps that was just wishful thinking on my part.

God, I missed him. So many times I wanted to pick up the phone and call him, but how could I do that now? He was as faithless as I had accused him of being, and looking at the inhumanly beautiful women keeping him company, I understood how it happened. I had never felt less attractive, with my body starting to swell. He was who he was and it was too late and he had moved on fast, which was another blow to my almost non-existent ego.

I was carrying his child, but the thought of telling him now scared me witless. I wasn't ready yet to deal with the fallout. I hugged my arms about myself and thought of myself with a new baby, like a talisman against the darkness. It gave me some hope for the future, a bright light to warm the frozen wasteland that was the rest of my emotional landscape. Once I was myself again, I would tell Anders, I promised myself, and I thought of the warm little incredibly precious being I would hold and love for the rest of my life.

After what I went through, I couldn't think of a baby as anything other than a miracle. Somehow, though, I couldn't force myself to picture raising my child in this house. Was it a sign? I didn't even believe in signs, but the thought of running away from everything and starting afresh no longer had the power to scare me as it once had.

Even though our affair was over, rumors still circulated, particularly on the Internet. There were mentions of us together in the Google search for Anders, though some of it was horrible, mostly on the sites that allowed comments at the bottom of the articles. Even though I knew it was going to upset me, I still had to look.

"She's so old and fat, I really hope they are not together!" sniped Sexxygirl9.

"I can't see what anyone sees in her. She's ugly and he could do soooo much better," agreed tabby14.

"What has she ever done? Why is she even famous???"

"God, I hate her so much! She is so dumb…"

"Her recipes are complete crap. I've heard she doesn't even write them herself…"

I pressed and held the computer's power button, wanting to get rid of the poisonous comments as quickly as possible. Shutting down properly would take too long. I was angry at myself for letting it get to me, and I was a fool to have looked. All it did was reinforce my own insecurities and remind me of why it would never have worked out with Anders, even if he hadn't been a lying son of a bitch. Actually, that was probably not fair to his mother, who could be perfectly nice. Sometimes you need to remind yourself of why you let that fish get away.

It was hard to get Anders out of my thoughts any time I was in London, though, seeing he was on every second bus dressed as Captain Milton. He had also just become the face of some men's fragrance, so he appeared in most magazines. Those I could avoid, and I had been lucky so far with the ad on TV, but I couldn't do anything about the buses. Or stop thinking about him in unrealistic scenarios where it was all a misunderstanding and he swept me off my feet into the sunset where we lived happily ever after. In reality, though, he was a million miles away with someone else, maybe several of them, probably laughing at my ridiculous reaction to him being with another woman, so hypocritical given I was married. If he thought about me at all.

I hadn't made any announcement about the pregnancy, but it was becoming apparent if you were looking. The rumors were unconfirmed, and being a food writer, there was more speculation that I had been overindulging in my own wares. I continued to do promotions for *The Temptations of Saint Kate*, the latest of which was a writers' festival.

I was part of a panel discussion on how to get published with other authors, which was particularly interesting as there were different genres present, not just food writers. It gave us all an opportunity to talk to new people that we didn't see at every event and who were amused rather than jaded by our practiced spiels about our own books.

I was seated next to a young English science fiction writer who introduced himself as Daniel Waterstreet. He seemed very serious about his stories of intergalactic robot wars until he smiled with a surprisingly cheeky dimpled grin. Strangely enough, he said he had heard of me, though he had never bought one of my books. I took that as a sign that Lindsay was doing an excellent job. We chatted away about random things while we waited for the event to start, and it was fascinating to hear how he came up with his ideas and his method of writing.

"How long have you been writing for?" I asked him during a break.

"In true geek style, I've been writing about aliens since I was seven. My first book was published when I was fifteen." He spoke so modestly of what was a huge achievement.

"That's incredible!" I smiled at him. "I think I was still playing with Barbies."

"Barbeques?" he asked puzzled.

"No, the doll!" I laughed. "I might be Australian, but we don't let children play with open flames."

"Oh, yeah, right." He laughed as well. "Lucky I don't have any plans for fatherhood just yet!"

"It's been a while since I've had small children too. Hopefully I don't let this one barbeque." I pointed at my slightly protruding stomach.

"You're pregnant?" he asked, seemingly taken aback.

"That or I had a very large breakfast. Speaking of which, I'm hungry now we're talking about food. Are they going to feed us at some point, or are they trying to starve us so we give a better show, like the lions in the coliseum?" I looked around the room.

"I've only seen tea and coffee so far. I have a muesli bar, if you want to share?" he offered.

"Thanks, I've actually got some healthy snacks in my bag that I packed in a fit of virtue this morning. I was hoping they'd give us something gooey and wicked, which is what I actually feel like." I gave a sad face. "Guess I'll just have to be healthy."

"If only you'd catered. I've seen the front of some of your books, and I've started salivating on the spot."

"That's sweet of you. By the time it gets into a cookbook, I'm usually so sick of tasting the recipes that they are the last thing I want to eat." I made a face. "The exception is chocolate, of course. I can always eat the chocolate things!" I sighed. "I so admire what you do though; the time and imagination it must take to write a book is incredible. I'm going to rush home and download you onto my Kindle!" I promised.

We smiled at each other. Something about him made me warm to him immediately.

"Let's keep in touch," he blurted out. "Are you on Facebook?"

"And on Twitter, LinkedIn, and any other social media outlet my PR people think I should be on!" I rolled my eyes.

"I hear you! My blog alone accounts for a ridiculous amount of time. I know it's necessary, but…" He shrugged.

I think most people felt the same way; the effort required to keep up with all of it took time away from getting actual work done and seeing real people. Still, it was useful and an easy way to keep in contact with people you just met without giving away too many details.

"Go to my private one which is under my maiden name — Winters. I'll look out for your friend request. I think we might be back on," I said, nodding to the organizer who had entered the room and was ushering us back onto the stage. My sons liked reading science fiction and fantasy, so they might have heard of him and be amazed that we were "friends." It was pretty hard to impress them, as they thought their parents incredibly uncool, but I liked to live in hope that one day I wouldn't be so frightfully embarrassing to them as I was now.

When I spoke to them on the phone from boarding school later in the week, it turned out they did know who he was, but I was still uncool.

Chapter Twenty-Two

The email, when it came, was devastating in its innocuousness. A simple request from Facebook from Daniel Waterstreet together with the message: "*I really liked you when we met at the festival. I thought you should know and, given your pregnancy, you may not. Look at Adam Mitchell in my friends. Daniel Waterstreet.*"

Curious, I friended him and went to look in his friend's page. I found Adam Mitchell and clicked on him. He was a slim, good-looking man in what appeared to be his late twenties. He didn't look familiar at all, and his information didn't give me much. I clicked on photos of him but had no idea why Daniel Waterstreet wanted me to look at him.

I flicked through the photos until I found the one that stopped my heart. The cup of tea fell from my suddenly-numb fingers, spilling all over my pants and the floor, but I couldn't tear my eyes away from the screen to see or care what it ruined. There was Jack, smiling happily into the camera, his arms around Adam. It could have been innocent, and yet it clearly wasn't. Their body language told the story of their intimacy. In the next shot, they were kissing—not deeply but this was no platonic friendship. There were so many pictures, the dates going back years.

My body seemed to shrink down into itself, collapsing until all that was left was a cold, hard ball. I concentrated on just breathing in and out. I'm not sure how long I stayed frozen in place, staring at the computer sightlessly. I should have felt relieved, the burden of guilt was no longer mine to bear alone, but all I felt was a lacerating betrayal, as if this were somehow worse than what I had done. He was gay! It fit in so many ways, yet I still couldn't believe it.

What I felt was beyond devastation. It was further down that dark spectrum that suppresses the ability to function or think rationally. I could only feel the deep hole I had fallen into as it closed over my head. Metallic shards of hurt pierced my vital organs, impaling me, and I was powerless for the moment to rationalize my way out of it. It wasn't another woman: it was a man, or more likely, men.

Jack had been living a second life, one that his respectable English family would not have been able to handle, and I was his cover. How could I have been so stupid to have not known? Clearly other people out there did. I had sat next to Daniel Waterstreet all day at the writers' festival, chatting happily, completely oblivious. He had known and looked on me pityingly, and I'd had no idea. How many other people out there knew? Feeling sorry for me or, worse, believing me to be complicit in his deceit?

My life was a fraud, and I had put myself out there, selling it. I was a fraud too for peddling something that at its very foundation was a lie. So many people had bought into it, this lifestyle I flaunted in my books and kitchen supplies. I had given up so much for Jack, for *this?* What a bad trade I had made. Jack could have said something at so many points along the way, but instead he clung to this dead marriage to cover his tracks. No wonder he wanted to stay married. *Bastard.* At that moment, I truly hated him.

"You lying arsehole!" I screeched at him when he came through the door. My rage, which had been building for hours as I waited for him, peaked as he closed the door calmly.

"What is wrong with you? Calm down," he said, his face showing his revulsion at my palpable emotion. Grabbing the nearest object, which happened to be a vase of flowers, I hurled it at his head. He ducked, and it crashed into the wall, sending shards flying and water cascading into a pool on the parquet floor. He stared at me, shocked and wary.

"What's this about?" he asked carefully.

"You fucking your fucking boyfriend, dickhead! Adam Mitchell? Ring any bells?" The vile language barely expressed the incandescence of the fury fueling my every action. I wanted to hurt him so badly. My hands were gripped into fists in an effort not to physically attack him again.

"Oh." He put down his briefcase and hung his coat on the rack. "Who told you?" he asked calmly.

I ignored his question; it was completely beside the point as the bleak devastation overtook me. A part of me had been hoping he would deny it and be able to explain the misunderstanding. That small hope was snuffed out, taking a surprising amount of wind from my sails.

"Everything you've put me through, trying to make it work again, and it was all a lie. There was no chance, ever, that we could make it work." The pain-filled bitterness in my soul showed in my voice.

"I'm sorry, no," he said brutally. Finally, all hope was gone. The sick feeling of having hurt someone I loved so badly was turned around. He had cast the first stone, not me, in this savage execution of our marriage. My brief affair was a pebble in comparison to the boulder of his. The guilt-lifting made me feel almost giddy. It tasted of freedom and, for the first time in a long time, truth.

"There was only so far you'd go, pissing off your family. Marrying me was the extent of it. Admitting that you fancy men would have been too much." It seemed bleakly funny, really. I'd been torturing myself for what I did to a marriage that was built on a big fat lie. "You're gay!"

A giggle bubbled up, out of my control, and suddenly I was howling with laughter, sitting on the floor, unable to move, with tears streaming down my cheeks. I laughed so I wouldn't cry, and even though my stomach hurt, still I couldn't stop. I laughed at the bitterness and humiliation, along with the irony of the way it had all worked out, until there was nothing left. No tears, no anger. I was just an empty shell. At some point, Jack had left, but I was senseless of when or where he had gone. He could have gone out the door or be somewhere in the house. I simply didn't know or care.

My uncontrolled laughter subsided into hiccups, and when even these had gone, I finally eased up stiffly from the floor. I felt cold all over, even in my bones. I went and took a long hot shower, deciding not to think about anything. I was tired of trying to work out what I was going to do. I had no answers, or the energy to even think through the implications. I was in my dressing gown, drying my hair with a towel, when Jack appeared at the doorway to our room. He stood uncertainly, not coming any closer.

"You must hate me. I understand that."

"What I don't understand is why you put me through that. Did it make you feel better to make me suffer?" I asked accusingly.

"Yes, it did. I know I shouldn't feel it, but I felt betrayed."

"What about your betrayal of me? You're such a hypocrite," I spat.

"I got so good at blocking off that side of my life that I just didn't think about it," he admitted.

"So, you've been living this double life for how long?" I demanded.

"Do we really need to do this?"

"Yes. How long has…this…been going on?"

"I met Adam about ten years ago. We've been on and off since then, mostly on."

"Ten years." That sent another knife-like stab through my heart, just when I thought it could feel nothing more. My stomach churned with bile when I realized the significance of that time frame. While I was barely functioning, going through the worst period of my life, he was "hooking up" with his boyfriend?

"What about before that?"

"Nothing really."

"What does that mean?"

He sighed and ran his fingers through his hair.

"I sometimes…did some things with…people…at school and before we were married, but I swear I was faithful to you until Adam."

I swallowed hard, trying to get my head around that. I thought back to all of Jack's school friends I had met, seeing if I could remember any strange reactions or looks. The only one that stood out was Andrew Plimpton. I think I just worked out why he stopped talking to me after that weekend.

"Well, no need to hide it any more. You're free to do what you want openly now," I said bitterly.

"That's not what I want. I still want to stay married," he said, an edge of panic in his voice.

"You're not serious!" I looked at him disbelievingly. "Why on earth would we stay married now?"

"I don't know that I am gay *definitely*. I like men, but I like women too. I've never…had sex with a man. It's never gone that far. I never cheated on you."

"How far exactly have you gone?" Morbid curiosity bloomed.

"Do we have to talk about this?" He squirmed.

"Yes. I need to know what it is we're talking about. And it does make a difference to me."

"Just touching and…oral," he finally managed with difficulty.

I didn't know how I felt about that. Should the fact that he hadn't had full sex mean that he'd done less than me and it wasn't as bad? Wasn't oral sex cheating anyway? Jack obviously didn't think so. I shook my head, trying to figure it out. It was all so overwhelming, this information, and I hadn't had time to process it. I rubbed my aching eyes with my hand. It still felt surreal to be having this conversation at all with my husband.

"But you were intimate with him. For ten years. That's a relationship. Do you love him?"

"I don't know…Maybe." He sighed heavily. "I don't think there's a label for it. We are friends but more than that too."

"I think that's being unfaithful. If you are emotionally intimate with someone else and it involves sexual touching, then it's definitely cheating. And you were doing it for ten years!"

"Yes, but it never went as far as yours. Plus, you're pregnant, and a child is going to last a lot longer than that!"

I opened my mouth to respond but didn't get a chance.

"I agree that I've been dishonest, but I don't think it matters who was worse." He held up a hand. "I think we should just try to forget what's happened and start again from here. We're good parents," he continued. "If we just take the sex part out it, what we have is fine. You don't have to have the baby on your own. We hardly ever had sex anyway, so nothing much would change. We're no longer in our twenties; it's not like we're at it like rabbits anymore, and how often do you want sex with a new baby?"

He had a point, but this was too weird.

"How would it work? Would you still be seeing your boyfriend, and we'd just be living together as friends?" Just the thought of him with someone else caused a stab of pain, even though I had no right to feel that way.

"No." His lips twisted in weary amusement. "I have no desire to 'come out' so to speak. I can only imagine what Mother would say."

"You want to stay married and raise a child that isn't yours just because you don't want to tell your mother you're gay?" Edwina may be a demon disguised as a baby boomer, but still. "You're nearly forty, for God's sake. Why do you still care what your mother thinks?"

"Because she still controls the money. She's threatened to cut off not only me but the boys as well if we get divorced. You know how she is about appearances." Yes, I did. "We need her to keep paying the school fees. I've looked at it, and there is no way we can afford it on our own and run the house, given that I'm not sure if I'm even going to have a job from one day to the next. Everyone around me is being laid off, and no one knows how long the credit crunch is going to last. Most of what we got for the house went on the mortgage, and if we paid the boys' school fees, it would severely deplete our remaining capital, as well as the cost of a second household."

He paused, letting the reality of the situation sink in. The boys liked their school and friends, and to rip them out of it and have their parents split was a lot to ask of them. They would be able to deal with it, but no one wants their children to have to bear that if they can find a way around it. My income added a significant amount, but it was not regular or enough to cover all the school fees as well as living expenses, and it had the potential to evaporate completely if I was no longer "happily" married to Jack.

"I know it's not ideal, but our marriage could still work. I do still love you…in my own way," he said quietly. I stared at him, not sure what to make of that. If only he hadn't added those last few words, it would have been temptingly easy to say yes.

"I'll have to think about it," I said.

He nodded and left, closing the door behind him with a soft click.

I was faced by an impossible choice. I could stay with Jack, who despite everything I think I still loved; otherwise this wouldn't hurt so much. But he would never love me the way I wanted, and it would break my heart every day to live in a pretend marriage, even though it would be easier in so many other ways. Or I could leave and try to manage it all and a baby on my own.

I didn't know if Edwina would actually follow through with her threat to stop helping pay the school fees if we disgraced her by divorcing. It was possible that she might, locked as she was in a time-warp where divorce was still a dirty word, rather than an unfortunate and painful event that was almost as common as marriage itself. Telling her that the reason we were breaking up was because Jack was gay and I had taken a lover was unlikely to help. I'm sure I'd still be blamed for not being a good enough wife to keep him interested in women.

Chapter Twenty-Three

Our next session with the counselor came two days later.

"Shall we look at the infidelity? Affairs involve sex, but it's not usually the real reason one has an affair. Do you know why you did it?" Faye asked, turning to me.

"Well, Jack and I hadn't been…intimate regularly for years. I guess we'd do it once every three or four months? So, I guess part of it was the sex."

"Yes, she's all about the sex," Jack said, rolling his eyes.

I took a calming breath before I exploded at him.

"What are your needs?" she asked me.

"I like sex," I said unapologetically. "Not all the time, but ideally once every few days. Jack used to want it, but then he stopped, and suddenly I was the one begging."

"Jack, what is happening for you?"

"Ah…um…" Jack was so uncomfortable, it was excruciating to watch, but I was fascinated to hear what he was going to say. "I enjoy sex, but I just don't want it that often. I'm stressed at work and tired, and we both have busy social lives, sometimes together, sometimes on our own. Sometimes it feels like the planets have to be aligned for it to happen. It's not that I'm avoiding it or don't want it, but it just feels like too much effort, and I'd rather go to sleep."

"Kate, how do you feel when you hear your partner saying that?"

"It makes me feel unattractive and unloved. How are you supposed to feel when your husband would rather sleep than have sex with you? It's also a lie. He's been fooling around with men."

Faye did a really good job of not reacting, though I could see her struggle by the sudden clenching of her jaw. I almost laughed at the horrendousness of the whole situation.

"Jack, would you like to respond to that?"

"No." He glared at me. Faye cleared her throat and soldiered on. I had to admire her composure; this had to be incredibly difficult.

"Kate, what else did you get from the affair apart from sex?"

"Why are we focusing on my infidelity? Jack was unfaithful too, but he gets to not have to talk about it?"

"We'll get around to Jack too. You seem a bit more ready to open up."

"I felt special and it was exciting, I guess. I enjoyed being intimate with someone. It made me really see how distant Jack and I had become."

"Jack, what is your reaction when you hear Kate say that?"

"It makes me angry. I thought everything was fine. She never said she was unhappy. Sure, we were busy, but that's just life. If she had needed something, she could have just told me."

"So, Kate, did you try to talk to Jack about it?"

"Not specifically. I don't think I was fully aware of how I was feeling before I met…before this happened." I nearly said Anders' name.

"Let's go back a bit. When do you think the intimacy problems started?"

Neither Jack nor I looked at each other. I thought back to the last time we had been truly happy, and the pieces fell into place. I understood the events that had started us down this path. I opened the box that I usually kept tightly closed, something that was the defining moment, the turning point for us: our daughter, Eve.

A miscarriage, such an innocuous word, sounds like it describes being too late for a conveyance of some sort that involved horses. Not so much. It is too bland a word to apply to an event so dark and bleak. The horror of labor pains too early, the unrelentingly cruel diagnosis, and the horrific pain of her death so close to what should have been a time of joy. My mouth twisted into a grimace with the onslaught of the tears, and my nose ran unchecked.

She was our dark-haired beauty who never had a chance. I held her in my arms, her tiny frail body, too red and listless, and felt her life slip away, and there was nothing I could do, apart from kiss the final warmth from her still cheeks. I could not deny her an escape from the needles and the pain, but I loved her so much I selfishly wanted her to stay. Jack and I cried out our heartbreak together, holding her so carefully until we had to leave her alone in the morgue, which was the hardest thing I have ever done.

It was ten years ago now, but the wounds were as fresh as ever. If I could have one wish it would be to have her back, healed and happy, and I would give my own life in exchange without a moment's hesitation.

Apart from our love for her, there was so little tangible evidence that she had ever existed, and we had buried her alone, Jack's family not making the effort to understand and mine so far away. Jack sat alone in her room for hours, slowly and gently dismantling the preparations we had started for her life with us.

The way I dealt with the grief was to bake. I baked everything, all day and night for months afterward. I ran out of recipes, so started creating my own. Inevitably, really, I became good at it. It didn't make things better, but it didn't make them worse, and somehow making other people happy by giving them a cake or a biscuit, such a small thing really, filled some of the void inside. That's how I got the name Saint Kate of the Cupcake; I would give away the endless things I had made to homeless shelters and women's refuges, and it was the name jokingly given to me by the director of one of the shelters.

The boys were only four years old at the time, so their memory and understanding of what happened soon faded, but they knew Mummy and Daddy were sad and did their best to cheer us up and make us laugh. I had to lock my grief away and carry on for them.

Maybe that made it worse somehow, not dealing with it properly, but I just couldn't do it. I felt that if I broke down I would never get back up again, and I couldn't do that to their childhood. They needed me to be there as their mother, not someone who never got out of bed. So, I locked it away for later, when I was alone in the dark, though there was not a moment that I forgot her. Slowly, the excruciating pain eased into something more bearable, but it never went away entirely. It never would. Even now, I occasionally woke up sweaty and cold in the middle of the night, disorientated and panting, in a panic because Eve was lost and alone somewhere and I couldn't find her.

Jack carried on too, but we were never the same again. We dealt with our grief in different ways. I mindlessly baked, and he went to work. When the cookbook became a success, Jack's indifference was the first real indication of the degree of separation between us. Both of us were swollen from sadness, but we were still functioning, and I had no energy left over then to build a bridge. We were not unhappy, just living in parallel. *Later*, I thought. There was nothing seriously wrong. But as time passed, it was still there.

The relationship we had before had morphed into something else, something far more solitary. When I stopped to think about it and mourn what we had lost, it was a dull hurt, and, in comparison, a mere brick in the house of pain where we dwelled. Rarely did we talk about Eve, as if we were both too scared to combine our pain as it might overwhelm us with its enormous weight, rather than lighten our own loads. So, we put one foot in front of the other and set off down the road to here, where we had both had affairs and our marriage was broken. We had become so good at ignoring things that were painful that neither of us had noticed until then. We had become too proficient at carrying on regardless.

We sat there silently in front of Faye, who waited patiently for us to open up the wounds we had so carefully concealed. I finally looked across at Jack and admitted to myself there was nothing left. All I felt was tired — tired of fighting, tired of trying to pretend everything might one day be fine, that we could go back to what we were before or find a new place where there wouldn't be so much pain between us. It wouldn't. It was who we were together, and to deny that was to deny Eve. I was ready to give him up, because that would keep her memory intact, which was the only thing I had left of her. A deep sadness settled into my bones, and all I wanted to do was sleep and make it go away. I put my head down in my hands and cried, dark, heaving, soul-wrenching sobs, unsure which loss I was mourning, my husband or my daughter.

I had finally reached the point where the thought of breaking up and moving on with my life was less painful than staying. It was never going to be anything more than what it was now: a complete façade, with no deeper feelings or connection. The difficulties from now — moving out of Clouston Hall, splitting the finances, the hurt this would cause both us and the children — I dreaded less than the feelings of drowning and disgust at the vision of my future if I stayed. Even if it meant the end of my career, it was a price I was finally willing to pay. I could see that, whatever justifications I had made to myself, I had stayed with Jack these last few months out of fear. I had been too scared of being on my own. The prospect of being alone still sent a chill through me, but if I imagined a set of scales, the fear no longer outweighed the relief of leaving.

And so, our dance that had begun with so much joy and enthusiasm at our wedding was almost done. There were only a few more steps until we finally reached the end of our song and the end of our marriage.

It took a week for me to get my head around the decision, and even then I struggled not to change my mind and take the "easier" path, the one where I had to do nothing at all, except live a lie. Jack seemed to have been avoiding me, without words asking me to pretend that nothing was wrong and to swallow this too. Unfortunately, all our issues had accumulated into a small mountain that was impossible to ignore anymore.

Jack had disappeared into his study after dinner and emerged only as I was turning the lights off, preparing for bed. It was time. I truly looked at him, tall and handsome, to all appearances the fairytale husband even now. I was struck by qualms over whether this was the right decision. It would be so much easier to stay with him. He'd left me with an option, one that would be mutually beneficial, but would mean a lifetime of no intimacy, only the pretense of it in public. I wouldn't truly know until I'd left him whether it was a mistake or not, and that was frightening.

What if I never found anyone else? It's not like single women were complaining that there were too many great men out there and they couldn't choose. I'd give up security and comfort, upset my children, and live a life of loneliness. On the other hand, the thought of only ever having *this*, of living the rest of my life in a barren desert of a marriage, was intolerable. Inside my head, I was screaming. I didn't want to bring my baby into an environment like this. Jack said he would be able to raise the child like his own, but would he when he was faced by a child who looked nothing like him? There really was only one decision.

"I'm sorry, Jack, but I can't do this anymore. I can't spend the rest of my life pretending everything is fine when it isn't and it's never going to be." My voice came out husky as I tried not to cry.

"It doesn't have to be pretend. I can take care of your…needs too." He seemed to squirm a little when he said that. It set me off, the thought that I was so repulsive to him, the sexual equivalent of eating a slug. I was sick of feeling like I was not normal and that wanting to have sex was disgusting. I think the pregnancy hormones might have been making me a bit touchy too.

"I get it! You're gay and you don't want to have sex with me! But this is *not my fault!*" I screamed, furious at him. I pushed past him to run up to our bedroom. I grabbed a suitcase from the cupboard and, randomly opening drawers, started piling things in. The dam wall containing all the hurt and anger was cracking, and it all came pouring out.

"I'm not gay!" he shouted as he came into the room.

"You want to fuck other men. That means you are gay, you idiot!" We were only centimeters apart, screaming at each other. His face was red, rage twisting his features until they were no longer beautiful and transformed into something ugly.

"That's all you wanted — sex, sex, sex. You're a fucking nymphomaniac!"

"What I wanted was a man, not a repressed mummy's boy who would rather lie to everyone than admit, even to himself, that he wants to fuck men," I hissed back. "That's it. I'm done!" I shook my head back and forth. "This marriage is over."

With an inarticulate roar, he grabbed me and threw me face down onto the bed.

I reached out with my hands to brace myself, and then he was on top of me, pinning me so I was bent over the edge, my face pressed into the mattress. I turned my head so I could breathe, but otherwise his weight held me immobile. I couldn't work out what he was doing, until I heard the sound of his belt buckle undoing. Even then I couldn't really believe what was happening. I felt his hands fumble with my underwear, pulling them down so hard it scraped my skin.

"No, Jack, don't!" I cried.

"This is what you want, isn't it?" he spat against my neck.

"Stop, please…" I pleaded, but he kept going.

All I heard was "hate you, hate you, hate you" in time with the bright starbursts of pain.

Finally it was over, and he collapsed on top of me.

"I love you," he cried, great heaving sobs escaping him as he clung to me. We slid backward onto our knees on the floor, Jack holding me against him as he wept. I felt numb, in shock. I didn't fight him, just sat there trying not to feel the different hurts—the stinging pain between my legs or the deep cramping ache inside from the brutalized flesh.

Warm rivulets of blood or sperm or a mix of both started running down the inside of my thighs. I pushed away from him, and he let me go. I went into our ensuite, locked the door, and stripped off all my clothes and ran the shower. I stepped into the warm water and began to wash myself. I scrubbed and scrubbed, trying to erase the feeling of violation like it was a mark on my skin.

Twenty minutes later I was still scrubbing and realized I was crying. I'm not sure when it started, but I couldn't make it stop. But it seemed distant to me, as if I was somewhere else looking in at my body. It was around an hour later I turned the shower off. Mercifully, the robot-like state continued, and I dressed and went downstairs. Jack was sitting on the couch, his head in his hands.

"You should leave," I said tonelessly. I think I was still in shock because I couldn't feel anything; there was no meaning somehow, even as I said the words. Seeing him look at me with hopeless resignation in his eyes, I felt nothing. It seemed impossible that he would even respond to them, when everything felt so insubstantial. I was hollow, just a paper shell, not enough mass to exert any influence on the outside world.

"I'm so sorry. I'll stay at the London flat until we can sort everything out."

"That would be best," I said, then turned and walked out. I went to the kitchen and started making myself a cup of tea, for want of any other ideas on how to keep my hands busy. I heard sounds of packing from upstairs, then footsteps descending the stairs and the front door shutting quietly. The end of an era finished with a soft click. My legs faltered, and I fell heavily into one of the chairs.

Chapter Twenty-Four

I sat in a stupor, unaware of my surroundings, staring at the small puddle of tea spreading and cooling on the table where I had bumped the cup. A rapping at the door startled me out of it, and through the frosted glass I could see Edwina's outline. *This was so not going to happen*, I thought fiercely. *There is no way I'm going to let the bitch see me like this.*

I rose, careless of whether or not she could see the movement, and went upstairs. I packed up what few things I absolutely needed into the car and, wheels spinning, tore past a startled Edwina walking back to her house. I returned to London and stayed in a hotel until I found a vacant rental house in Clapham that I could move into immediately. I bought some furniture that arrived the same day I did, took off the wrapping, hired a divorce lawyer, and then I fell apart.

I have no clear recollection of the next few weeks, as if someone had turned off the lights and I sat in darkness. Gradually the numb feeling left and the pain and loneliness set in. Despite everything, I missed Jack. He had been part of me for so long, and that part was gone, painfully and messily hacked off. I grieved for him, myself, and us.

The child inside me remained, unaffected by the assault or my emotional state. I had wondered what it would be like to be alone. Maybe one day it would reach that comfortable stage, but right now it felt like a life sentence in solitary confinement. I lay in bed, watching the drapes that enclosed it move in a slight breeze, the light changing as the days passed, unable to summon the will to move. I ignored the phone and the knocks on the door. They seemed irrelevant. There was nothing anyone could say that would make a difference, and I couldn't handle anyone seeing me like this. Pity or sympathy right now would make me physically sick. I sent text messages when communication with the outside world became unable to be refused. I pretended I was starting a new book and was deeply absorbed in preparation work. Nothing could be further from the truth. I spent all day in my pajamas doing nothing at all, day after day. I wept. I slept. That was all.

The only one persistent enough to break through my bubble was Bats, because she literally broke into my house. I had shambled from my bed to the couch, where I flopped listlessly, watching God knows what. I didn't care enough to notice what was on or whether it was those infomercials that usually annoy the bejesus out of me. I was wearing a pink fluffy dressing gown that badly needed a wash, and my hair had become solid. I vaguely registered the tinkling sound of breaking glass, but I didn't think to connect it with my house. Footsteps down the hall sent a chill of adrenaline like a splash of icy water, and I sat bolt upright, frozen with indecision: try to hide or get out of the house.

"Katie?" I heard Bats' voice shouting from half way up the stairs and almost wept with relief that it wasn't Jack or a burglar.

"In here," I said weakly, my voice cracking with misuse. I cleared my throat and repeated myself a bit more loudly.

"Dear God! What has happened to you?" she said upon seeing me through the open door.

"I...well...Jack..." I tried to start explaining but just burst into tears.

Putting her arms around me, she shushed me gently.

"I love you, but you need a bath desperately. I don't know if I can handle a long story if I have to be this close," she said kindly as she firmly helped me up off the couch and steered me to the bathroom. She turned on the shower and pushed me in, clothes and all.

"Strip off, and I'll put them in the wash." Dutifully, I followed her instructions, handing her the sopping garments. She disappeared briefly and returned with a towel and some clean clothes.

"I'll make some tea while you finish up here. Wash your hair and clean your teeth too!" she ordered, and then she disappeared back around the door.

Dried off and in clean clothes, I felt much better. Somehow the logic that I needed to wallow in my misery by not taking care of myself had gone a bit far. Hopefully, liking being clean was the herald of a new, less painful stage. I took a deep steadying breath and went downstairs.

Bats had made me something to eat and a cup of tea. I was so ridiculously grateful, I could feel tears coming again. She carried it over to the table, and we sat down. I took a sip of tea, which was hot and perfect on my tongue.

"So, what happened?" she asked. I told her almost everything, what I'd done, what I'd found out about Jack. But not about *that*.

"You never suspected anything?" Her brow furrowed slightly.

"No. Should I have?" I looked at her closely, to see if she had known. It would be so much worse if everyone else was in on it and I was just the poor deluded wife who had subconsciously refused to see what was obvious to everyone else.

She held up her hands, palms outward, to show no offense was meant.

"I had no idea, but then I wasn't married to him. Frankly, you never know what's going on in a relationship from the outside."

"No one else knows, then?"

"I hadn't heard even a rumor. He must have been pretty careful, because you know how everyone gossips. There hasn't even been anything in the media, unlike your little fling."

"Yes, I know. Completely stupid, but I don't really regret it, even now. Well, maybe a little bit." I grimaced slightly. "Part of me knows that having an affair didn't cause the problems with Jack, that there were other issues that were seriously wrong, but it was the catalyst for bringing it out into the open. Maybe I could have kept my head in the sand a bit longer, or become braver and confronted it on my own. I'm sure it would have been better if I could have taken the moral high ground."

"Maybe, or maybe you both being in the wrong meant you could talk on an even footing without someone playing the victim."

"That's not how it went," I whispered, unable to meet her eyes. I burst into tears, ashamed of what happened. Could I tell Bats? Or should I keep it quiet?

"So, it's really over?" she said gently. "There's no chance of you getting back together?"

"No." That's all I had to say. There might be a time when I could speak about it, but not yet. "This is going to be hard for you; you and Jack grew up together. I'll understand if we can't be friends anymore."

"Are you asking me to choose between you?"

"No, but Jack might."

"We'll deal with that if it comes to it. Don't borrow trouble from another day."

Bats gave me a long hug, and I wiped away the tears, determined to pull it together and do better.

The human body is amazing, and I had no lasting physical effects from the assault, but in my head at odd moments, I kept flashing back to Jack on top of me, remembering the words of hate. It was being powerless to stop it that was almost worse than the thing itself. I knew I would have to see him again because of the boys, but I couldn't just yet. I knew he was sorry; it said so on the card with the flowers I threw straight in the rubbish bin. He tried to call a few times, but I screened the calls, allowing them to go through to voice mail but deleting them unheard.

I shouldn't have been surprised when the television deal fell through. Stupidly, I somehow thought that the world could stand still while I went into hibernation, somehow able to sense the devastation in me and back off for a while, even though, of course, they knew nothing about it. Unfortunately, the world doesn't work like that, and after numerous desperate phone calls from Lindsay, the phone went quiet. When I finally called her back, her voice was cold.

"Where the hell have you been?" she demanded.

"Dealing with my marriage ending," I shot back, quick to anger these days.

"I'm sorry to hear that," she said stiffly. "Don't you think you could have let me know? Do you know how many times I pushed back the deadline on the TV deal, trying to keep it alive? You made me look like an idiot. I don't like looking like an idiot."

"I'm sorry, Lindsay. To be perfectly honest, I wasn't thinking much outside my own stuff."

"If you want to have any hope of continuing you career, you're going to need to put in some serious rehabilitation to your image. I'm not going to even bother if you're not committed."

"Trust me, I'm committed. I'm raising the baby on my own, so I need an income more than ever."

"We're going to need to get your story sorted. Is Jack going to have a problem with saying the baby is his?"

"I'm sure we can come to an arrangement." I shuddered at the thought of having to see him again.

"Are you going to be able to get back to work soon? We'll do a photo shoot with you pregnant and then plan to have something new to release after you've had the baby. How soon after the birth are you going to be able to do publicity?"

Dread filled me at the thought of having to leave the baby with a nanny for the length of time required to publicize a book, as well as being vulnerable to the media to ask me whatever questions they wanted. There was nothing for it; I couldn't go back to work as a lawyer after all this time. I had to make this work or I would be without an income.

"I'll get started on a new book. Any chance of getting the TV deal?"

"No, not now. You've screwed that up."

"Sorry."

Lindsay sniffed. "I'll try to get you some appearances and paying gigs. It's going to be harder now you're not with Jack. How long can we hold off announcing it?"

"No hurry. I don't think Jack wants it out there."

"This is good. Try to keep it quiet for as long as you can."

I knew I needed to pull myself together for the baby and get my life back on track: eat, shower, brush my hair, etcetera. It took me a month to start the day with a shower, rather than random times throughout the day or night. I was shocked to look at the calendar and realize that the boys would be home for the holidays in three weeks. I wanted to see them, but not in the state I was in. I pulled myself out of bed and forced myself into preparations. I cleaned the house, did the laundry, set up the bedrooms even though it felt like there was a weight on my back, slowing me down and making every job that much harder.

Lindsay managed to book me for a photo shoot and interview with a particularly sympathetic reporter who worked at a glossy magazine, and I was amazed that with hair, makeup, and lighting I could look like a normal human when I felt like a disintegrating zombie. Lindsay had some major pull with the magazine because the article was flattering to the point of gushing, making a huge deal about "our" excitement about the new addition to the family. No mention was made about my last pregnancy, only the boys. There was also a heavy plug for my previous books. Lindsay must have called in serious favors, and I owed her.

I went to pick up the boys up from school, summoning as much energy as I could to meet their buoyant enthusiasm. I told them I was housesitting for a friend to get some peace and quiet while I worked on another book. It wasn't the time yet to tell them while they were sitting in the car. I had really missed them, and I found myself tearing up and having to cover it by looking away and busying myself with something.

"Mum, what's wrong?" Charles asked as I sat quietly in the breakfast room, eating my toast the following morning.

"What do you mean?" I asked surprised.

"We know you keep crying. We can see it, you know." He sat down next to me. I know you're not supposed to have favorites, and I loved Edward to the last beat of my heart, but there was something about Charles I just got. It wasn't that he favored me in looks — both boys took after Jack — but even when he was little, I understood him a bit better. Clearly, it went both ways.

"Your father and I are separating. I need to talk to Edward too. I wasn't sure when to do it," I said sadly.

"It's okay, Mummy." He gave me a hug. "We thought you guys were going to eventually. It was a bit of a giveaway that you're living in a different house," he continued dryly. "Why would you have some of our things here if you're only housesitting?"

"Really?" I was shocked. "I didn't think you'd recognize any of it." I hadn't brought much with me, though I guess I hadn't been thinking too clearly because my favorite painting that I had bought on our honeymoon was in the sitting room, and it was fairly distinctive.

"Yeah." He rolled his eyes, in a typical "whatever" teenage way. "Besides, you're one of the few parents still together, and it's not like you guys were super affectionate or anything."

"I'm so sorry. I wanted to give you both good role models, but I guess we didn't do a great job. It doesn't have to be like this, you know. I wish I could have shown that to you."

"Don't worry about it. We'll figure it out. It's not like you were horrible to each other or anything." Little did he know, and I was thankful for that.

"So, are we going to get a stepfather soon? Were you really hooking up with that Norwegian actor guy?"

I couldn't believe we were having this conversation. On the inside, I squirmed uncomfortably.

"No. No stepfather," I said bluntly, and thankfully, he just nodded and didn't ask any further questions. I'd spent way too much time dwelling on what a cock-up I'd made of my life, without having to try to explain it to my fourteen-year-old son.

Looking back, I could see that I'd never really given Anders a chance. I didn't seriously consider his offers of a real relationship, not being able to trust that he was genuine or that I'd ever have the freedom to pursue it. Maybe that's why he felt the need to take the drastic action of leaking stuff to the media and springing photos of himself with someone else on me with no warning. Not that that made it okay, but I had to accept that my actions had contributed to the situation. With Anders, I'd at least had the chance to have at something genuine and fulfilling, rather than the fraud my precious marriage had been. I had thrown away any potential happiness with Anders out of fear and pride, and it was too late now to go back.

Chapter Twenty-Five

Having the boys at home turned out to be just what I needed. They took me out of myself and forced me into genuine recovery, seeing friends again, going to the gym, grocery shopping, ending my self-imposed exile. I even told Bats what had really happened and had to stop her from going off to hunt down and shoot Jack, which was nice in a homicidal way. She urged me to go to the police, but all I wanted to do was put it behind me and move on with my life. There was no way either of us were going to get up in court and regurgitate the events of our marriage for the entertainment of the general population. No matter how confidential you tried to keep it, details would always get out. I had a baby to support, and that sort of bad publicity could kill what was left of my reputation.

"So, moving on with your life, huh?" She gave me a skeptical look.

"Well, not just yet. I think the overly large stomach might put off any potential first dates."

"Okay, after that?" she conceded. "Will you marry again?"

"It might be a bad time to make any firm judgments, given that I'm so horny due to the hormones. At the moment, all I want is a man who can fuck like a bunny and doesn't talk. He will only be able to speak a few words of English, maybe with a fabulous accent—something Latin and sexy. Strangely too, after watching an equestrian program on TV, I've been having fantasies about men who ride horses. It looks like they'd been able to do a good job, so to speak. So my requirements are: young, sexy, Latin, and can ride a horse. That's it."

Dear God, it had been a long time since I had sex. I had never been so sexually frustrated and hormonal at the same time. I was ready to jump the next man who was nice to me. Flirty butchers beware…

"I know you. You're a relationship person. I can't see you doing the casual sex thing. You'll meet someone who will love the baby and you, and you'll be ecstatically happy while I'll be green with envy."

"No. I don't have the energy for it, even if I could find someone who'd be interested." I sighed. "I'd have to wax."

"Maybe you can become a trophy wife and get someone to take care of you."

"Nope, then there's no sex because they're too old. What I need is a young, fabulously hot guy who's ridiculously rich and wants to take care of a knocked-up old lady!" I laughed.

"Hmm…maybe a South American polo player? I'll keep a lookout. You're not old," she said belatedly.

"Thanks." I rolled my eyes.

The boys decided to go to a friend's house in France for the rest of the summer holidays. I missed them, but it was great to see their happiness and enthusiasm, even for such a short time. They were growing up, strong independent teenagers, and they didn't need me so much anymore. It was a bittersweet moment, but it put my pregnancy into perspective. I should have talked to them about it, but the moment never came. As teenagers, they were completely oblivious to the possibility, given I was so ancient and wore nothing tight fitting anyway, and the shock of the separation was enough for the moment. The school fees were paid up until the end of the next school year, but after that, who knew what Edwina would do.

Gradually life resumed, though different from what it had been. I wasn't particularly good at navel gazing, and it was unlikely that I would be repeating the circumstances of my marriage, so I wasn't sure what lessons there were to be learned from it all. Don't marry gay men? Have sex on the first date to make sure it all works properly? Never assume you're infertile?

My new life had its good points and its bad. I wasn't particularly happy on my own. I wondered how I was going to manage a baby by myself and what kind of childhood I could give it. Would I still be able to take it to Smith & Gardener with me for a haircut, or would I be surviving on a much-reduced budget by then? We would be living on whatever I could earn, and the next few months would probably be the decider. I hadn't kept as good a handle on our finances as I should have. I knew what I made, but Jack had handled the mortgage and the proceeds from the sale of the house. We still had the joint accounts, but that would change sooner or later. *God, I wish Picasso's hadn't closed down.* I was craving one of their bacon sandwiches really badly right now, flashing back to my previous pregnancies when I had gorged on their salty bacon-y goodness. There was a café on Northcote Road that did them, and they were pretty good, but just not the same.

At night, there was no one around, and the house felt empty. Strange noises in the night kept me awake with a pounding heart, bracing for the sound of footsteps on the stairs that never came. On the upside, I was able to get a lot of work done and cook in the early hours when I couldn't sleep without fear of disturbing anyone. My cooking felt stilted and robotic, though, and I struggled with ideas. I was also overly obsessed with bacon. Could I do a bacon cookbook? God, I loved bacon. And orange juice. Together was the ultimate. I was on a tasting mission to find the best bacon available in London and was steadily working my way through all the sources. I was also pairing it with new combinations of sauces: maple syrup was divine, though tartar sauce was very odd in a strangely compelling way. Tomato sauce was good too.

Trying to work this time around was a completely different experience from my previous books, especially *Temptations*, which flew out of me with virtually no effort or stress. The only idea I thought might work in my current frame of mine was a book on fast and easy family meals. My working title was *Quick Roasting in the Fires of Hell*. I was thinking I might need to change it before it is published. *If* I got it published. I was hardly a "family" icon now.

A lot of our friends dropped off the radar, clearly deciding that staying friends with Jack was more important. I wasn't really surprised. At least I knew now who had liked me for me. Bats stayed with me, but her life was busy, and I had a lot more free time now. As hard as I tried, I was lonely.

Somehow I couldn't see myself on RSVP or speed dating. Being pregnant was a handbrake when it came to getting back into the singles scene. Plus, it had been so long, the thought of dating terrified me. Also, the only person I had been intimate with in years (other than Jack) was Anders, and how could anyone compare with that? Nothing in my life before had come close to it, no one had ever wanted me like that, nor had I wanted someone with that intensity. What were the chances of feeling a spark like that more than once in your life? Or maybe it was just the hormones talking. I wouldn't know unless I saw him again, but that wasn't going to happen unless I sought him out. I wasn't going to, at least not yet. Maybe when I had it a bit more together. Mentally right now, I was in a bad place. To feel I could hold my own with Anders and the world he lived in, I needed to be confident or I would sink under the weight of my own insecurities. My self-esteem was barely treading water as it was.

Bats came over every Wednesday for dinner, pretty much the highlight of my week. At the sound of her knock, I hurried to open the door, but I could tell immediately that something was wrong by how tense she was.

"What's up?" I asked after pouring her a glass of wine and myself a sparkling water.

"I think you should be sitting down." She gulped down a slug of wine. "Jack has started seeing Caroline."

I gasped, feeling like I'd been bitch-slapped. "You are fucking kidding me!" Thinking back to how she treated me when Jack and I had first started seeing each other, it seem almost like it was a deliberate move on Jack's part.

"No, unfortunately not. Frankly, even I was surprised at the speed at which she dumped her husband once Jack was free. I didn't know him well, but he seemed nice enough, and it is him I most feel sorry for. On the upside, from what I hear, Edwina is so very happy with Jack because he's finally with the 'right' type of girl, that she's going to keep paying the school fees for the boys. At least that's what she told Mother."

Oh, good God. I should have pitied her for what she was getting into, but really just then, I hated them both: Jack for being a hypocrite and a coward, scurrying back into the closet as fast as his rat legs would take him, and Caroline for just generally being a completely heartless bitch. Her poor husband. At least they hadn't had children.

The thing I most regretted about our breakup was how public it had all become, now that we were unable to keep it just between ourselves. Everybody thought they knew what happened, or some version of it, from the Internet and gossip magazines. Of course I'd borne the brunt of the blame, despite Lindsay's best efforts.

I was now seen as a slightly notorious scarlet woman, though I tried to pay as little attention as I could to horrible things that were being said about me. It was hard to see the headlines on the weekly magazines everywhere, screaming that you'd been dumped by both your "brave" husband (who had finally found love again with his childhood sweetheart) and your "sexy" younger lover (who had been busy living it up with the loveliest young Hollywood things).

Jack hadn't publicly denied that the baby was his, but neither had he said that it was, which they used for fuel, speculating on the deeper meaning of his silence. I tried not to let it get to me, telling myself that the interest in us would pass soon enough and the vultures would be on to their next victim. Despite all the rumors, there was no actual evidence that I'd had an affair with Anders, so there were no photos of us together or other proof to regurgitate endlessly in the media. It was too easy to deny it ever happened, which shouldn't have made me sad but it did.

Standing in what was now my bedroom, I looked at myself in the mirror. I dropped the towel that was wrapped around me after the shower and stared appraisingly. I had lost weight with the stress of everything, and more bones showed than I think ever had in my life before. My ribs stood out, my thighs had a gap between them, and my cheeks were concave. Only my belly was rounded, and my breasts had their pregnancy fullness.

Aesthetically, I had probably never looked better, though I had never felt less attractive on the inside. *I might be the closest I've ever been to Anders' skinny-minny type, but here I am, thirty-eight, pregnant and alone,* said the quiet unhappy voice in my head. *Shut up, voice,* I told myself. No one was responsible for my situation but me. So I stuffed things up with Anders, but it wasn't like I'd known about Jack then. And, frankly, at the time, I hadn't been willing to admit how broken my marriage was. Any regrets were pointless.

Before I could descend into the waiting bottomless abyss of self-pity, I scrambled into my gym clothes. As part of getting back to myself, I needed to improve my mood and get out of the house, and exercise was the best way to do both. It was my third week of the new routine, and already I felt better, stronger. *I think I should treat myself to some cake on the way home,* I thought, and found a small bit of my optimism coming back.

It was a simple thing, but taking pleasure in the small things like cake could get me through this bad time too, even if I wasn't making it. I had to force myself to cook, and then only as much as I needed for work, as it brought back memories of how happy I had been with Anders in the cocoon of our hotel rooms and rented apartment, eating and having sex lustfully and with abandon. Lately, my hormonal mind had been revisiting those times with even more frequency. I missed Anders, and Jack sometimes, but there was no way we could go back. Some things weren't fixable. Once the trust was gone, it was virtually impossible to get it back. I don't think any of us would be prepared to work that hard.

Still, all things considered, I almost felt like myself again. I guess having worse things to compare it to made my current unhappiness more bearable. The end of my marriage was awful, but not a tragedy. Losing a child is a tragedy, and I had survived that, so I could survive anything. I walked out into the crisp morning, feeling like I could cope with the day, admiring my new glossy red door. I had always wanted a red one, but Jack had insisted on black. I liked the way it brightened up the white entrance and contrasted with the black and white diamond tiles on the steps.

"So, it's true. You are pregnant." A man's voice came from the footpath. The words were innocuous enough, but the anger behind them wasn't. I looked up from the keys in my hand and saw Anders standing there. I was half way down the front stairs and hesitated, not knowing whether to go back up or make a run for it. In my indecision, I stayed where I was on the middle step. I was in my gym gear, which showed the bump, so there was no point in denying it.

"I had to read about it on the Internet. Is it mine? I can count, you know," he said, loudly and accusingly, oblivious to anyone hearing.

He stalked over to stand at the bottom of the stairs, his eyes on my stomach. His eyebrows drew together in a harsh line. He looked furious, but I grabbed his arm and dragged him back up the stairs and into the house quickly before a more public scene could ensue. Who knew how many neighbors or lurking paparazzi had caught that! *Bugger.*

I took him into the lounge room and tried to think how to begin as he just stood there fuming.

"Yes, the baby is yours," I blurted out, for want of a better way to phrase it.

"Were you going to tell me?" he asked, his voice somewhere between irate and exasperated.

"Maybe. I don't know." I shook my head, unable to look at him. "Later."

"So, all that angst was a sham." He exhaled sharply, sitting down on the couch and burying his hands in his hair. "I'm so stupid." He shook his head. "I should have seen that I was just the stud service. Did your husband know all along?" He glared at me.

"No!" I exclaimed. "That's not it at all. Please let me explain." I sat down opposite him and tried to cam my own anxiety. I took a few deep breaths and rubbed my damp palms on my legs. He moved forward to perch on the edge of the opposite sofa, looking down at his tightly clenched hands like he was ready to take off at any moment.

"Jack and I hadn't had a…real marriage in a while." I couldn't face telling him that Jack was gay and I hadn't known. The humiliation of that would wait for another time. "We had difficulties getting pregnant after the twins and used IVF to fall pregnant again. The second time, we lost the baby at twenty-six weeks. A daughter."

He looked up at me, puzzled as to why I was telling him this now.

"I don't think we ever really recovered from that." I steeled myself to keep going. "We're not together any more, regardless."

I let a shuddering breath out. It didn't sound so bad now I'd said it out loud. I kept going, holding up my hand when he was about to say something. If I didn't get it out in one go, I might not be able to.

"I honestly didn't think I could get pregnant. I'm older now, so less fertile even than then, and we only had unprotected sex once. When we ended it, I thought that was it. I didn't think being pregnant was even a possibility, so I didn't realize until I was three months along. I couldn't terminate a child, not after having gone through so much to have Eve. I wanted to have the baby. I didn't tell you because I wasn't sure how you'd take it. We had ended things, and you seemed to have moved on. It would have been unfair to force you into being a parent when you were so far away and we weren't together anyway. You have your life in LA, doing the single man thing, and it was my choice. I'm prepared to accept the responsibility, and I will manage it financially. I know what I'm getting into. I would probably have told you eventually, though, when I had a handle on it. I'm sorry you had to find out this way."

He came over to me and knelt next to my chair.

"I want babies!" he said fiercely, in contrast with the large gentle hands he placed on the curve of my belly. "I can't think of anything I want more than to feel you rounded with my child inside you. Why would you think I wouldn't want that?" His voice sounded puzzled. "I told you this is what I wanted from us. I've missed you so much. Why didn't you call me? I would have dropped everything to be here for you. You didn't have to be on your own."

I looked down at him, his face completely changed, earnestness mixing with joy.

"But that was before…"

"Sure, I like sleeping in and traveling wherever and whenever I want, but I would give it up in a heartbeat." He laughed softly and placed his hands on either side of my face, kissing me with a tenderness that was as beautiful as it was unexpected.

I pulled back and searched his eyes, unable to take the surprised look from my face.

"What? You don't think I mean it?" he asked in disbelief. "You don't trust me?"

My silence was answer enough.

"I have never lied to you. When I met you, something changed. It felt like…coming home. All I could think about was making a life with you, seeing you every day, getting to do all the mundane things I couldn't because you were already doing them with someone else. Getting you pregnant and having a family was what I wanted, but you said you didn't know if you wanted that, and I never really thought you'd leave Jack without a push. I know I shouldn't have tried to force the issue, but I couldn't think of another way to shake you loose from him. I love you so much it makes me crazy."

I melted inside, needing to hear that more than I could possibly have imagined I would.

"Jack's lawyer told my lawyer he doesn't want a divorce and wants to try to work things out, for the boys' sake." I still couldn't believe Jack was hoping for a reconciliation. He'd been pushing hard for a face-to-face meeting, which I'd told my lawyer to do everything she could to prevent.

"Do you want to do that?" he asked, his expression suddenly uneasy.

"No." I shook my head. "It's not going to work. We want different things." Actually, the problem was we wanted the same thing: a man in our bed. "But you…you were with all those other women. I can't trust you not to do it again."

"But I didn't, not on my own time. It was only for work," he insisted. "Do you know how many jobs I turned down so that I'd be free to fly over here to see you every few weeks? I would do *anything* for you. If you're happy to be poor with me, I'll give up acting and become…a waiter. They don't have to kiss other women to get paid."

I held his face in my hands and shook my head. I was never one that needed romantic declarations, but he was saying everything I wanted to hear, and it was like a balm on my rubbed-raw heart. I didn't want to ask, but I had to know. "I don't understand, though. You meet and get intimate every day with such perfect, beautiful women as your job, how do I even compete?"

"You're smart and beautiful and *real*. You make me feel things, good things. Other women are place-fillers. I wouldn't know or care whether they were there or not. And I know you want me for me, not to enhance your career."

"No, I guess not. It would probably be better for your career if you were dating one of those girls."

"I've done that before, but it's horrible. I never wanted to be magazine fodder and harassed by the paparazzi like that." He shuddered slightly. "You stole my heart and ran away with it. I had no choice but to follow you. These last few months have been hell, thinking of you with him instead of with me. When I found out you were pregnant…" He breathed out heavily "…and that it could be mine, I didn't know whether to be happy or kill someone. You are finally free, and there's no way I'll accept anything less than you being completely mine, in every way."

It was so caveman, but in an utterly delicious way that made me swoon just a little. I wasn't going to doubt it and look for ulterior motives like I usually would. I could let him finish the healing I needed to function again properly; all I had to do was trust him. *Take a leap*, I said to myself with wry humor. Only this time, it was less of a leap. I'd already lost what I had previously been hesitant to gamble.

"No, I know you love what you do. I get it, really I do, but it caught me by surprise. I can handle it, as long as you let me know when it's going to happen before I see it on the Internet."

"So, can we make this work? Will you move to LA with me?" He smiled widely, showing a lot of white teeth. *Like a wolf who's going to eat me up,* I thought, distracted yet again by his mouth and the things he could do with it. Forcing myself away from my hormonally-charged thoughts and back to the very serious conversation we were having was hard.

"I don't know. The boys are at school here, and I can't leave them here on their own."

"Could they move to the States?"

"No, it's not fair to upheave their entire lives. My life is in England, yours is in the States, and that's not going to change for at least the next five years until the boys leave school."

"But they're at boarding school! It's not like you have to be there every day to make them lunch. They can come to us in the holidays. I'm sure they'd like the heat and sunshine."

"That's true, I guess," I said doubtfully, but seeing the truth of the argument. I wasn't required to be here every day. It would take a bit longer to get to them if anything happened, though. "I don't know anybody there, and you'll be away so much. It's a huge decision, and we really don't know each other that well."

"We have something between us that's special. We both know it," he urged. "And we're having a baby! I'm not really away that much, just a few weeks here and there, and you can come with me. They have kitchens there, big ones, and lots of people to feed too," he teased. "You can write your cookbooks there just as well as here. The sun will also do you good. You look pale."

I smiled despite myself. He pulled me up so he could wrap his arms around me. My arms willingly encircled his hips, holding onto the hard muscles of his back.

"Imagine relaxing by the pool in the warm air during the day, cuddling up to me at night, not having to rush off home or hide anything. Just us, as much as we want." His voice deepened and went husky. The picture of life with Anders sounded good. "I want to come home to you and the baby every day," he said softly and more seriously. "I don't want to be a stranger that sees it once or twice a month."

"I know what we're having. Do you want to know?"

He nodded.

"It's a girl." I told him.

He grabbed me tighter in an exuberant bear hug. Being held by him felt so good. I breathed in the distinctive sunshine smell of him, with a slightly woody note, feeling something tight inside me relax.

"We'll make it work. I'm not going to let you go again, even if I have to tie you to my bed and make you come so much you can't walk straight enough to get out the door." I could feel his smile against my forehead. "You can't leave me again, not now," he whispered against my hair. He lifted my face with his large hands and kissed me like he was trying to drink me down and absorb me into himself. "Promise me."

"I love you, Anders." I sighed and pushed back against him, so that we touched along the length of our bodies. I could feel the round hardness of our baby in between us, sharing in the love. I could finally admit to myself that despite the improbability of it, with Anders, I had come home too.

Was he my happy ending after all? No, this was not the end, and we had no way of knowing what was in our future, but more importantly, he gave me hope that we could have a new beginning that would overwrite the mistakes of the past. I had a lot to look forward to.

Epilogue

Jack looked at the smiling picture of his ex-wife as she sat on a picnic rug in the sunshine, a plump blond child on her lap, the big man next to her looking at her with clear adoration as he cradled the newborn. He knew he should be happy for her, but he couldn't. The darkness within him wouldn't let him.

In the beginning, she had pushed it back, but over time even her light had been unable to prevent its return. Nothing could. It was passed down their family like a cursed inheritance. *His family.* What a joke. His mother was in denial, as usual, but it was clear to everyone else that Crispin would be going to jail this time. His father had all but disappeared now, his silence and withdrawal almost complete. With work and running the estate as well, at least Jack was too busy to think.

He ripped the page from Caroline's magazine, knowing she had deliberately left it open on that page for him to find. Her revenges were petty but still cut him deeply. Slowly he tore the page into tiny pieces, leaving a trail to the bathroom, where he closed and locked the door. He turned on the shower and undressed quickly, bracing under the punishingly cold water. Only then did he let the tears fall, the loud torrent of water muffling the deep hacking sobs of his loss.

If he'd been the type, he would have ended it all. But he wasn't, so he didn't. He just retreated inward and did the best he could. Adam had broken up with him not long after Kate left, tired of waiting for a commitment that would never come. He understood, but it was yet another piece of him lost that would never be recovered. What he had left to give would never be enough for his girlfriend, but if she left, he would be alone, and that was intolerable. So, he put up with her jealously and cruelty — it was what he deserved — and locked away his heart, which still and would always belong to Kate.

Acknowledgments

Thank you also to Anna, for giving me insight on how celebrities are managed and not even letting me buy her lunch. Also to Jess and Emma, who shared their experiences living in London.

Thank you also to all the amazing people in the UK who opened up their lives and homes for me to peer into and steal details to make this book at bit more real: Eden, Tory, Will, Evanna, Alice and Gillian.

To Fiona especially, who took me under her wing and shared her love of Chelsea and its surrounds. Hopefully I have used the information wisely!

About the Author

L.C. Fenton lives in Sydney, Australia, with her husband and two children. In addition to her cake-making business, she works as a freelance copywriter and pens occasional articles for various online magazines.

Not being one of those people who had a burning desire to be anything in particular, L.C. worked her way alphabetically backward through the available degrees at Sydney University. Surprisingly, given the amount of fun she had at school, L.C. finally managed to graduate with a completely unemployable degree in philosophy. A law degree soon followed, however, simply to make it possible for some organization to hire her.

After ten soul-destroying years, lost and wandering aimlessly in the corporate wilderness, L.C. threw it all in and reassessed. Deciding to bring the "one day I will write a book" idea to the present, she started and hasn't stopped. As a huge fan of the romance genre, she writes the kinds of books that she enjoys to read.

In her spare time, L.C. Fenton…actually she has no spare time. She either sleeps or reads copious amounts of romance novels instead of sleeping. One day she hopes to have nothing to do and to take up reading full time, after completing all the levels of Candy Crush. Not likely to happen any time soon, but everyone needs a dream.

◄────►New Adult◄────►

Three Daves by Nicki Elson
Streamline by Jennifer Lane
The Shades series: *Shades of Atlantis* by Carol Oates
The Heart series: *Beside Your Heart* & *Disclosure of the Heart*
by Mary Whitney
Romancing the Bookworm by Kate Evangelista
Fighting Fate by Linda Kage
Flirting with Chaos by Kenya Wright
The Vice, Virtue & Video series: *Revealed* (book 1) by Bianca Giovanni

◄────►Erotic Romance◄────►

The Keyhole series: *Becoming sage* (book 1) by Kasi Alexander
The Keyhole series: *Saving sunni* (book 2) by Kasi & Reggie Alexander
The Winemaker's Dinner: *Appetizers & Entrée* by Dr. Ivan Rusilko & Everly Drummond
The Winemaker's Dinner: *Dessert* by Dr. Ivan Rusilko
Client N° 5 by Joy Fulcher

◄────►Paranormal Romance◄────►

The Light series: *Seers of Light, Whisper of Light* & *Circle of Light*
by Jennifer DeLucy
The Hanaford Park series: *Eve of Samhain* & *Pleasures Untold* by Lisa Sanchez
Immortal Awakening by KC Randall
The Seraphim series: *Crushed Seraphim* & *Bittersweet Seraphim*
by Debra Anastasia
The Guardian's Wild Child by Feather Stone
Grave Refrain by Sarah M. Glover
Divinity by Patricia Leever
Blood Vine series: *Blood Vine* & *Blood Entangled* & *Blood Reunited*
by Amber Belldene
Divine Temptation by Nicki Elson
Love in the Time of the Dead by Tera Shanley

◄────►Historical Romance◄────►

Cat O' Nine Tails by Patricia Leever
Burning Embers by Hannah Fielding
Good Ground by Tracy Winegar